Finding

Makeba

ALSO BY ALEXS D. PATE

LOSING ABSALOM

G. P. Putnam's Sons   New York

Finding

Makeba

ALEXS D. PATE

G. P. PUTNAM'S SONS
Publishers Since 1838
200 Madison Avenue
New York, NY 10016

Copyright © 1996 by Alexs D. Pate
All rights reserved. This book, or parts thereof,
may not be reproduced in any form without permission.
Published simultaneously in Canada

Library of Congress Cataloging-in-Publication Data
Pate, Alexs D., date.
  Finding Makeba / by Alexs D. Pate
    p.   cm.
  ISBN 0-399-14200-2
  I. Title.
PS3566.A777G63   1997
813'.54—dc20   96-18418 CIP

Printed in the United States of America

10   9   8   7   6   5   4   3   2   1

This book is printed on acid-free paper. ∞

Book design by Gretchen Achilles

FOR
GYANNI, ALEXS
AND CHEKESHA

The secret of fatherhood can only have been revealed to men by the women themselves . . .

THE WOMEN'S ENCYCLOPEDIA OF MYTHS AND SECRETS
by Barbara Walker

Standards for fathers are not so high. Drunkards, adulterers, child-beaters, even criminals are supposed to have a "right" to fatherhood, to say nothing of millions of men who treat their children with a neglectful indifference that would bring down society's wrath on a female parent. Possibly men should be taught to regard fatherhood as a privilege to be earned, not as a right to be abused.

THE WOMEN'S ENCYCLOPEDIA OF MYTHS AND SECRETS

The hearty ringing laugh of a child is sweet music to the ear. There are three most joyous sounds in nature — the hum of a beem, the purr of a cat, and the laugh of a child. They tell of peace, of happiness, and of contentment and make one for a while forget that there is so much misery in the world.

THE COLLEGE OF LIFE OR PRACTICAL SELF-EDUCATOR:
A MANUAL OF SELF-IMPROVEMENT FOR THE COLORED RACE *(1898)*

Finding Makeba

Prologue

Makeba looked across the aisle of the train and found the eyes of a thin-faced man. In the shadowed light of the train he was almost an apparition. His skin was bad, like the gray rocks she used to collect from the railroad beds near Rock Garden, a place of her childhood in North Philadelphia. Her grandmother had called them "funk rock" because if you rubbed them against each other or against cement, they would crumble and emit a nasty odor. The man swam in a shiny blue serge suit. A frayed, dingy white shirt stuck to his body. There were other people on the train, which traveled the Main Line route to downtown Philadelphia, but Makeba could feel only his eyes.

She straightened up. Why was he staring at her like that? Did he know what she was about to do? Could he tell how uneasy she was? She had purposely dressed to avoid the boring gazes of the men who rode trains in the middle of the day. She wore a set of baggy, faded blue denim overalls with a long-underwear top underneath. On her feet were a set of black combat boots. She couldn't be attractive to him.

But he wouldn't turn his head. He seemed to be staring into her chest. Makeba wished she had worn her baseball cap. With that she could have blocked him out. Simply pulled the bill of the cap down over her eyes. But her close-cut hair was no protection; indeed, it was but a frame for her soft, youthful face.

She was already in a steady tremble, a string away from tears. She wasn't even sure she could stand up to get off the train when it arrived at Suburban Station. All morning she had been conscious only of herself. Her thoughts. She had walked past her mother and her stepfather—mindless, oblivious to them, as she left the house. No one had intruded into her consciousness until this man's wild-eyed stare.

Makeba carried a large black shoulder bag. She pulled it onto her lap and looked inside. There was a sixties-style brown suede, fringed purse which held fifty dollars and a loose collection of photographs. Resting against the purse were two books and a small stuffed lion, its frayed cotton fur worn nearly to skin. The face of the lion smiled up at her. It was the kind of encouragement she needed.

With a sigh she leaned back into her seat again. She wasn't afraid of the man across from her. Not today. At best he only symbolized the disconnection that was a part of her life. He could sit there and put his eyes on her and she was powerless to stop him. But he didn't matter. He would eventually get off the train. He would eventually pass into meaninglessness, just as most of the people in her life did.

Makeba took out her journal and a green felt-tip pen. She opened to the first blank page. She did not want to review what she had written the night before. She was afraid that if she turned back to that page, she would not follow through on her mission.

So many things could turn her back. And she had promised herself: Today she would do one of the most difficult things she'd ever done. On this day her life would change. How it would change she had no idea. Maybe there would be no tomorrow. Maybe when she was done doing the thing she had to do, the feelings of fear and dread which had been with her since she was a child would finally be exorcised and she would simply collapse and die.

Makeba felt the rhythmic sway as the cars rocked on their feet. But she had completely missed the moment when the train ducked into the tunnel that led into downtown Philadelphia. Makeba had traveled this route many times and was always fascinated at the moment when daylight became darkness. When the space of suburbia was immediately replaced by the density of the city. The interior lights of the train only heightened the effect. She tried to write but nothing came. She stared at the white pages, trying to block everything else out of her view. Especially the man across from her.

The train stopped briefly at Thirtieth Street Station. As the brakes engaged, the man stood and crossed toward her. The doors opened but he stood staring at her. And then, suddenly, he opened his mouth. "You're a very cute young woman." And then, for the first time, there was a crooked, brown-toothed smile. "Have a nice day." He breathed through his teeth, and stumbled out the door.

Makeba didn't respond. Didn't move a muscle. Wasn't soothed by his good wishes. In fact she wanted to scream at him. To curse him. He was what she hated. Men full of insincerity and lies. He didn't know her. What could he know about her day? What he had said under the guise of cordiality wasn't for her. It rolled off of her. It meant nothing.

She looked again at the empty page and suddenly felt like writing again.

But instead of making her pen put words down, she watched the new passengers board for the short ride from Thirtieth Street to Suburban Station. The train was dotted with businesspeople, more symbols of the lies and exploitation that were all around her. Everyone looked scrubbed and buffed and ready to make more money.

Outside, the May day was bright and warm, one of the first days of the year that hinted at the heat of the coming summer. And then her body was shaking again. Fear came over her, unannounced, like rain. It was a serious journey she was on. And there was no thought which allowed her to escape it. Years of dread were compressed in her thin body. It erupted into anxiety without warning. That was what this trip was about. She was going to the source of everything. The point at which her life, through no fault of her own, had been stuffed full of disappointment.

As a child she had always had flawless cinnamon skin, a shade lighter than her mother's, but now at nineteen, there were the shadows of pimples that had plagued her over the last year. Whenever she became emotionally uncertain, the bumps would rise on her skin like flowers. The small dark spots marked the remnants of the last outbreak.

The train squealed into the station. Makeba closed her journal and replaced it in her bag. She carefully stood up; her heavy combat boots scuffed the floor as she grabbed her bag and slung it over her shoulder.

Makeba found it hard to walk as she left the train and climbed the steps into the station. Her legs felt tired, as if she had run all the way into the city from the suburb of Malvern.

Now, even though she was aware of many more people around her, all of them going somewhere, all of them rushing, she could make out no details.

She wanted to turn around and go back home. What she was doing was crazy. Even though this had been carefully planned, she wasn't sure she could go through with it. Her stomach was lurching. She passed by the concessions and shops of the station like a waif, lost in thought and with increasing fear.

As she emerged from the station, the sunlight surprised her. She had almost forgotten what time of day it was. She pulled out an old pocket watch, given to her by her grandmother. It was nearly two o'clock. Makeba made her way to Chestnut Street. She *wanted* to be late. It would be very dangerous to arrive early and then have too much time to wait. If that happened she might back out. No, actually she wanted to get there just as everything was ending. That would be the right way.

Makeba walked with a loping gait, an imitation of a boy she knew. It was a walk that waded through the center-city crowds in oblivious determination. She waited for no red lights, lumbered through the traffic, weaved her way to her destination.

And then, suddenly, she was standing in front of the bookstore. She froze. Her trembling got worse. Maybe she really *couldn't* do it. And then she saw it. His picture sat in the window like a huckster waving the customers inside. *He* was the reason she had tried so hard in school, only to feel stupid. Had searched so hard for a man to love, only to suffer loneliness. *He* was the reason her speech was subdued and slow, to the point that sometimes even her friends thought she was chronically depressed. *He* was the reason she never felt safe and why nothing ever felt good to her. She had to go in.

Inside the store there was a strong murmur emanating from the back. She moved in that direction. Her mind was blank now. This was what plans were for. They move you even when you cannot think. This was well rehearsed. Instinctive.

She took up a place at the end of the line. She hoped no one would come up behind her. She wanted to be the last. He wouldn't be able to see anyone after her anyway.

The line moved briskly. Makeba was careful to stand behind the woman in front of her so that she could not be seen by the man who sat at a small table, the place where the line ended. And she really didn't want to see him either. Not until she was right in front of him. She heard him laugh. And then others laughed. His voice was complex, soft and compelling at the same time. It was a voice you wanted to listen to.

And then she was one person away. Makeba could now hear the dialogue.

"Do you always write stories about families?"

"It's what I've been thinking most about lately. I've got other stories to tell, but right now, I just believe it's what I have to do." Ben shifted in his chair. "What's your name?"

"Madeline Jones." Madeline was a middle-aged white woman who Makeba thought must have been a teacher. There was a faint hint of chalk sprinkled throughout her navy wool suit with a pleated skirt.

"May I ask you a question, Mr. Crestfield?" Makeba wanted the woman to get her book autographed and keep moving.

"Of course."

Makeba lost her breath again. That voice. She knew that voice even though she had not heard it in so many years. Her knees started to buckle.

"Is this your story? Is this autobiographical in any way?" Makeba stared at the woman's back. That was a dumb question. Of course the story was autobiographical. Someone would have had to live this story. You couldn't make this up.

Ben Crestfield's voice rose in animated laughter. "I get asked that a lot. And I answer it by simply saying that, yes, there are parts that really happened to me and other parts that I made up. But that doesn't mean all of it isn't true."

"I see. Is that why the main character has your name?" Makeba was growing impatient. The woman's questions were so stupid.

"Well, Madeline—it's Madeline, right?" The woman nodded. "Usually, writers change the names and keep the situations true. I just did the opposite."

"I see. Well, after reading your book, I felt like I knew you."

Makeba could feel the air tense a little. Ben Crestfield paused, trying to decide what to say. "Well, Madeline, I take that as a compliment. I hope you feel the same way about my new book, which, by the way, is not about me."

Makeba felt the finality in his comment. Madeline's audience with the author was over. But she made no move to leave. Makeba felt nauseous.

And Madeline *didn't* leave. She leaned over the table, bending at the waist. "Mr. Crestfield, is it possible I could talk with you sometime? Not here, but somewhere else. I think we have a lot in common."

Makeba was instantly frightened. Even though she was trying to keep her head down, she couldn't help but catch a glimpse of the man just beyond Madeline. He was heavier than she remembered. Rounder. He was almost bald, with just a shadow of hair covering his head. Still, even in this subdued atmosphere of books, the smell of dust, paper and ink permeating, the flash in his eyes held her. And just like always, there was somebody between them.

"I'm sorry, Madeline. I'm leaving tomorrow. I don't get to Philadelphia very often. But next time I'm in town maybe we'll run into each other." Makeba looked at the floor. She wasn't sure but she felt like the newly famous writer was trying his best to see over Madeline. Trying to see who his next fan was.

Madeline finally pulled away, leaving Makeba, face pointed

downward, standing in front of the author. She took a deep breath and steeled herself. She knew he was looking at her but she didn't move.

"Yes?" He was speaking to her. "Have you read my book?"

Makeba held each word. She had promised herself that before she spoke a word, she would remember all of the times when she had wished, with all her strength, to hear his voice. And now, those moments were zipping through her head like shards of light. She struggled to hold herself together.

And then, slowly, she reached into her bag. She knew he was watching her. He was silent now. Without looking up, she pulled out a copy of his book. She held it in front of her face and opened it to the page where the dedication was.

Ben looked at the young woman. She was the youngest person who had come in for the book signing. His interest always grew when he came in contact with younger readers. They held the strongest pain. Just the week before in Buffalo he had spent three hours with a young woman who couldn't stop crying. Her father too, gone into the shadows.

But he sensed something about this woman. Some deep signature of pain marked her. And she still hadn't held her head up so he could see her. When he saw the book he smiled.

"Did you like the book?"

"Like it?" Makeba hadn't expected that question.

"Yes, that's what an author asks someone who has read his book." Ben wondered why she wouldn't look at him.

"Well. . ." Makeba stumbled. "Like that woman, I guess I wasn't sure what was real and what wasn't." She paused, uncertain again of her determination. "I just came to the conclusion that it didn't matter, that wasn't the point."

"Yeah, that's the way I wanted it." Ben pulled her copy of the book closer to him so he could sign it. "What's your name? Who should I sign this to?"

"To me." Makeba looked up; now she was a thin light without a body, hovering there. She forced herself to speak. "Make it for Makeba Crestfield." Ben looked into his daughter's eyes and felt his body short-circuit. He leaned back in his chair. Yes. That was his forehead. That was his nose. He knew her soft-featured face. That beautiful brown skin. This was his daughter. He felt his body quaking.

Makeba's eyes were clouding; she knew this would challenge all of her strength, her resolve. She struggled to hold herself back.

Ben was trying to breathe. He was aware he hadn't said anything, and searched inside himself for a voice. But before he could speak, Makeba's hand emerged again from her shoulder bag and offered a second book. This one was black with gold trim embossed on the borders. It was very slim and felt like a hymnbook in his hands.

He opened the cover, a sheet of paper fell out. The script was tight and thin:

Dear Father?

I've been so quiet most of my life. Do you know that? What do you really know about me? You've created this character that is supposed to be me, I guess, but how can you create something you don't really know about? It's not fair. It doesn't really matter if I understand why you left or not. I know I expected you to come back. I know that. And every day, for a while, I thought you would. And then there were months and then, well, to be honest, I stopped thinking about you so much. I could go months without remembering that someone I had loved, my father, was completely gone out of my life. You may have been thinking about me, which I have to say I don't believe, but whether you were or not, I wasn't always thinking about you.

But still, my life has brought me to this moment where I need to talk to you. I need to hear your voice. No matter how hard I have tried to completely push you out of my mind, I have to admit that I still have a hole in me. Maybe I did need to know why it all happened. And maybe I needed to tell you that no matter how you tell this story, it could never adequately explain away the most important fact: You left me. You did. I loved you, yes, but it was more than that. You had a deep effect on me. You thought I was beautiful. You thought I was so smart. You gave me books. (By the

*way, when a boy buys me a book, he's halfway there.) Anyway,
I've changed everything in my life now. I'm going to go to school
next year and get myself together. I've been lost for so long. Lost
and trapped at the same time. Trapped by something I didn't have
anything to do with. But, to be honest, reading your book has
made a difference.*

*I came into town last month and passed by the bookstore with
your picture in the window advertising the book. It upset me. I
recognized you right away. Until that moment, you were a feeling.
Like someone who had died a long time ago. Somebody you might
have cared about but who you just had to go on without because
they weren't coming back. When I bought the book, finally, I had
something—something from you. I carried it around in my bag for
almost a week. And when I started reading it, I decided to start
writing again. If you could do it, so could I. So I kept a journal.
After each chapter, I wrote whatever came into my mind. And
now, you are reading it.*

Makeba

Ben looked up from the letter into his daughter's eyes. He
thought about the agonizing nights he had spent trying to feel her
presence. How he had been driven mad by her absence, his absence.
How he had slowly taught himself to live without her. It had been
like a mythological journey. From safety to terror and back again. He
had come the full distance and, like Odysseus, washed up on the
shores of sanity again. And he had the golden fleece.

When he wrote the novel she held in her hands, he had used his
longing for her as both the reason to tell the truth and the fuel to
keep going even when facing her presence in his fiction made him
physically ill. He had almost died trying to finish that book. It was
truly a letter to her. It held the answer to the question he knew she
had to be asking. It held the answer to the question "Why?"

One

Love starts small. In the beginning it is a tiny, nearly invisible blossom. Yet in a short time it can take you over. Overrun you like you were a building and it was ivy. It has its own life. Love grows. Envelops you. Suddenly there is no escape and you are trapped. It becomes so thick you lose control of your own faculties. Finally you are within it.

There, too, is an unseen force. His name is Mates. In the first moments of love, Mates has no substance. But he is there. If you have been in love, especially if that love has ended, as love eventually does, you already know him.

Mates is guilt in waiting. He knows that in every relationship someone will eventually break a promise, or do something which irrevocably destroys that love. He is there to punish that person. He hangs there, waiting—in the space, in the shadows, everywhere.

When called, when things are just so, Mates is able to metamorphose out of the shadows. Some then see him as a wolf, others as a dog. A black dog. At those times his teeth and claws have substance. Then he is able to do his purpose.

His purpose? Well, many, even though they may deny it, have felt his strong jaws clamp down on them. Others, only the sound of his paws forever on their heels. Mates can chase you to the end. To the place where there is only a gasping for breath. The last step before nothing. It has been said that he feeds on the dead, that he eats the hearts of those he pursues and then carries them away into the netherworld.

But you must understand that he is there at the moment when love becomes itself. He knows what we don't. When love dies and one person looks at the other and accuses them of some ugly action, he knows that that guilt has been there all the time, first as air, later as frustration and finally as anger and pain.

Mates was there the day Makeba's parents, Ben and Helen, met. It was at a Saint Valentine's Day party in 1975. Chance. Neither of them knew that on that February night they would begin a falling flight.

As Ben drove his yellow 1970 Volkswagen Bug away from the center of the city on his way to the party, he struggled to keep his eyes focused on the street. A light snow had fallen and he was already high enough to race a cloud to heaven.

He had been with his friend Ramsey, who was still at the Thirteen Bar, eyes glazed and focused on a topless dancer, where Ben had left him. Ben had lied and said he had to go home. Instead, now enfolded in his VW, he was headed to a party in West Oak Lane. And he wanted to go alone.

When Ben and Ramsey were together, they unconsciously stopped each other from approaching women. Together, they sat on the sidelines and exchanged a satiric running commentary as if neither of them were actually interested in the women. Ramsey would find something wrong with every one of them. After all, in the years Ben had known the man, Ramsey had never had a serious girlfriend. He would occasionally meet someone, but after one or two dates she would usually break it off.

Ben suspected that the real problem wasn't Ramsey's weight but his personality. He was rough. Like a chunk of coal. It was just a matter of time before he offended or hurt someone. And, Ben figured, that was why Ramsey always put women down. Ramsey talked about wanting to be in a relationship with a woman, but he wasn't willing to do what that required. Namely, treat women with respect.

Ben went to the go-go bars and he participated in the juvenile banter, but underneath, he did not hate women the way he felt some men, including Ramsey, did. That was the thing, he could feel the hatred that radiated from men toward women. The need to possess, to use, to abuse, to discard. He was aware and he fought those urges whenever they arose in him.

Besides, he was planning to be a writer, at least that's what he was studying in school, and he was becoming more and more consumed with his own identity, his own process of determining the meaning of love. And that was why he had lied to Ramsey about the party. He was tired of going places, being around the social swirl without actually being in it. On the rare occasions when he would break away and try to talk to a woman, Ramsey was always there waiting to make fun of him. He would say things like, "What you want with that girl? I told you, man, they just want your money," or, "Why you want to talk to that bear?" And Ben would stifle his anger, play it off as just another episode of macho ghetto humor.

So he had taken to lying. It was the only way he would ever meet anyone. The only way love could ever come to him. And on this night Ben felt desperate. He knew there was someone out there for him and he wanted to hurry up and meet her.

In the small car, Ben filled all of the space made for the driver. His solid five-foot-nine-inch frame found just enough room to maneuver. He was twenty-two, a recent veteran of the Navy, where he'd met Ramsey, and was laboring through his second year as a part-time English major on the G.I. Bill.

Somehow that night, as he cut through the snow and the cold blowing wind, he found the right block of Sharpnack Street. Ben saw the lights through the frosted window of the house and knew he was in the right place. He parked a half block away. As soon as he opened his car door, he heard the thumping bass twisting through the heavy night air.

Fortified with alcohol, Ben stumbled up the steps to the West

Oak Lane row house. He shivered. He had taken off his leather coat and left it in the car. He never took his leather into parties where he would have to lay it on a mountain of other coats. He wasn't about to give some opportunistic fool the chance to exchange a cheap light-weight London Fog trench for a two-hundred-dollar leather.

The windows of the house were glazed over but he could see the shadows of people dancing inside, defying the cold temperatures outside.

Unlike the house in which he had grown up in North Philadelphia, most West Oak Lane houses had front porches. It was one of the features that the upwardly mobile looked for. And West Oak Lane was the first neighborhood that black folks from North Philly headed for when they got some money.

It was late, a little after midnight and therefore after the proper celebration of Valentine's Day. Ben rang the bell but no one came. Through the haze of the small window on the door, he could see the people dancing. He could hear the music. But none of the dancing bodies was willing to break from the beat and open the door for him. He banged on the door with his fist. Finally, a man dancing closest to the door reluctantly tore himself away from the jam to let Ben in.

Ben quickly pushed through the threshold. It was dark. There was a small lamp sitting on a table at the end of a gray sofa. In it a dark blue light burned. It glowed. It made the room bluedark.

Ben couldn't tell how many people were moving with Earth, Wind and Fire's "Shining Star." You could always count on Earth, Wind and Fire to raise a sweat in the February freeze. The heat that came from the dense layering of bodies rippled in the thick air.

He was struck by the way black folks created heat. They wanted to create heat. That was a part of the process. Dancing without heat was what white people did. And it was hot within the sea of people. It was hard to believe that it could be so cold outside and so smoking inside. From the moment he stepped into the room, he felt the sweat break free and seek the air.

Ben weaved through the crowd. There was a complex odor coursing through the room. A composite smell of individuals. And he could smell each one. Each one a separate celebration of life and energy. The styles and steps formed a raw strength. If dancing were war, African people would rule the world. If dancing ever becomes war, look out. He felt the complex energies of the city. As he passed among the folks, he felt middle-class energy, poor-working-class energy, gang energy, high yellow energy, gospel energy all swirling on the dance floor.

Underneath the blaring stereo a different noise hovered about the dancers. It was like a buzzing whistle that darted between the loud music and the empty space in Ben's head. Like a whirling plastic toy sold at circuses and carnivals. People weren't talking, there was little evidence, even in the cornflower light, of smiling faces. Just serious attention being paid to the rhythm, the beat and the moving body.

He couldn't distinguish faces and so he didn't know if there was anyone there he knew. Ben moved by instinct to the kitchen. In the kitchen he knew he would find the people who wanted to be seen. People who were not afraid to be under the light. Of course he had been to parties where the people in the kitchen were the ones doing the illegal drugs. But that was uncommon. Most people honored kitchens and wouldn't permit foul shit to go on in them. In most houses the kitchen was a respected place.

He worked his way through. As he broke free of the throng of dancers, darkness and sweat, his eyes were unprepared for the bright light of the kitchen.

There he knew he would find Geri and her friends, a small number of women, "girlfriends" they called themselves, who often gave parties or knew where there was one.

Geri was the primary "girlfriend." Every Friday Ben would call Geri and ask what was up. She'd have a list of parties that stretched into the next week. Parties of all sorts. She'd have parties in the serious hoods, in North, South and West Philly. She'd also have another list of parties in Germantown, West Oak Lane and Overbrook. She'd know where they were doing drugs and which party had good food and which one had the best music for dancing. Geri was party central.

But on this night she was having her own set. A Valentine's Day jam. Lovers and folks looking for lovers.

Ben felt the rum running through him. He practically leapt into the kitchen, catching everyone, including Geri, by surprise. The light blinded him. Everything wavered like an underwater image. He could tell there were a lot of people standing around, but suddenly he couldn't see very well.

Geri was breathtaking. Her walnut skin was like velvet. Her penetrating eyes cast a sweet shadow on the sunflower walls of the kitchen. At the time, she had one of the largest Afros he had ever seen. Her body was long and strong. She wore a multicolored tank top and tight white Levi's. Her black platforms set the outfit off.

She was quickly at his side. "Ben? I didn't know you were here yet." She put her fluorescent-red lips on his cheeks. Her face wrinkled. "Are you drunk already?"

Ben didn't feel drunk, but he couldn't explain why he suddenly wrapped his arms around her and pulled her close. So close he could smell the Ambush perfume painting peach on the inside of his mind. So close he felt her breasts against his chest. Lost in the moment, he reduced himself and curled up next to her. Unconscious of everyone around. Unconscious of everything and everyone except his need to be enveloped. He let his fingers meld into the cotton of her tank top.

This is what happens when you are lonely. You find yourself pulled unexplainably into situations you would not normally be pulled into. Like the softness of Geri's body. Ben knew it wasn't right. He could feel Geri tensing up under his clutch. But she felt so good to him. So comfortable. And on this night he felt pliant, malleable.

He should have known better. He knew Geri. He knew she didn't play that. "What's wrong with you?" She gently pushed him an arm's length away.

Ben was instantly shaken back into himself. Whatever traces of him couldn't make it back into his body remained on her. He tried to clear his head. "Nothing. Ah . . . nothing's wrong, Geri. I'm just buzzing a little, that's all. Everything's cool."

She looked at him and laughed. "Cool? You come in here grabbing all over me and you got the nerve to say 'everything's cool'?" She paused. "I ain't your property."

"I know, Geri. I told you, I'm just lunchin', that's all. I didn't mean no harm." As he fumbled with his words, Ben suddenly realized there were three women standing around them. He had obviously interrupted a conversation. Now he became more nervous. Maybe he *was* drunk. He had forgotten for a moment that he was at a party. That people were all around him. He felt them laughing, hiccuping lilts in the yellow kitchen.

Geri smiled, ignoring him with a flourish of her moving hands, simply said, "Ain't no thang, Ben. I was just messing with you. Long as you keep them hands to yourself. I got enough problems tonight without having to fight you off."

Ben knew he'd never have a chance with Geri. She was the first woman the men went after. Somebody was always trying to hit on her. He knew she never considered him as a potential lover. He was too plain. Not flashy enough for Geri. To her, he was a good friend, a brother. Geri would sometimes get mad at him for making simple things complicated. "Damn, Ben," she would say, "I don't know about all that book learning you gettin' at that damn college. You can't make up your mind about shit anymore. Stop making everything so damn hard. Just do what you supposed to do, that's all." That was Geri, fast and to the point.

She introduced him to everyone in the kitchen. He said hello but he couldn't focus on faces. Soon silence surrounded them. The five of them stood there, shifting weight, awkwardly staring at each other. But whoever was controlling the music box was on the money. The Isley Brothers kept the dancers churning.

Finally, to break the silence around him, Ben asked Geri to dance.

"Oh no, Ben. I'm not dancing with you tonight."

"Why not?" Ben's vision had started to work better.

"I've already got a big problem out there. Both of my boyfriends showed up. They're out there waiting to find out which one I'm going to be with tonight."

Geri turned to her friends and made an overly dramatic gesture with her arms as if to say, "I just don't know what to do."

The woman standing next to Ben broke in, "Oh go on with that shit, Geri. You know exactly what you're gonna do. You know who you want." The other two smiled in agreement.

Geri waved them off, her mind moving faster. "I've got an idea." Geri looked at Ben and slowly turned her head in the direction of the woman across from him.

He followed her eyes into the clean caramel picture that was Helen. Standing in her red pumps she was about the same height as Ben. Thin, with a head full of straightened, cascading hair, Helen had a smile that stopped people cold. She would never again be as beautiful to him as she was on that night.

Her eyes gave permission. Ben took her hand.

"Be careful, Helen, Ben's one of them *artistes*, you know," Geri called out as they started for the living room. "He'll be talking 'bout how he wants to invite you home for a poetry reading or some shit."

Helen smiled and Ben quickly ushered her out of the kitchen and into the dining room cum dance floor.

"Are you a writer?" Helen asked as they walked into the darkness.

"I . . . ah . . ." Ben hated that question. He knew what he wanted to be but saying it was difficult. He was just beginning to meet writers at school. He was just beginning to take literature and writing seriously. He thought he wanted to be a writer, but . . .

"Yeah, I guess. I mean, I'm writing a lot of poetry and stuff I . . ."

"That sounds interesting. I've never met a writer. I would never have expected Geri to even know one."

Ben chuckled. "Yeah, I bet that's right." He couldn't help smiling as they took the floor. His head was spinning just a bit and Helen was fine fine fine.

And once they were within the clutch of the steaming, shaking room, they too joined the freed souls. They danced together all night. They spoke without words, only swinging hips and strutting feet. They twisted and skipped. They called the Yoruban spirits. They danced gospel. And finally they swooned into each other.

James Brown, War, Santana, Osibisa, the Spinners, New Birth and Bobby Womack serenaded them. Called them to movement. Ben felt himself slipping into the folds of enchantment. Her softness. Her smell. The way she fit into the groove of his body spoke to him in a language his body understood. It was beyond the intellectual. He wasn't thinking. It was in the energy between them. It was silent and yet it spoke loudly. It told him that she was made to be next to him. So his hands found the places where her skin was exposed and anchored themselves there.

They instantly became the beauty and the curse. When Ben and Helen came together, there was no sky and no ground. Everything around them, above and below them, was only swatches of color. They became eagles, black eagles, entangled in their own wings.

On a slow record he whispered into her ear, "What are you? Are you some kind of spirit? Do you have some sort of magic? Why can't I let you go?"

Helen didn't move her head. "Because I don't want you to. I want you to hold me like this and never let go." The music punctuated her sentence and they danced until the record ended. Then, as someone searched for the next song and there was a hushed murmur throughout the room, Helen said softly, looking directly into his eyes, "If I really got any magic, you can bet I'm gonna try and use it on you."

The entire night was awash in blue lights and soft skin. Eventually they kissed and were swept away by the circumstances of giddiness. They held hands and drank spiked punch. Danced some more. He knew he loved her. He wasn't lonely anymore.

Langston Hughes called it the little spark that danced in the dark. The beginning. The way love starts.

Makeba's Journal

I thought this was supposed to be a novel. But as I flipped ahead I was completely shocked when I saw my real name. And Mom's and Nana's. I thought in fiction you had to make up new names. Now I'm really scared. I didn't think you could do this in a novel. Does it mean that everything I read actually happened? How did you know what she was thinking? How could you write about things you don't know? I don't understand.

What is the truth? That's what I want to know. Who is supposed to tell me the truth? Everybody lies. Everybody is afraid of what happens when you tell the truth. It's strange too, because adults always ask you to trust them. Trust them to do what? is what I want to know. I can trust them to mess up my life. I'm nineteen and I feel like I don't know anything. I always want to know what people don't tell me. I used to ask my teachers about the years that weren't on the history charts. I mean, like what happened to people on an average day. On a day when there wasn't a war or a volcano eruption or something. Do you know what I mean? What is the truth?

Everything happens inside me. I watch other people open their mouths and say things. They just say things. I might have wanted to say the same thing. But I hardly ever talk. I'm one of those silent faces sitting in the back of the room. People thought I was stupid. I know they did.

But, in a strange kind of way, I never got down on myself. I think I wrote poetry to prove that I had stuff to say. Sometimes I would forget that you wanted to be a writer. Occasionally I'd be in my room, trying to write my feelings down, and it would hit me that you might be somewhere doing the same thing.

I had this teacher in the tenth grade that really scared me. His name was Mr. Saunders. He was always bugging me to speak up in class and all that stuff. He was one of those weird white guys. Tall, thin, big glasses that were always sliding down his nose. He tried to act like he was in the know, but he was very lame. Yeah, everyone called him "Spastic Saunders" because he was always bumping his knee on the desk. He was the perfect nerd. Just what you'd expect an English teacher to look like.

Now I should tell you, because you don't know this, I was not a good student. I know you probably imagined that I was smart and all, and maybe I am, but I never tried to show it. In fact, I tried my best to hide it. Why? I don't know. I really don't. My parents—yeah, they are my parents, both of them—would get on my case but I would just stare at them. And later, in my room, I'd find myself crying because I couldn't figure out why I never tried in school. Even when I wanted to. Homework was a big problem. I hardly ever did it. They tried everything: punishment, beatings, everything. But, like, it was my thing to figure out ways to keep from doing what people wanted me to do. Still, I wrote those stupid poems that I thought were so good. And I read. That was the one thing I know you gave me. The books. Can you remember the first book you gave me to read. Can you? It was *The Hobbit*. I still have it. I still read it from time to time.

Anyway, one day, just to shut him up, I gave Mr. Saunders some of my poems to read. He had told me that he was interested in what was going on in my head. He knew I read a lot and I think he thought I was smarter than I acted. And, in a way, he was the first person to pay any special attention to me. Usually when teachers saw I wasn't going to do my homework, they left me alone. Most teachers didn't want the hassle.

God, it took him three or four days to read them. I couldn't believe how upset I got waiting. Then, at the end of class one day he asked me to stay a little later. When I walked up to his desk I could feel my legs shaking. I remember how he smiled at me. At first it was like he was seeing me for the first time. And then he handed the folder to me. When I opened it, all I could see were red marks and notes. Capitalize this, misspelled words circled, punctuation problems. I felt the tears seconds before they rolled up in my eyes. That smile hadn't meant what I first thought. When I looked up at him it was clear to me that it was pity, he felt sorry for me.

I left him sitting there like that. I cut his class so much I think he eventually forgot about me. Got a D in that one. But the grade wasn't the thing. Mr. Saunders took something away from me. Aside from Ka, I had almost no friends. But until that day, I really did believe in myself. He took that and I hated him for it. I hated him and I hated you for making me depend so much on him or anyone, for what you were supposed to give me.

Still, the way you write about meeting Mom is nice. It sounds like love at first sight. Aunt Geri is something else. It's good to know that you loved my mother. That's something.

Mom doesn't even know about this book. I've got a feeling she's not going to like it. But I'm not going to tell her about it until I've finished.

What are you trying to say with this Mates thing? I think it's very cynical to think that every time two people fall in love there will always be someone who messes it up. Just because that happened to you doesn't mean it's true for everybody. Don't get me wrong, I'm cynical too. But it seems to me that the whole idea of it is rotten. People are always looking for someone to take care of them.

Two

As the morning opened its eyes and peeked into the West Oak Lane house, it found Ben and Helen curled up on the floor in a corner against the wall. The music had long since evaporated, as had most of the people. Geri was on the couch with one of the two men who had come there each assuming she was his girlfriend. Her other suitor had quietly left an hour earlier when it became apparent that he had miscalculated his importance.

Helen and Ben sat silent, watching the blur of moving hands as Geri and her chosen lover clutched and kissed and discovered the regions beneath the surface. She moaned loudly as he, eyes closed, moved like a surgeon.

"Do you think they're going to come up for air?" Helen whispered into Ben's ear. He barely heard her words. He felt the heat of her breath. He was already riveted with excitement. He was swimming in his quiet, unprofessed emotion. He wanted her. And if that wasn't possible, he would take what he could get. If tonight all he could do was be close to her, to sit next to her, to watch her red dress grow brighter and more wrinkled in the waxing sunlight, he would accept that.

Helen smiled at him. She didn't feel quiet. She wanted to talk, to laugh, to hold on to the exploding fire of the night as long as she could. She didn't want to know what the day would bring her. She didn't want to know what plans Ben had for that Saturday. She would have loved to stop time. To prevent Saturday from ever arriving.

"I've got a mind to go over there and give that girl a chance to get some air. They need a station break or something."

Ben smiled. "Helen, if I were you I'd leave them alone. In fact, I don't see anything wrong with what they're doing. In fact"—he reached over and cupped her brown cheek in his hand and turned her face toward him—"I think, if we were doing what we should be doing, you wouldn't know so much about what they're doing."

Helen stared into his eyes. "And what should we be doing?"

He placed his lips on hers. They exchanged the inside air, the taste of each other. His tongue explored, lapped at her.

Helen's breath flowed hot into him. She felt herself letting go. Felt herself giving in to the feeling. At nineteen she had never given herself to anyone. She was suddenly overwhelmed by her own body.

She abruptly pulled away.

"No, Ben. Not like this. Not here."

Ben recaptured himself. For a moment he had sailed out into the deep. "I can't believe the way I feel right now. I just can't believe it." Of course he wanted to make love to her. What else was there to do at this moment? He couldn't think, there wasn't much more he could say. There wasn't much else he knew except to try to pass through her defenses.

"I know. I think I feel the same way. But . . ."

"But what?"

"I'm not like that." She looked over at Geri, who was now naked from the waist. The dark-skinned man on the couch with her was bent over, his mouth kissing and sucking her breasts.

"Is there somewhere we can go?" Maybe if they could be alone, maybe Helen would see that there was nothing else left between them.

"For what?" Helen was nervous. She knew what he wanted.

"I want to make love to you." What else could he say? Even

though he was comfortable with words, he didn't want to explain how bottomless he felt. How vulnerable, how small he felt in her arms. Like a little boy.

"I don't know. Why? Why do you want to make love to me?"

"Because . . ." Ben had begun the sentence without knowing what he would say. He knew what he wanted to say. He wanted to say that his body was telling him that they should make love. That if Geri and her friend could, they could too. Neither reason sounded strong enough actually to say. So he stopped and said nothing. He hoped her question would dissipate like morning fog.

"I'm a virgin." Helen pulled back six more inches to see his face in the early-morning light. She could still smell the paper plates strewn about with remnants of a spicy potato salad and fried chicken.

"So?" What difference could that make?

"Well, I just want you to know I don't know anything about sex and stuff like that."

"But Helen, the way I feel about you . . . Right now, after only knowing you for four hours . . . I know I want you. I want to touch you, to kiss you all over. Show you what love is." His words were traveling faster than his mind. That is what happened when he got confused. He wanted to know just the right thing to say. He wanted to do whatever he could to show her that this newly discovered desire was genuine and overpowering.

"I know what love is, I just haven't made it, that's all. I know what love is." Helen watched his eyes. They were still dancing. Like two black fires they glowed. His brown face, just a shade darker than her own, looked good as it pressed close.

This was like a harmonic convergence. Two people who were in exactly the same place at the same time, looking for the same thing.

"Until you make love, you *can't* know what it is. You have to feel the sweat and the energy running through you."

"I just met you. It's happening really fast, you know."

Ben felt her pulling away. "I know it's fast but that's what love is. That's the way it happens. You have to pay close attention to it when it's happening or it just goes away."

Ben looked over at Geri and her boyfriend. They were now

throwing light from the couch. They were dancing on each other's bodies. He was sitting up and she was straddling him. Ben could see her coffee-colored back glistening in sweat as she moved. The outline of her breasts was barely visible on the sides as she rhythmically rose and fell.

"That's what love is." He nodded in their direction.

"That's not love, Ben. I'm not that stupid. She really loves Jesse, the guy who left."

"Then why isn't Jesse here making love to her?"

"Because he couldn't take the pressure. He didn't want to find out who she wanted the most. He was afraid it wasn't him. So he left."

"But that's no reason to fuck the other guy."

"I know that. You know that. But Geri doesn't. She's just having fun. She could give a shit about Ralph. He was just here. That's all it is."

Ben sighed, accepted his defeat. "Damn. That's deep."

"So don't tell me about love. Sometimes what you think is love ain't it at all. I'm not stupid, you know. Sometimes it's just somebody fucking with you. Trying to see what they can get." Still, Helen was weakening. She wanted to feel him around her. He was bright, poetic, romantic. Not many of the men she had met seemed as soft as him. She had never known her father, who had been killed when she was a child, but her mother had filled her head with stories of his gentleness. So she knew there were black men with soft, careful, tender touches. But she had never met one, until now.

"But I'm not like that." Ben wanted to tell her about his future, his dreams. His flight away from the inner city. His determination to go to college. His desire to tell the stories of black people. Yes he wanted to make love to her. But he wanted her to know that he was different from the other men she'd met.

"Do you love me?"

Ben was stunned by the question. He had felt the answer in his throat all night. He had almost uttered those words earlier but stopped because he couldn't believe it himself.

"I . . . ah . . . I . . ." Helen smiled at him. "Well, maybe I do.

Maybe I'm falling in love with you right now." He knew that he was lonely. That there was something missing and that her smile and the warmth of her body filled up the empty space.

Helen looked into his dirt-brown eyes. "Maybe you are, Ben. I hope you are, because I'm falling in love with you." She paused. "But I'm not Geri."

Ben looked again at the couple on the couch. Geri was moving frenetically now and moaning loudly. Wiggling beneath her, Ralph added his voice to the sounds. They obviously didn't care that they had an audience.

Helen reached over and turned Ben's face back toward her. "I'm not Geri and I have to know that you love me before I'll be that way with you."

Ben felt a wave of emotion sweeping through him. He reached out and pulled Helen close. Into her ear, he whispered, "I love you. I know I do. If it takes a while for you to see that, I understand. I don't want you to be Geri. I want you to be Helen. That's what I want." As he finished, a scream erupted from across the room. They both looked over as Geri leaned backwards, her Afro now reduced to black flames. Her mouth upside down locked in grimace.

"One day, maybe I'll be that for you, Ben," Helen said as fatigue claimed her. She put her head on Ben's shoulder and closed her eyes.

But she could not sleep. Almost as soon as she felt his skin she pressed her lips to his neck and nibbled it. Her mind was a flurry. But it cleared as she imagined her mother seeing her cradled in a man's arms. Helen stiffened just a little. Her mother had tried her best to keep this moment from happening. When Helen was eight years old, her mother gave her the lion's share of the responsibility for the care of her sisters. Helen was already a surrogate mother.

Now, finally free of her mother's list of chores and responsibilities, she knew what she wanted: her own family. Sometimes Helen couldn't tell how much of that dream came from the feeling that her mother, a housekeeper by trade, had neglected her. But it was an understandable neglect. Her mother worked nights and days. Which left Helen in charge of the house. During Helen's childhood, her mother was preoccupied with making enough money to support the family.

Still, Helen really did love children. When she thought about a career she imagined herself as the director of her own day-care center. And she couldn't help but feel excited about the idea of being someone's wife. Of having her own family. Being with a man who cared about himself. Who had a real passion for life. Not just another hurt and confused black man, but a man on the move.

In a night of bluelight dancing and red-lipped kissing they fell into the cauldron of mutual need. Her body was so soft, provided so much strength. Helen spoke rivers of silence about family. Ben needed it.

Finally, nearly limp from exhaustion and the perpetual excitement, Helen suggested that they go upstairs to the guest bedroom where she was to sleep. Ben, his eyes heavy, tried to smile but couldn't.

Across from them, Geri and her boyfriend had fallen into a post-Valentine sleep. They drooled on each other. Ben could see a white trail in the corner of Geri's mouth as they seemed like two dead people.

He and Helen climbed the long stairway to the second floor. Once inside the dark bedroom, they found themselves standing over the bed, holding hands and looking out at the early-morning winter sun.

"Do you want me to stay?" Ben fidgeted. He wanted to sleep, to make love, to move past this point.

Helen looked into his tired eyes. For the first time in her life she contemplated going against her own rules. She had promised her mother and herself to be careful. But she also knew it was inevitable. She had to open herself to someone. She couldn't stay within the confines of her own body. All of her friends had children. Most of them were married. She couldn't keep turning everyone away. And Ben felt good to her.

Still, this wasn't the way she had envisioned it. If anyone had asked her how she would meet her dream man she would have said without hesitation that he would find her in church. They would be standing next to each other at choir practice or paired together in a sack race at the annual church picnic. Not at a party. Not high.

"Do you want to stay?" She stared out the window.

"Come on, Helen. You know I want to be with you. But I don't want to mess things up. I want to stay if you want me to."

Helen was so tired she felt her body breaking apart, as if it wouldn't wait for her to give approval for rest. She heard herself say, "Well, Ben, I don't think anything's going to happen tonight."

"Then suppose I stay. Suppose I just get into that bed and lie beside you and hold you tight for a little while." He smiled into her ear. "You know, I would love to write a poem for you. That's what I'm going to do. I have to get this down. Tomorrow, just for you." He pointed his finger at her. "I can feel you."

"How do you know what I'm feeling?"

"That's what a poet does, Helen. I just know. I want to be able to write about all the things I feel. They act like a black man doesn't have feelings. But I do. So I just know how you feel. I know that you have something that I need."

Helen smiled and turned her head away from him as she slid, fully dressed, into the bed. Ben got in and put his arm around her. "One of the best things about my parents, Helen, is that they always told me that I could do anything I wanted to. They always told me that I was going to be great one day. But you know what?" Ben paused; he started speaking again before her tired mind could respond. "One of the things they never prepared me for was being by myself. I don't like it."

Helen heard him but didn't answer. She was tired. She pulled him closer and slipped into the euphoria of developing love. Neither of them spoke another word.

Makeba's Journal

I don't know if I can read this. I didn't know this part. I mean, I know what
happened, but Mom never told me about how you two met. If this is the
truth I guess I don't understand. Why were you attracted to her? You knew
you wanted to be a writer. I don't blame her. You must have seemed really
cool at the time. She was a country girl. I know she was pretty, she still is.
Is that what it was? Was she so pretty to you that night that you just fell in
love with her? I don't think it was a good idea in the first place. I met my
first boyfriend at a party too. But I'm not stupid, I'm not letting no man
mess up my life. I've learned the hard way.

If it was up to Mom, I'd be just like her, a little country girl in bows
and dresses and shit like that. That's why she and my stepfather still live
out in the boondocks. They think living out there will keep me out of the
world. Not me. I can't live like that. They want me to be some little
"thing" with a dress on. But I'm determined to break out. I don't feel like I
have a choice. I'm trying my best to be my own person. It's hard though. I
always hear Mom's voice in the background. Evaluating me.

So, little by little, I'm trying to show her that I am my own woman. I
appreciate who she is. I really do. God, think about what would have happened to me if she wasn't who she was. Obviously you weren't ready for
it. You obviously had more important things to do. Don't you see, that's
the hardest part: accepting that you had something more important to do
than be my father.

Anyway, I'm going to try not to just rag on you. I could probably fill
this entire book up with stuff like that. What I'm trying to say is: I know I'm
confused. I know I don't know much about a lot of things. But I do know

that I want to be Makeba, whoever that is. And Makeba is not going to wear miniskirts and low-cut dresses and high heels. And she is not going to spend hours in the mirror trying to get right for some "catch." That is not me. I'll never dress for men again. This is one young black woman who ain't going for it anymore.

People think I'm out of it, but I don't care. That's just where I'm at. I've had it with the dating game. I don't know where that's going to take me but I'll figure it out as I go. I know one thing though, when you look at all the so-called couples around, you have to wonder. Nobody's happy. Nobody stays together. It's all bullshit.

There was a time when Mom and I did everything together. It was right after we moved back from North Carolina. She was very weak then and Nana had stayed down South. I remember coming back to Philly in October. It felt really weird. Everything seemed so dark and dirty. But Mom tried to put on a strong front. She would wake me up in the mornings and drag me all over town. We went to lunch together, to museums and movies. At least once every day for about a month she would grab me by the shoulders and say, "How are you doing, kiddo?" I never knew what to say except, "Fine." I wasn't fine. Neither was she. But what else could I say? I knew what she was asking me. And I knew why. She wanted me to have hope. She wanted me to believe that things were fine. I knew that she needed that from me.

Believe it or not, for at least a year she really thought you were coming back. That we were going to be a family again. There was this one time not long after we got back to Philly and we were staying at Aunt Geri's house, when we were having dinner and she asked me did I miss you. I said yes. And she said she missed you too and that we just had to hold on. That you were probably gonna come to your senses soon. We were eating meatballs and spaghetti and she just sat there for the longest time with a meatball on her fork, holding it up in the air.

"Aren't you going to eat?" I asked her. And then I saw the tears. They were streaming out of her eyes, dropping in her plate. "Don't worry," I said. "Daddy will be back." I told her that and I reached over and wiped her eyes. She was so sad. I remember it like it happened yesterday. "Daddy will be back."

She told me that she knew that but that she got tired of having faith in other people. That was when she told me that I was the only one she knew would never leave her. It was her and I. I guess I never felt that bad about it because I was so worried about her. She was all I had.

Where were you then? I couldn't believe that you were still alive. That you could know we were somewhere and you wouldn't come back.

Three

In the days that followed, Ben could think of nothing but Helen. He was either at Geri's, where Helen had extended her visit, or he was on the telephone talking to her. For the first time since he had left the Navy, he was not interested in his studies. He was not hustling at his job driving a cab. And he couldn't write. What he first thought was inspiration had turned into paralysis. He never wrote the poem for Helen. It was present in his head, and he spoke the words to her, but he never put it on paper. He was too preoccupied with being in love to do anything else.

All of the emotion that Ben felt about Helen was now focused on sex. Somehow sex had become the most important thing. Ben knew better. But he couldn't help it. A budding love has to grow. And to Ben, the blossom of love was sex. He had cajoled, begged and, once, even cried in an attempt to get her to open herself to him. But she always changed the subject. Helen had decided on the night she met him that she would sleep with Ben. But she would pick the time. She knew what would happen to her. She knew she would be caught in a vortex of stored-up energy and emotions that would be hard to disentangle herself from. She had been waiting for this love. She was ready to dance but she wanted to call the tune.

So instead of her body, she fed him food. Every time Ben came over, Helen's table revealed the success of her tutelage under her mother. They ate and kissed and hugged and pushed each other to the brink of restraint.

And then, finally, three weeks from the night they met, she called him. That alone was surprising because she never dialed his number. Helen's mother had taught her never to call a man. But she did.

"What are you planning to do tonight, Ben?"

Ben laughed. "What do I do every night, Helen? I come over there or we talk on the telephone all night."

"I love our conversations." There was a breathless quality in her voice.

"Me too."

"Well, Ben, when you come over here tonight, what are we gonna do?"

Ben laughed again, but this time it was a nervous laugh. He couldn't tell what she was getting at. "I don't know, Helen. Maybe what we always do. I beg you and you act like you don't know what I'm talking about."

"Maybe I haven't said much, but I know what you've been talking about. And tonight I don't want to hear it. I want you to show me."

Ben sucked in all the air around him. He teetered. The telephone was delicate in his hand. He tried not to act excited. He didn't want to scare her. "Well, fine. I'll be there at ten. Maybe nine-thirty. Soon as I get off work." He hung up the phone quickly.

And then, within hours, he became a splash of color inside her. And once there, he painted his name on all the walls, in corners, on the floors, everywhere inside her that there was a clean space, he put his name.

They professed undying. They gathered themselves and their spirits and danced a skin-to-skin, heart-to-heart dance. Smokey Robinson flowered the air with "More Love" and they gave in to each other.

Helen felt herself holding him so tight. Her fingers seemed to plunge past his skin into some region that was without flesh. Her fingers played with the air in his limbs. She dug as deep as she could. She pulled as hard as she could. She wanted to mark him.

After all, he was in a place that no man had ever visited. He had to be invited there. He had to immerse himself in her. And he had to bear the mark of his adventure. She would have it no other way.

And Ben was lost in the overwhelming cascade of hope and strength he felt in her. He tried to hold back, to be the center of power, to move her. But her energy was too strong. He could only accept the feeling of being lost in someone. Of swimming in a pool without walls. Of needing that someone desperately.

And he did. There was no floor beneath his feet. No walls. Nothing to hold on to but her. No other foundation than her sounds.

He felt her hand on the small of his back, instinctively pulling him deeper into her. He felt her long fingernails piercing his skin, plowing it like a field of rich black dirt.

He felt her thighs against him. The soft wetness that held them. He whispered pictures into her ear. And she heard him. And Smokey creened, "More love. More love."

Makeba's Journal

THIRD ENTRY

The first time I had sex I was drunk. I was young, too young to be drinking, too young to be with this guy. I barely remember the details. You probably don't want to hear them anyway. But I remember that the next day I was so sad. Mom kept asking me what was wrong. I couldn't tell her. But you know Mom, she came right out and asked me if I was still a virgin. I tried to lie to her. I knew she would freak. But she just kept on me until I told her. I realized as soon as I told her, I had *wanted* to tell her all the time.

She jumped all over me. She made me tell her who the boy was and everything. And then she called him and told him he had better never see me again. I was totally embarrassed. I mean, I knew she was right, but . . .

Anyway, I guess the hardest thing was how I felt. I was sad for a long time. Mom said it was because fifteen wasn't old enough to deal with sex. She said that if you didn't love the person sex could make you feel lonely. And that I was too young to know how to love somebody. It made sense to me but it didn't make me feel better. If you feel sadness because you're alone and sadness after you make love to someone, then where is joy? I don't understand that.

But guess what? It's to the point that I like it. I'm comfortable when I'm sad. I'm feeling sad now. I knew I would.

Four

As Mates watched Ben and Helen make love he knew there would be trouble. He pitied people who fell in love. They made love with the hope that the intensity of their feelings would forever enfold them. But he knew, and he suspected they knew, that everything changes. Still, his purpose was not to pass judgment, only to haunt the guilty one.

And it didn't matter to Mates whether the person was black and American and suffered from the ravages of slavery. It didn't matter that there was this urgent need for an entire race to seek unity and healing in the cliché of the strong family. And yet, Mates knew, the need for family did not make it any easier.

In the throes of love Ben made many promises to Helen. With his mouth, with his hands, with his entire body he pledged himself to her. He fell fully. His four lonely years in the Navy and the years since had rendered him powerless to the desire of love. He remembered, as he kissed Helen's soft brown skin, what it felt like to be out at sea, the ship rolling through the valleys of the Atlantic, with no one back home missing him.

The thing about being away, especially in the armed forces, is how quickly you realize how much you need someone waiting for you. Someone standing on the pier as your ship comes in.

Ben had returned from three Mediterranean cruises and one in the Caribbean to a pier full of strangers waving flags and blowing kisses. He had always wanted someone there waiting for him. And Helen felt like that person. She was the one who should have been there for him. She felt like home.

When he looked at her sleeping he saw his future. Ben had been energized by the political energies of the sixties. He had flirted with the fervor of the black revolution. Now, as a developing writer, he was an invisible Young Turk in the blossoming Black Arts Movement. Even though he had not published a single poem, he was reading everything he could get his hands on. And suddenly, there was so much work by African American writers available: Baraka, Madhubuti, Sanchez, Reed, Evans, Troupe, Toure, Webster and countless others. Fire and righteous thunder from the modern-day *niggerati*. Suddenly, being a writer seemed possible.

Buried in the rhetoric, the strident pronouncements of black power and black chauvinism, was the notion of family. That the real power of the African American community was in the love found between black men and women, the children they brought into the world and the community they lived in. There was a way in which the struggle for unity and healing was screwed into the cliché of the strong family.

And when Ben looked at Helen his stomach quivered from the realization that he had met someone who could give him everything he didn't have: love, companionship and the promise of significance.

We hardly ever examine the way promises are made. The way we commit ourselves. As if each promise is equal. There are times when our lives are turned by moments of confusion, when the thrill of commitment is reached in a veritable dust storm of feelings. The truth is that judgment is displaced by drugs or alcohol, by fear, by loneliness just at the moment when we must promise someone something. And these promises exist with the same weight as any other, regardless of whether they were made drunk or in the palpable need to be held.

Many men suffer through this dance with life. They promise. They leave. They try to act like they don't hurt. But they do. If you are a child of a missing father, you already know this. Then again, maybe you don't.

Makeba's Journal

FOURTH ENTRY

Reading this almost makes me silent. So many things are flashing in my head that it's hard to keep writing. Maybe it wasn't a good idea. You have your own pain. This story is about you. About your feelings. None of us have had a chance to speak. Not me or Mom or you. I never knew this stuff. I never realized how much you must have loved her. I mean it's a goddamned love story.

I don't have one of those yet. Now that I'm older I *can* have sex if I want to. And sometimes I do. But I don't think I'm going to have a love story happen to me. People like me don't have love stories. I have no patience. I have never met a man worth believing. Nana says the same thing. She's the one who's got it in for men. She hates them. But I think you know that. I don't know what happened but you did something to her that made her really hate you. We can't even talk about you with her in the room. She just goes off.

I knew the day Mom came home and told me that she had met this guy that everything was going to change again. We had moved out to the suburbs by then but we still spent a lot of time together. She was helping me with school and everything. But suddenly she was always going out. She would take me back into Philly on Fridays and pick me up Sunday night. I was staying at Aunt Geri's all the time. And then, when Nana came back to New Jersey I spent a lot of time there too. His name is Dwight Stones.

In one year I lost you and in a way, I lost her too. I could tell the moment he came into our house that it was no longer just her and I. She waited on him hand and foot. Now I think Mom thought that it was her fault you left. Something she did or probably didn't know which drove you away. And she wasn't going to let that happen again. You have to remember she didn't have anything. We had nothing. We were getting government assistance. The telephone was always getting cut off. I know she always talked about starting a day-care center but she didn't act like she was going to do anything. So she needed him, or somebody, to help take care of me and her.

But when he came over he was the most important. And he was so different than you. It was like he just sat back and accepted all that attention from her. I guess he was thinking, if you didn't want it, he'd take it. And all I could do was watch.

At first I was never in their plans. It was like they forgot I was around sometimes. One night after he came over they left to get some pizza. I was supposed to be asleep, but I heard them leave. I was terrified. I just lay there in the dark waiting. I know I probably wondered why I was so alone. I was always thinking that. Then they came back and ate. They ate the whole pizza. I could hear them in the living room, laughing and eating. It was like Mom had suddenly just stopped being sad. And then I didn't hear anything for a long time and I got scared again. So I quietly got out of bed and walked to the stairway. I slowly went down the steps until I could see them on the couch. He was on top of her. I could see his long, narrow back full of sweat. I didn't realize what I was doing but I just kept walking toward them. I was like a spirit or something. Before I knew it I was standing right over them. I heard him breathing and saying "uh . . . uh . . . uh . . . uh." I don't know what came over me but I just starting hitting him. My hands were fists and I was pounding on his back. For a second he didn't know what was going on. But then he turned around. I'll never forget his eyes. They were shining like a cat's. It was like I woke up from a dream right then. I turned and ran back up the stairs, into my room and under the covers.

Mom came up and sat on the side of the bed. She explained all that love stuff. That "we're adult" stuff. She didn't want me to be upset. She wanted me to like Dwight. He was thinking about moving in. She was thinking about it too. She asked me to also think about it. That was when I began practicing silence. I didn't say a thing. I think I went to sleep.

Five

Ben was with Helen every moment he could break free from his studies and his job driving a yellow cab. Helen had stayed at Geri's, taking a spare bedroom in the three-bedroom house. She was in no hurry to go back to her mother's house in Woodbury, New Jersey, where she had grown up. She had found a job working at the telephone company and Geri had welcomed her like a little sister, encouraging her to explore her new-found freedom.

But Helen limited her exploration to Ben. With the whole world to traverse, she was happy, blissfully happy, working in Philadelphia and living in Geri's house, waiting for Ben to come to her.

She and Ben had quickly settled into a routine. Helen was home from work every afternoon by four-thirty and Ben would often meet her at the front door. He was fresh from the university, bursting with creative energy, talkative and fiery. They would eat and frequently make love after. Later he would leave to drive the night shift. At about one-thirty in the morning, he would return and they would lie in her bed and watch the moonshadows and the creases of golden light that were present in Geri's house.

And then one day everything changed. Helen was pregnant.

"Girl," Geri nearly screamed, "I know you ain't gone and got yourself pregnant already. You was just a virgin a month ago. I told you you had to do something 'bout that."

Helen had just returned from the doctor. She was churning with confused energy. She was pregnant. Her first sensation was intense joy and then she thought about Ben. She wasn't sure how he would take it.

"I know," Helen said meekly.

"Then how come you're pregnant? Ain't nobody ever told you nothing about birth control?"

"I know about birth control, I just didn't think I was gonna get pregnant so quick." Helen felt dumb.

"What do you think happens when a man sticks his dick in you? Huh? Babies, Helen. That's what happens, babies. And you can't tell me you didn't know that."

Helen looked away. "I know that, Geri. I know that. But I never made love with nobody else. I just never put it all together."

"Didn't Lena teach you about sex and babies?" Geri stared at the side of Helen's head, which Helen held perfectly still. "You mean your mother hasn't told you about all this?"

"You know my mother. She acts like she's afraid to talk about it. The only thing she always said to me was, 'Keep your legs closed.' That was the main thing. 'You just keep those long legs of yours closed and you won't have no men problems.'" That was why she hadn't gone back home. Helen knew that when her mother looked into her eyes, the image of Ben lying between her legs, sweating and moaning, would reflect out.

Geri stared at her, then burst into a muffled laugh. "That's probably why you got two sisters that Lena don't know what to do with. I swear, I can't believe it." She paused again. "So you two never used nothing?"

Helen shook her head.

"And what about Ben? What the hell has he been saying? Seems like to me he should know better. It ain't all your fault. The only problem is you're the one stuck with the baby, not him."

Helen was silent. Geri made her feel simple, like the country girl she was. Why hadn't she thought more about birth control? Why hadn't he?

Geri gathered her coat and scarf and headed for the door. "Anyway, I think you better tell him fast and decide exactly what y'all gonna do. This ain't no joke, girl. I knew ya'll was up there burning up the sheets but I had no idea y'all was two fools. Anyway, you can always take care of it."

"What do you mean?"

"You know what I mean. Don't look at me with those dumb eyes. You could get an abortion."

Helen's face froze. It seemed to take the air out of her body. The image of her mother loomed in front of her.

"My mother would die. She would put a curse or something on me and then she'd just die. I can't do that, Geri."

Geri shook her head, silently put her coat on and left.

Their conversation played over and over in Helen's head as she waited for Ben. She raced from euphoria to anger to panic. When she heard Ben at the front door, her heart ran ahead.

Ben was tired. There was a hint of blue under his eyes. His Tootsie Roll face was dull, its vibrancy drained by the long schedule of lovemaking, studying and driving the taxi. He collapsed next to Helen on the sky-blue couch.

"You look tired."

"Wiped out, baby. I'm totally wiped out. And I've got to get up early tomorrow to study for a sociology test."

Helen put her hand on the soft outline of his short Afro. Her fingertips played on the edges. "I guess this isn't the best time to tell you."

Ben couldn't tell whether it was a question or a statement. "Tell me what?"

"Ben, you have to promise me that you won't hate me."

"Hate you?" Ben immediately went with the feeling. Had she already met someone else? Was it ending before it actually began? He felt his breath leave and not return. His body hardened and grew a protective moss. "What's going on, Helen?"

"You know I love you very much, don't you?"

"Just tell me, Helen." Ben was suddenly very afraid. His fatigue forgotten, he wanted to get up from the couch and head back into the night air. In the short span of their time together he had discovered safety. A place so strong, so completely sheltering that he could be safe there. It was inside Helen. Not sexually inside her. Not in the juice of her life that flowed between her legs. But in her heart. In the cavity where life is pure, and cloistered.

Helen knew how to make him feel quiet. She knew how to provide the night moments all day long. That time when you know nothing is searching for you. Nothing wants you. Where there is no fear. She knew how to give that to him without saying anything and without him having to articulate the need for it. In fact, he had never known that he needed it. This quietness, this peace, was so unknown to him that he would never have thought to ask for it.

And in those moments when he was mindless, within Helen's environment, he could discern the beauty of silence. He could actually know peace, even in the swell of anxiety that accompanied the growing brutality of the Philadelphia police. He could overlook the confused looks of his younger classmates who knew somehow that they would graduate and go on to dominate his life. When he was with Helen those feelings dissipated like the image of O. J. Simpson running for a touchdown.

He looked at her, her fear crackling like sparks between them, mingling with his fear and the long awkward pause to create a volatile, combustible energy. Suddenly he realized he didn't want to face a life without her. Without that protection. He didn't want to think about Helen leaving him.

Helen stared at him. "I don't think I can tell you, Ben." She quickly averted her eyes downward.

In an uncontrolled moment of terror, Ben's body began to prepare for trauma. He felt his stomach lurch. Water collected just below the lids of his eyes. "Helen, I can't take it. Will you please tell me. Is it another man?"

Helen was swimming in her own sense of dread when she heard the question. It snapped her to attention. She put her face close to his. "Ben, I don't think I'll ever want another man, ever."

Ben breathed. He sat forward. "Then, what is this all about?"

"I'm pregnant. I'm going to have our baby."

Ben grew wings. He slid through a narrow opening in the doorway that led into the basement. He fluttered down the stairway and circled the dark, stone-walled room. There were old paint-flecked bicycles and rusted garden tools and tan cardboard boxes all around. The musk nearly choked him. But there was no opening; the cellar windows, narrow and rectangular, abutted the ceiling and were sealed with cardboard to block out the weather.

There was no way out.

And then he found himself drawn into the light. He moved closer and closer, mindless and given up to air. He closed his eyes and passed into the fullness of Helen's lips.

Helen opened her mouth to speak and Ben found himself staring into the eyes of a woman who offered him life. He pulled her close.

"I'm going to be a father?" He put joy into his voice because he knew he had to. He felt her fear and he knew that this was a big moment. He couldn't believe that he hadn't thought about it. Of course, he and Helen had already talked about the possibility of marriage, and she had made it clear that she wanted children. And yes, he had agreed that when he got married, he wanted children. But he hadn't *really* thought about it.

Already Ben began to recognize a pattern in himself. He wanted to ask her whether she really thought this was the right time to have a child. He wanted to talk about the responsibilities that having a child would place on both of them. He wanted to say that he wasn't sure this was the right time for him to become a father. He knew that he should have thought about this earlier. This was his fault. He knew that Helen would be very disappointed if he expressed the slightest hesitation. And he knew enough about her already to know that she wouldn't really consider having an abortion.

And he loved her. Her growing dedication to him was over-powering. No one had ever completely succumbed to his presence before. He was usually drawn to women who held their nurturing urges at arm's length. Women who were more interested in their own careers, their own dreams, not his. But Helen seemed to be saying

47

that his aspirations, his dreams, his life could be hers. That she would be the force in his life which ensured his success, and that that role would make her happy.

So he took a deep breath and injected all the joy he could find into his speaking voice. "We're having a baby. A baby." He said it over and over into her ear. Each time with a different inflection. Each time discovering more happiness, more anticipation. Until it sounded exciting. Until he was swelled big with the energy of impending fatherhood.

Helen was now crying and laughing at the same time. She was spent, relieved. She buried her head in his chest and sobbed directly into his heart. And his heart heard. He held her tightly and looked at the ceiling. His arms were not wings and there would be no flight from here. Instead the chant "We're having a baby" continued to flow in his head. And he felt the moving chest of this warm woman in his arms and he wanted to make her happy.

He was a proud man. He could come through for her. He would show her that a black man could stand up and be responsible. For the first time in his life he thought about morality. This was what the shouting was about. How could a man create a life and then not be there? But this was exactly what was going on. There were men who could boldly tell television reporters that they liked to have children by different women. That it was a badge of masculinity.

Not Ben. He would do the right thing.

Later that morning, just as the sun came up, Ben asked Helen to marry him. She quietly said yes. She kissed him and held him tightly. A sense of relief cascaded through her body. And in the next instant a picture of her mother, Lena Brown, flashed in her head. They would have to go through Lena before there were any ceremonies or any birthings. Helen stiffened.

"Ben, you've got to meet my mother. We've got to go see her."

He felt the tension in her voice. "I never said I didn't want to meet your mother. In fact, I think it's about time."

Helen got up from the bed and walked to the window. "My mother is a little weird. She's . . . ah . . . well, she's just different, that's all."

"Is she going to want to kill me?"

"She's going to want to skin you alive." Helen laughed. "On the outside she can be pretty tough, but inside she's a sweetheart, really."

"Well, that's good to know. Because I don't want to have to fight with your mother."

Helen slowly turned around to face the bed where Ben lay, bathed in the first dusting of sunlight. "She's kind of religious," Helen said meekly.

"How religious are we talking, Helen? Southern Baptist?" Helen was silent. "Pentecostal? Voodoo? Apostolic? Santeria? Holiness? What are we talking about here?"

"She sort of mixes up a bunch of different religions. She believes in a lot of things."

Ben was uneasy. "Well, does she believe in God?"

"In a way. I guess. In Lena Brown's world God is everywhere. She used to be a righteous Christian but somewhere along the line she fell out of it."

"It doesn't matter, I'll be very nice to your mother." Ben smiled. He was not the type who had problems with the mothers of his girl-friends. They were almost always impressed with him. He knew how to present just the right image: sensitive, intelligent, serious.

"I'm not joking. Don't play around with my mother. Be straight with her. Because if she thinks you're making fun of her it could get very ugly. She's my mother and I love her to death, but I swear she's a very unusual woman. Sometimes I think she really has some kind of power or something." Helen crawled back into the bed as she talked.

Ben was suddenly very curious about Helen's mother. "You can't stop there. What kind of power are you talking about?"

"Not now, Ben—I don't want to go into it now." Helen closed her eyes. "I'll tell you later, maybe after you meet her. Just telling you what I've already told you makes me nervous. I want you to like her."

The next day Ben took off from school and work and Helen stayed home from the telephone company so they could drive to Woodbury to see her mother.

As they turned off the freeway and headed toward the street of Helen's mother's house, Ben was keenly aware of the landscape. The dense standing structures of the city had completely given way to the brown scruffiness of the Jersey country. The trees stood bare. The ground showed its scuff marks. But it was different from the shadowy gray of the inner city.

They surprised Helen's mother, who was sitting at the dining room table cutting coupons. Lena Brown was thin and short, two shades darker than Helen's coffee complexion. She sat in a chair at her dining room table in the tight two-bedroom A-frame house. The room, like the house, was thick with the clutter of pictures and bric-a-brac. Ben thought the house smelled like peanuts and uncooked fish mixed together. He was immediately uncomfortable as they walked through the small living room. He noticed the painted porcelain figurines posed all around them. Doilies of petrified snowflakes lay under them and every other standing inanimate object that crowded the room. The exact same large gold-painted Crucifixion cross, with Jesus attached, bowed and bleeding, appeared on the three walls surrounding the large table.

Lena looked up at them. She looked first at Ben. Then she quickly turned her eyes to Helen. She smiled. "I got a coupon here for Van de Kamp's. You want it? Fifteen cents off."

"No thanks, Mom." Helen pursed her lips with a smirk and bent down to meet Lena's cheek. "Hello, Mother. How are you? It's good to see you too. Oh my, what a surprise. It's so nice of you to drop by," she teased.

Lena kept her smile. "Don't be foolin' with me, girl. You know I'm glad to see you. I just looked at you standing there skinny and all and I thought you'd be needing this here coupon for some food or something."

"No, Mom, I eat fine. Geri always has a full refrigerator. Everything's fine."

"That's good, Helen. That's good. I want my little girl to be fine."

Helen looked back at Ben, who kept shifting his weight as he stood in one spot. "This is Ben, Mom. I brought him with me so you could meet him."

Instead of looking up at Ben, Lena looked back at her stack of torn-out newspaper pages with blocks of coupons on them. Ben and

Helen now stood side by side and waited for her mother to say something. But the small woman took her time. She fished through the sheets of paper. Finally, she said, "I kind of figured you wanted me to meet him. Otherwise there'd be no reason to drag him all the way down here."

Helen stared at her. "Well?" Ben instinctively grabbed Helen's arm, hoping she'd take the sting out of her voice.

"Well what?" Lena looked up at her daughter. Helen took in a breath. Ben felt his body tense. Lena stared directly into Helen's eyes when she said, "So you want to marry my baby?"

Ben heard her, saw her lips move, but because Lena was looking at Helen he missed his cue. Finally, Helen looked at him. "Ben?"

"Huh, ah yes? Yes." He grabbed Helen and pulled her close. Suddenly he realized what Lena was waiting for. "Yes, Mrs. Brown, I love her."

Lena still stared at Helen. "You want to marry him?"

Helen smiled. Her mother was stubborn and whatever process she was intent on would be exactly the way it would go. Lena could "work" on somebody until they came undone.

Lena had a habit of talking a subject into the ground. If Helen forgot, for example, to wash the dishes on a given night, or to make sure one of the other children did, Lena would wake her up early the next morning, fussing. And she'd fuss all day long and into the night. Even as Helen stood at the sink washing the second night's dishes, Lena would still be talking about how lazy and forgetful Helen was. Maybe the next day, Lena would suddenly grab Helen's hand and say, "You're a fine girl, Helen."

Helen wondered what Ben felt as they sat down side by side at the table. He stared at her with a blank face. She knew he had no idea what to expect from Lena. But even Helen, who had lived with Lena all of her nineteen years, couldn't predict the way her mother might act.

And now, looking across the table, she realized from the iron-cast features that Lena would play it to the fullest.

"You know I do, Mom. We wouldn't have driven all the way down here if I didn't want to marry him."

"Why? What makes you think you love this boy?" Lena, still ignoring Ben, looked at her daughter.

"Because, Mom, Ben is one of the nicest men I've ever met. He's smart. And I love him. I just know it. That's enough."

"You think that's enough?" Lena still showed her emotionless face.

"Yes, I do."

Lena turned to Ben. "This is my baby girl. You understand that?"

Ben stared into her stone-brown eyes. "Yes, Mrs. Brown, I understand."

Ben felt her right up in his face. Even though she was across the table he felt the heat from her body. He felt his hand being grabbed. The touch was warm and thin. He could feel the hint of strength on the surface and the frailness just below. But the grip was solid. He couldn't let go. Suddenly he couldn't see or feel Helen's presence. The room seemed filled by a silver-gray haze. With his free hand he rubbed across his eyes.

"We must pray." Ben recognized the sharp voice as Lena's. "Dear Mother, you know my body is your vessel. And this girl, who knows my insides, wants to give herself to this man."

Ben felt fingernails scratching the back of his hand. He wanted to look down and see what held him but he was frozen.

"This man. You know who this man is, don't you? You know where's he's been and what he's made of. You know everything about him. But I don't know nothing about him. Only that he wants my baby. And he has come here to get my approval. How can I approve of this man taking my daughter? What woman would give her girl to a man from nowhere? Especially when you know what's in store for her. But I know that if I try to stop her she will go on and do what she wants to anyway. Yes, I know she'll just do what she *thinks* she wants to do. So I can't stop her.

"But you can put the mark on him. You can put the fear in him that will let him know that just because he's a man don't mean he's holy. It don't mean he can treat my daughter any which way. It don't mean nothing except he's got something hanging out of his stomach.

"I want to you scare this boy out of my house. Make his hair turn white or even fall out. Make him wish like hell he'd never met Helen or come here to see me. Give him to somebody else, Lord. I don't need him. Neither does my girl.

"But if you won't do that, if he ain't gone in two shakes, running up the road toward Philly after I'm done, then I'll accept your will. I got to. You are what makes me happy. Living in your light."

The hand let go, the room cleared and Ben instantly turned his face to Helen's. He wanted to see if she'd seen or heard what he had. But Helen was staring at her mother. When Ben looked at Lena he realized that she was talking. Her voice seemed to grow in the air as if someone was controlling the volume.

"It's a struggle, Helen. You know that," Lena was saying. "Staying together nowadays is a real test."

"I know, Mom," Helen said. "But I really feel like we can do it. Don't you, Ben?"

Ben nodded. He tried to remember what he had heard. The exact words. But he couldn't. The message was clear though. Now he wanted to get up and leave. He didn't feel right. The thought of a lungful of fresh air seemed good to him.

"Helen." Ben leaned into Helen's ear. "Can we leave? I need to get out of here."

Helen continued talking as if he hadn't said anything. She turned to Ben and tried to tell him with her eyes that she wasn't ready to leave. If they got up from the table now, her mother would have every right to be angry. She wanted Ben to read her eyes and relax. Based on the range of responses her mother was capable of, she felt everything had gone rather well.

"Ben's going to college and working full-time. He's a very talented writer, you know. And I've got a new job. I just feel like we're going to make it."

Ben couldn't sit still. He slid the chair out and stood up. Lena put her eyes on him. Helen kept talking. But Lena watched Ben, who was now walking around the room. He picked up a small white porcelain unicorn. It was the newest of the figurines in the room.

"We're going to have the best family. I just know it."

Ben started walking toward the door. He couldn't listen to any more. The whole thing suddenly seemed ridiculous. He was sweating profusely. He wanted to get out. He reached for the front door.

"Ben," Helen shouted. "Mom's got a sweet potato pie. We are not leaving until I eat me a piece of this pie. And I know you want one, so get your butt back in here and find some plates in the kitchen."

Lena's eyes had followed him all the way to the door. Now she looked at him straight on. They were frozen together. No words passed. Helen was up at the breakfront slicing the pie.

"Ben, if you don't get in here and get us some plates I'm going to get mad at you and you know you don't want that."

Lena still stared at him. His body wanted to leave. But he couldn't leave without Helen, he didn't want to do that. He looked at her, immersed in the cutting of the pie. Then back to Lena, the trace of a smile gracing her lips. He felt suddenly light-headed, the tension crumbled. He exhaled a strong shallow breath. "For a minute there I thought I left my keys in the car. But now I see they're on the table. Did you say sweet potato pie? You know those are magic words. Ain't no telling what I'd do for a piece of homemade sweet potato pie." He grinned. Lena winked at him. There was a glint in the crease of her eyes.

"So, Ben, Helen. I guess you might as well tell me now about my new grandchild." The pie knife fell out of Helen's hands and hit the wide-slatted wooden floor, sweet potato pie splattered. Ben walked by Lena and into the brown kitchen as if he hadn't heard her.

But he had. As he gathered three small plates for the pie he tried to quell the disturbance that clanged inside him. How did she know that Helen was pregnant? Why hadn't Helen heard what he had? What was he in for? He thought about his classmates at school and what they would have thought about Lena. Not many Ivy League students would have to deal with a mother-in-law who had "powers."

Ben and Helen were married in May, three months after they met. Makeba was already deep in Helen's womb. It had been a whirlwind. A relationship of cascading waves. Like sugar and water, they had instantly become a confection.

Makeba's Journal

FIFTH ENTRY

I hated this chapter. It explains so much. I feel like that hesitation that you felt is in my blood. Somehow you gave that to me. It's a part of how I am. Tentative, nervous, certain that I am wrong.

You should have spoken up. Maybe I was a mistake. Maybe you could have stopped it. You didn't have to be so proud. You could have just said, I don't want to have a child right now. Maybe she would have done something. At least she would have known how you felt. Don't you see? I can never make a direct, decisive move. I always feel like I'm making a mistake. It comes from you. It makes everything so much clearer. I know you loved me, but every child should be wished for. That's what I think. Not discovered.

Good old Nana. She knew what was going on. I believe that part. She tried to help. I bet she scared you good.

Six

Mates was nearly rolling over with laughter. Ben should have gotten the hell out of there. Lena was trying to warn him. She tried to tell him that there was something, something hidden in the airborne particles that fluttered around him, just beyond his eyesight, that was watching him. That something was Mates.

Mates was amused by the arrogance of people. They think that the worst can't happen to them. They always walk into his open jaws.

What was it people sought in marriage? What were they looking for? Mates knew that the creation of family satisfied some raw emptiness in their lives. Marriage was the way they were taught to make family. It was the cornerstone of faith. It was the frame around the picture. Still, it seemed, if they were aware of how difficult it was for two people to live together, wouldn't you expect that there would be many fewer marriages?

There could still be family without marriage. There could still be that fulfillment of the human drive to keep themselves going. They could still make babies.

Ben had been terrifically shaken by his visit to Lena's. When they were in the car he asked Helen if she had heard a voice while they were in the house. She shook her head. But Ben couldn't let it go. "Are you sure you didn't hear your mother say anything weird or anything?"

"What are you talking about? I think my mother handled it all very well."

Ben focused his eyes straight ahead. "And you didn't hear her get into that prayer thing or about God or somebody scaring me out of her house or anything like that?"

"Ben, this isn't funny."

"I'm not laughing. When we sat down at the table I heard her start this long prayer about how you were her little girl and how could she give you to me and all this shit." Ben paused. "You mean you didn't hear any of that?"

Helen didn't say anything. She wanted to say he was crazy or hallucinating, but she could tell by his voice that it would be a mistake to do so. Instead she thought about the odd things she had experienced growing up with Lena. But more than anything it was the way other people had treated them. Everyone was fearful of Lena. Helen had heard rumors of hexes and curses that Lena had put on people, but she had never heard her mother utter one unpleasant thing about anyone.

She *had* seen her mother heal a blind woman once. The woman, about sixty, dark-skinned with graying hair, had been brought to Lena by her daughter. Helen had watched as the younger woman gave Lena two hundred dollars. After she had taken the money Lena realized that Helen was standing in the kitchen doorway watching. She shooed Helen upstairs, but Helen had crept halfway down the steps to see. Lena sat in candlelight with the woman in front of her. Helen couldn't hear what Lena was saying but she did see her put her hand over the woman's eyes. The woman instantly fainted.

While she was unconscious, Lena had wrapped a bandage around her eyes. When the woman regained consciousness, Lena then whispered some instructions, gave the daughter a small bundle and ushered them out of the door.

Two weeks later the two women came back screaming with joy and praise. They swore that it was Lena, not the doctors, who had brought the woman's sight back. Lena just smiled and said how happy she was that she could help "in any small way."

"Look, I know my mother is different but she's not bad or anything. I didn't hear her say anything like that. I'm sorry. Maybe I was cutting the pie or something. I just didn't hear her."

"She scared the shit out of me. I almost lost it in there."

"Well, it's over now. We've got her blessing."

"I don't know. I'm still pretty shook up." Ben couldn't lose the feeling that something was wrong. It wasn't supposed to be that way. At the moment a person knows they are in love there shouldn't be a feeling of foreboding. And that was what Lena was. Foreboding.

The next day they visited his parents, Margaret and Benjamin Crestfield, Sr. Margaret was a social worker for the Health Department and Benjamin was the foreman for a construction company. They had long since left the tightness of the inner city and moved to the outer reaches of Mount Airy.

Sitting together on the mauve sectional couch in their sunken living room, both Benjamin and Margaret smiled approvingly at Helen. They were smitten by the way she acted as if she already knew them. They could sense her desire to make Ben happy. And they liked that.

Benjamin was the first to speak after Ben had announced the marriage. "To tell you the truth, honey, I'm pretty damned happy. I thought this boy of mine was never gonna do a damn thing with his life. Least I can tell he's got good taste."

"You ought to hush, Benny." Margaret poked her husband in the side. "Don't mind him. If you two think you can make it, we're right behind you."

After they were married, Ben threw himself into their new dream: the family. They lived in a cavernous Victorian house on the 4500 block of Sage Street in University City. By August he sat at the dining room table fanning a stack of bills to ward off the heat as he struggled with numbers on a pad of paper. There were two thoughts crowding his mind at the same time. He still had not been able to write. He was barely keeping up in school. And in his African American Poetry class he was actually falling behind. He didn't understand what the problem was. Since he had decided to become a writer he had never experienced a silence like this.

He began to think that whoever said writers had to be unhappy to create might have been right. He was happy. He enjoyed getting into bed with Helen. He enjoyed knowing she would be home when he got back from school or work. Her smile was larger now than it was when he met her. And that smile was so sweet, so joyful that it was hard to feel anything but happiness. Still, when his mind turned to writing, no stories, no pictures were there. And there was one other thing which he had slowly begun to realize. Helen didn't know how important writing was to him and didn't know how to stimulate him in that way. He counted this as a minor thing, something that would change or that he would learn to accept. He knew she loved him. And that love, expressed by her as "an unqualified love," was more powerful than anything he'd ever experienced.

But the other thought that fought for his mind's attention was their growing economic crisis. They were broke. He tried to still the uneasiness, the stress of not having enough money, but it wasn't easy. He told himself that if they could just hang on until he graduated, everything would work out fine. Luckily he had a job and his tuition was covered under the G.I. Bill, so the basics were taken care of. It was the unexpected bills that were wearing them down. His car had sucked up a lot of the money lately and Helen had taken to buying things he hadn't known she was going to buy. He wasn't angry, just nervous, worried that they would collapse before he was able to properly provide.

Still, he wanted to let her know that they were living dangerously. He looked at the list of bills. There was another mysterious payment.

"Hey Helen." He heard her upstairs cleaning the bathroom. It was Saturday morning and time for cleaning. He imagined her up there, on her knees, creating white clouds of Comet as she scattered the cleanser over everything. Then she followed it with a wet football-shaped scrub brush and a strong circular motion, spraying water about like fireworks. The only thing she'd leave behind was a thin white film of cleanser residue.

Ben heard her drop the brush into the bucket that sat beside her.

It was already hot. The late-morning August sun caressed the white enamel windowsill and threw the remaining brilliance throughout the small bathroom. Already she had cleaned the kitchen and the bedroom.

Kneeling in the bathroom, Helen watched the water settle into the yellow plastic bucket. She felt her daughter shift positions in her stomach. Yes, she loved the act of cleaning but not in the way that Ben thought. In a way, he seemed to be almost ridiculing her when he teased her about her methodical and painstaking effort. As if to take care, to make something glisten, was somehow wrong. It seemed at times that Ben could be moved by a lecture in behavioral psychology to criticize her for being anal or insecure.

But cleaning her house was one of the things in her life that she loved. She loved its transporting energy. It almost always took her back in time. She couldn't help but think of her mother, probably in her room with the door closed reading or sleeping. Her sisters in the yard playing. Gospel music on the radio. The smell of ammonia, soap and sweat. The swinging light of a high sun. Those were peaceful, tranquil times. She loved the feeling of being solid, persevering— always able to change the reality of poverty with a shine and a smile.

Since she was a little girl, she'd been preoccupied with family. Perhaps it was because hers was so porous, so incomplete. She'd never really known her father, a construction worker who died at work one day when she was three. Her mother rarely talked about him and had never brought another man home.

Helen had grown up in a house of women. And although she was always conscious, especially at school, that she didn't have a father, life at home had always been decent. It was true that her mother did very little in the house. Helen cooked, cleaned and tended to her sisters. But in a way, it was smooth. Normal. What was joy anyway? Where could it be found outside the walls of her home? They all played together, including her mother. They ate together. Danced together. And no man ever crossed their threshold except to share a meal or fix the toilet.

Yes, there was public assistance, and food stamps and times when the electric or the telephone was disconnected. There were those times. But mostly it was a life of labored joy. There was no wild-eyed euphoria but neither was there abject sadness.

Still, Helen had always felt trapped. She'd been only a fair student in school. Had no patience whatsoever with what she considered mental masturbation. What she wanted was real, not theoretical. What meant something to her *happened*. Anybody could talk about *things*. Her mother had taught her well: Talk meant nothing. It's about what you do.

And now she was married. She was who she had wanted to be. A mother-to-be. A wife. Of course, Ben wasn't the kind of man she had expected. His weaknesses were many, but she liked his sense of humor. His passion. And, God forbid, in spite of her mother's admonitions, she liked his words.

She had heard Ben call her name, but decided to finish wiping the sink. After she was done, she walked to the top of the stairs. "What do you want?"

Ben looked up at the narrow oak banister with its white, one-inch-square spokes ascending alongside the stairs. "What're you doing?"

"I'm cleaning this house, that's what I'm doing. What kind of a question is that? It wouldn't hurt if you found something for yourself to do."

"I *am* doing something. I'm down here trying to pay these bills. Can you come here a minute?"

"I told you that I was busy. I can't be running all over the place for you."

But even as she said that, Ben heard her begin her descent. He watched her move down the stairway. The yellow flowers in her dress picked up the sunlight and made her fairly glow in contrast with the white wall behind her. Her tall cinnamon body, full with the fresh flush of pregnancy, her bright overlarge smile, her swirling hair, bounced down the steps. He couldn't help but meet her smile with one of his own.

"You been cleaning the bathroom?" Ben knew what she had been doing, but couldn't stop himself.

"No, I been swimming in the pool." She winked and sat down at the table. There were beads of sweat on her temples.

"Well, just knowing that my baby is busy trying to make this house a home gets me right here." He touched his heart.

"It don't get you in the right place if you ask me." She held his eyes in her soft hands.

"What's that supposed to mean?"

"It means that when a newlywed couple moves into a new house, both the husband and the wife are supposed to work to make it livable and nice." She turned to face the living-room window, looked through it and out onto Sage Street. "You've been sitting here at this table for quite a while now."

Ben couldn't tell whether she was joking or not. "I'm trying to get these bills organized. I can't believe it got this bad this quick. We're already sinking." The plan was that he would finish his education and then she would get hers. They would do whatever they had to to make ends meet. Still, Helen had insisted that she quit her job at the telephone company. During the early days of her pregnancy, Helen was sick nearly every morning and getting to work had proven too difficult. Ben had reluctantly agreed that she should stay home. He loved her. And even though he knew better, sometimes their love felt like enough. A guarantee that everything would turn out good.

"I'm sure you'll figure out what we have to do. That's why you're the one doing the bills. Right?" Again she smiled an ambiguous smile. Being coy was one of Helen's great pleasures. It was a power. She realized how weak Ben was. She understood his insecurities. She met his arrogance with bewilderment. His seriousness with playfulness. She smiled to herself at the wonderful way love accommodates. "Anyway, why did you call me?"

"Well, I just wanted to know what this bill was for." Ben held up a blue sheet of paper.

She didn't even look at it. Instead she turned back to the window. "Which one?"

Ben couldn't help but laugh at her attempt to play him off. This was one of those little moments. One of those barely perceptible little spurts of growing love.

Ben held the bill up and waved it in front of her nose. "This one right here."

But she still wouldn't take it. She wouldn't even look at it. She just stared at him, smiling. She tried to act like she could care less about what he was saying.

"Woman, will you take this piece of paper and read it please? Then would you tell me what you spent twenty-two dollars on?" Ben mustered as much strength as he could. It was a game. They were playing with each other and in the playing was every inflection of love.

She finally took the bill out of his hands but still did not look at it. "I don't remember buying nothing from Kresge's."

"Did you look at it?"

"Well, no. Not yet."

"How did you know it was Kresge's? Will you please just take one little peek at it and tell me if you know what it's for." Ben's smile grew tired on his face.

But Helen held her ground and didn't look. "Oh yes, I think I remember this bill. Twenty-two dollars did you say? Yes. I remember it." She got up from the chair and headed for the stairs.

"Helen?"

She climbed three steps, then stopped and spoke deadpan into the dense air in front of her. "Yes dear?"

Ben could barely make out the tight roundness of her ass underneath the yellow flowers. "What the hell is it for?"

Still standing on the steps, she turned toward him and said in an oblivious, matter-of-fact way, "The wallpaper for the baby's room." She tapped her stomach to punctuate the sentence.

"We could have waited at least another three or four months before we spent money on wallpaper. I don't have time to wallpaper nothing now anyway." Twenty-two dollars was a lot of money. Ben felt a tightness in his head. They couldn't do everything. They couldn't buy it all at once.

Helen held her lightness. She smiled fully, flashing a sugared smile that was like a poisoned dart. It was her smile that thickened Ben's tongue and made him giddy.

"I suppose we could have waited," she said simply.

"Then why didn't *we*?" He tried to ignore her standing smile.

"It was on sale. Is this what you gonna do to me? You gonna constantly be asking me about everything I buy?" But before Ben could respond she added, "Anyway, why wait? The wallpaper was on sale this week. I swear. Why wait another two months when I'll be so pregnant I won't feel like messing with no wallpaper? We can't afford to pass up a good buy when I can find one."

Ben picked up the stack of bills and scattered them across the table. "If you looked at these bills, you'd know we couldn't afford no kind of buy. Good or otherwise. We just have to be careful, that's all. That's all I'm saying."

The smile disappeared. He tried to hide the strain sweeping across his face. Suddenly, at precisely the same time, they were both tired of playing.

"I don't think I did anything wrong." The words rolled like stones from Helen's mouth and at Ben.

She turned around and came back toward him. For a moment Ben was paralyzed. He wasn't sure what she was going to do. But the smile came back. "I'm sorry, sweetheart." She slid herself into his lap. "Are you mad at me?"

Ben could smell the acrid perfume of cleanser on her. It reminded him of many Saturday mornings spent scrubbing the stone steps in the front of his family's house in North Philadelphia. "No, baby, I'm not mad. I can't be mad at you. We just have to be careful, that's all."

"Well, when you're out of college we'll be doing just fine. We won't have to worry about a thing." Helen believed what she was saying. She expected them to be happy. She gently trailed her hand over her softly swollen belly.

"Guess what?" Her voice was now recharged, the twenty-two dollars gone into the distance.

"What?"

"I was thinking about names for the baby today."

The baby was still an abstract idea to him. But Helen felt the growth of life inside her. She journeyed through the physical kaleidoscope of changing shapes. She felt the sweep of emotion, of love, of dedication, of reverence, of revelation. Ben tried to sink into her so he could feel the same things. He tried to understand what was going on.

Men struggle with the concept of childbirth. They are challenged to love and bond in spite of it.

"I know it's gonna be a girl. I just know it. So, I was thinking about Makeba. What do you think about Makeba?"

He liked it. He knew that Miriam Makeba, the South African, was one of her favorite singers. Miriam Makeba could conjure heavy duty. Spirits flew when Makeba sang. "Makeba sounds real good to me."

Helen faced him and moved her full red lips close to his face. "I'm so glad I met you. I think we're gonna make a great team, you and me."

Ben turned into her open hearth. The wallpaper forgotten. The bills still unpaid.

He kissed her softly, reached his hand under the dress and felt her breasts, heavier now than ever before. "When I asked you to marry me, it was because you were just what I had been searching for. We belong together." He kissed her again, allowing his tongue to run into her mouth. He tickled the underside of her tongue.

"Besides, you've got a part of me in there." He poked her lightly at the navel. "Now, who else could be the father of your child? Who else could get that close to you?"

She pecked him on the cheek and got up from his lap. "You know there will never be anyone else. I love you."

Ben took a deep breath as she stood and glanced at the table where the Kresge bill stared back at him. "And don't worry about the bill, sweetheart. I think we can take care of that."

She kept moving toward the stairway without turning around. "I wasn't worried," she said into the stairwell space.

Makeba's Journal

How strange. How completely strange it is to read about me. To read how unsure you were. I don't understand what you mean about men and childbirth. All you have to do is love your child. What's the big deal? You didn't have to tell me about Mom. I could just see her acting like she was a queen or something. You were her knight. She thought you were the man. Yes, I could sure see her thinking she was in seventh heaven. She acted like that with my stepdad sometimes. Not that much though. He's okay—very different from you. I've never seen him *write* anything but checks and money orders.

I have a whole collection of Miriam Makeba's tapes. I'm hoping I can see her perform sometime. For a while I followed everything she did. She's an incredible woman. Her music is a religious experience. My favorite song is "Pata Pata Pata." I don't know why. Maybe it's because she makes me feel so happy, so strong. But you know, whenever I think of you I always end up wondering what happened. What happened? I thought you were coming back.

There were times when we didn't have anything. I mean nothing. We'd eat pork and beans three times a week. I got so sick of pork and beans that I couldn't stand to be in the same room with that sweet cinnamon smell. To this day, it makes me throw up. And whenever there was no money there would be arguments. There were times when I heard Mom and my stepdad fighting and prayed for you to come and rescue us. And when they argued I couldn't help but think that he was always mad because I was there. I was another mouth to feed. I wasn't even his daughter.

What happened? You were supposed to come back for me. You promised.

Seven

Mates knew from the beginning that Ben and Helen would have a tough time. They were trying, but there was something in the air, in the texture of the connection between them, which made him anticipate trouble. He didn't know how long it would take but he knew there would come a time when he would move into physical existence. When he would become the flesh he now began to long for.

Mates wondered how long a relationship that began in the clutch of sweat and music could last. Add the responsibility of a child and you had a problem. Then, of course, there was Lena.

Mates could now hear Ben's thoughts. He knew Ben wanted to write. But the world Ben lived in didn't make a space for that kind of desire. Ben was going in the wrong direction. His loneliness had led him to Helen and now he was fixed on living out an expected role.

But Helen was clear. Her focus was on Makeba and her family. To Mates this tension was like the smell of fresh meat.

During her pregnancy Helen sucked in everything related to new life. She grew plants and tended her flowers in the backyard. She continued her household routine as long as she could and she began to fashion the world of motherhood.

Ben stood back. He tried to be helpful. He watched Helen's stomach grow. He kissed her often and told her how beautiful she was pregnant. And she was. Helen couldn't understand why some women felt ugly when they carried their children within. How could they not understand the changes a body *had* to go through for the sake of the next life. It was a chain to God. A God's life. An internal vision realized.

Her mother had worked too hard. Had shunted Helen off in domestic service to her siblings. But she vowed, from the moment she awoke with a queasy stomach, to dedicate herself to being a real mother. A modern mother.

She felt Ben's hesitation. He stuttered sometimes when talking about the baby. About the lump in her stomach that kicked and cried loud enough for her to hear. At night, when she turned for two, trying to find the place that two could lie comfortably, she had to reach over and grab his hand and place it on her stomach.

"Feel that?" she asked.

"Is it moving?"

"Yes, she's moving, Ben. Right here." And she moved his hand again. "There. Feel her now?"

Ben felt the tremble. The rumble. The small bulge in the pit of her stomach. It was like a small ball rolling slowly. And when he did feel it, it shook him. "That's our baby. That's our baby, isn't it?"

"Yes. That's Makeba."

"I wish you wouldn't make such a big deal about it being a girl. Suppose it isn't? I don't want to have a boy who you thought should have been a girl."

Helen sighed. "First of all, I know it's a girl. I just do. Second of all, even if it is a boy, he will know the only sense of true love he will ever experience, with me."

Ben chuckled. "You think you're going to be the greatest mother that ever lived, don't you?"

Helen shifted her weight. Makeba stirred again. She was comfortable there in the womb, in the position that Helen was now in. She slipped again into anticipation. Helen smiled. "Of course. What do you think? Do you think I'm not going to be the best damn mother a child has ever known?"

"No doubt about it, Helen. No doubt. If ever there was a woman ready to love a child, you are it."

Helen looked at him in the darkness of the room. "And you? What about you? Are you ready to be the best father in the world?"

It was something that Ben had been thinking about. He was anxiety-ridden. He had promised Helen's mother, Helen, his parents, himself, everyone, that he was ready. He could take care of a family. He was ready to be a father.

Everyone expected as much from him. He absorbed the expectations and put them into himself. But in the darkness he shivered. It seemed so big. And Helen's serene confidence rattled him.

"I'm going to try, Helen. I really am."

"Do you love her?"

"Who?"

"Makeba. Do you love her?"

"I'm trying, Helen. I love you. I love what we're doing here. I love being with you and expecting a child. Of course I'll love her." Ben felt frustrated. How could he talk to her? She seemed the blessed one. The loved one. She exuded the knowledge of fullness.

"I love her now. Right now." Helen placed her own hand on Makeba's small back.

"I know you do. I can see that. But you are her. You have her right there inside you." Ben stopped. This was the stuttering conversation that Helen was growing to hate.

"What are you saying?"

"I don't know." He paused. "Sometimes I feel left out. You and the baby have so much together. I don't know how to get in there."

Helen laughed out loud. "You do so know how to get in there."

"I'm not joking. Sometimes I feel so separate."

Helen closed her eyes. "Separate? Well, I guess you are. I'm a mother. This is one of the reasons I'm here. To bring Makeba into this world. And I loved her from the first thought. From the first instant I knew she was there."

The room fell silent. Then, after a long wait, Helen finished her thought. "I feel sorry for you. You will have to learn to love what I have loved from the beginning."

"I will though. I will." Ben felt a sense of desperation. He didn't want her to think he was incapable.

"Oh, you don't have to reassure me. I know you will. We could not conceive a child that you couldn't love. So I'm not worried about that at all. Plus"—she leaned over to kiss him—"you're just about the sweetest man I ever knew and I love you very much. Any daughter of mine will love you too."

Ben slipped into a sleepy reverie with a fresh coat of security. Just before passing into the mists he said again, "I love you."

Makeba's Journal

It seems like you were really weird about her being pregnant. What's the point? Babies come from women. That doesn't mean men have to be separate. But that's the way you felt so I guess that is the point. Are you saying that's why so many black men aren't with their children? I don't think so.

And you don't have to tell me that Mom loved me. I know that. She's always been with me. She's been with me through everything. Even when I made it hard on her. And I did make it hard on her. I blamed her. Still do in a way. That's partly what this journal is all about. I'm trying to figure out what to do with all my feelings about this. But she was there and you were gone. So I blamed her. She told me it wasn't me that made you leave, so I figured it must have been her. Sometimes I just totally acted out. I'd do anything to make her angry. My secret weapon was silence. I'd go days without talking. She'd totally freak out. You know her. The one thing that drives her absolutely buggy is not talking to her. She can't stand it. I'd just sit in my room and read. Sometimes I'd write poetry. I guess that was how I kept my connection to you. I'd write stupid little poems about every little thing. Sooner or later she'd come into my room and try to get me to talk. I'd make her sweat. I knew the thing she feared even more than my silence. Losing me. If I turned against her, she would have died right there on the spot. I held her life in my hands. If she got on me too tough, I'd threaten her with silence and make her wonder if I had stopped loving her. Make her wonder if I wouldn't rather be with you. She was terrified of that. She never said it, I just knew it.

Anyway, when I turned sixteen, I took all the poems, a big stack of paper, out into the woods near our house and made a little fire and burned each one. I just didn't want anyone to see them. They made a pretty, light blue-gray smoke. It was like a ritual. Just me and the fire. But I decided then that I would never use you as a threat to her. I love her unconditionally because that's the way she loved me.

Eight

It was 3:23 on Monday morning, December 15, when Helen shook him roughly. She was ready to go to the hospital.

"Makeba's coming today," was all she said as she went down the steps.

In the waiting room Ben found a seat in the corner. In 1975 men still paced the room. There was the gratuitous path worn into the carpet. Men still followed the pattern of their fathers and found consolation in the isolation from the miracle of birth. They smoked cigarettes and read sports magazines.

Ben was in a room with five other men. None of them talked. They smoked and walked. Smoked and read. Drank coffee. Had no idea of what was going on down the hall. Didn't see the sweat, hear the grunts, smell the thick floral smell of new birth.

Ben didn't hear Helen's gospel screamshouts of anguish, pain and purpose. He didn't know that she wanted him to see her there. He didn't see Makeba when she was pulled two hours later from her temple. He wasn't there to hold Helen's hand as she prayed silently when she saw the top of her daughter's head.

Even though he didn't smoke, he bought a pack and lit a

cigarette. It fell out of his mouth when a nurse came to take him down a long hallway to see a molasses drop swaddled in a pink blanket.

He lost his breath there. He pressed himself against the glass and felt something deep within him. He waved and kissed at Makeba. She smiled at him. Now, he was a father.

Makeba's Journal

Wow. I was alive. And you were there. When I was the size of a loaf of bread, you held me in your arms. And you kissed me. And you smiled at me.

It was such a short chapter.

I'm sure you know about Kwame. Well, I think that when Mom got pregnant with him everything changed again. I was always the one who had to make adjustments. I was the one who had to figure out how to deal with the way things were. Mom tried to act like she really cared about me. I know she loved me. I mean, nobody could probably have a better mother. I knew she wouldn't abandon me. But I lost something in her when you left. She seemed so desperate. Every problem was a disaster. I was constantly worried that she was just going to have a breakdown. Maybe she did anyway. Now that I'm thinking about it, and with what I know now, I think she did have a nervous breakdown. She would just start crying for no reason. And until she met Dwight she never took that damn housecoat off. And even though we were spending a lot of time together, I remember being more sad than anything. Nothing felt right.

One time we went to a play. I don't even remember what it was but it was supposed to be funny. We sat behind this other black family and the man kept putting his arm around his wife and hugging her. It was so tender. So sweet. After a while I could feel my arm shaking. Then I realized it was Mom, she was trembling. I looked at her and saw her trying to hold back the tears. Some days I really hated you. I couldn't believe how you destroyed her like that. You were everything to her.

Anyway, it wasn't long after Mom and Dwight were seeing each other, maybe seven or eight months, that they took me out to dinner. We went to that restaurant we used to go to on Chestnut Street in University City. You know, the one with the prime ribs. I can't remember the name. But anyway, we got all dressed up. Dwight is really skinny. He's tall but almost like a stick. And he's bald too. So I remember thinking he looked like an undertaker in his black suit that night. He can be really stern too. Rigid. But that night he was smiling and laughing. And he called me Buttons. I could see why Mom liked him. He was serious about family stuff. He couldn't understand how any man could leave his children.

He told me that he loved Mom and that they wanted to get married as soon as they could. I remember staring at Mom, wondering what in the world was going on in her head. What was I supposed to say? She had made me promise to keep hoping you'd come back. I went to sleep every night for at least a year praying that you would call or something. So I was stunned. I was too young to understand what was going on. I couldn't know how lonely, how frightened Mom must have been. I could tell, sitting there, that she was really nervous about my response. There was such a pressure on me. I didn't dislike Dwight, but I didn't want another father. I didn't know what I wanted. So I shrugged my shoulders and kept eating. They talked at me all night. When I got home I grabbed Ka and went to sleep.

But what I didn't know was that Mom was already pregnant with Kwame. About two weeks after the dinner, Dwight and I went for a walk. He told me then he wanted me to call him Daddy. He said he was going to be my father and that he'd never leave me or Mom. And then, when we got back home, Mom came up to my room and told me she was pregnant. I was numb. Empty.

Níne

It amused Mates that Ben and Helen were so impressed with Makeba. They thought her life was something special. Something that would solidify their relationship. Actually it added a weight that they had to shoulder. The delicate equation of love, marriage and family would be too much for them. How did he know? He listened to the way Ben thought. Ben was already fighting himself.

Still, Mates also knew there was a light that shone on a facet of life that could only be seen by those who had created children. It was a brilliant light, pointed always to tomorrow and the journey of growth. Parents saw the subtle tightening of bone. The slow movement of hair. They were sometimes frightened by the brightness. Sometimes suffocated by it.

The decision to have a child should be cause for serious thought and consideration. But it often isn't. More likely the fact of pregnancy is present before the parents have fully contemplated their lives, as it was for Ben and Helen. People meet, they fuck and then, suddenly, they must learn to love the idea of parenthood.

Ben was scared. With Makeba's birth, he was suddenly aware of what he had helped to create. He was now responsible for another person's life. And he was committed to becoming a writer. Both were intense and uphill. One had to do with real life, the other with an imagined one.

Ben was open to obsession. It had become apparent as he delved into black literature. He read voraciously, trying to catch up on the continuum of African American literature. He read Zora Neale Hurston's *Their Eyes Were Watching God* and lost himself to the sweet smell of Florida and cane fields. He felt the thick drape of accents and the southern struggle for survival. It was Zora and then Alice Walker in her collection of short stories *In Love and Trouble* that revealed the truth: Black writers could write stories about black people for black people. This is what he wanted to do. He wanted to explore the details of black life in the same way that white writers could for white people. He loved the way D. H. Lawrence, for example, could get under the skin of sensuality and reveal the complexity of feelings while at the same time providing a critique of the life-changing Industrial Revolution.

From the abstractions of Ted Joans to the earthy truths spoken by Amiri Baraka, Ben absorbed everything. And because he was in school, his elective reading was always forced into the context of Western culture. Shakespeare and Hansberry, Frost and Hughes, Faulkner and Wright—everything ran together.

This was one obsession. The other was fatherhood.

The *idea* of being a father wasn't what frightened him. He had become used to that. He was actually excited about that. The problem was more connected to the *reality* of being a father. The expectations that he provide, teach, be present, be "in" the world for his child were etched in his mind. He wasn't sure he could do it. And the more he learned about the lives of the writers he admired, the more he wondered whether it was possible to be a good father and a writer. His life, if lived true as a writer, would be a struggle itself.

His loneliness had led him to Helen and now he was fixed, in a way, set in a place. The same magic which swooned him now defined him. And when Makeba was born, though his obsessions were a part of the air, there was a joy, like strong hands, holding him up in the rarefied atmosphere of parenthood. He and Helen would sit in the hospital room and just stare at the little girl that was them. Suddenly, for Ben, there was little thought of anything but his daughter and Helen.

Makeba's Journal

NINTH ENTRY

I'm trying to hold on to the belief that I've always had that I wasn't the reason you left us. But it's difficult the way you've written this. It was me that made you afraid. It was me that made you worry. Your two obsessions? Right from the beginning you were pitting Mom and me against writing. And I never even understood what was going on. I don't think Mom did either.

Ten

Mates lived with them. He watched them. He never slept, always observant. He shared with them the joy, though he knew it was only a flash, of their new family. He marveled at the transformations people must make for their children. When a baby is born, the concept of love is defined. No matter the circumstances of the mother and father, the birth of a child grabs everyone by the collar and shakes them. And even the confused can feel, at the witnessing of birth, the sharp clarity of love.

And then new decisions must be made. The people who created the child must decide individually how they will live out their love. People who are not fathers or mothers don't have this demand put upon them. Their lives are not awash in the bittersweet colors of parenthood.

Makeba's birth was the culmination of the euphoria that accompanied the joining of two people. In her, both Ben and Helen could see themselves, and the promised idea of love and marriage became reality.

Helen was only in the hospital for two days. During that time she had many visitors, but Lena never came. Helen had talked to her mother on the telephone, but Lena would not set foot in the hospital.

On a brisk Wednesday morning they brought tiny Makeba home with them to West Philadelphia. When they reached the front step of the house they were surprised to find Lena waiting for them on the porch.

As soon as Ben saw her, his heart stopped. Lena frightened him. At the wedding, Ben had felt her eyes tearing holes in his back as the minister conducted the ceremony.

After the vows were given, Ben remembered turning around to face Lena. He almost walked into her eyes. He wasn't threatened, just admonished. He saw her nod at Helen, who shook stardust every time she moved. Their new house was charged with happiness.

Now Lena sat, clad in a heavy gray coat, in the only chair they had on their porch. It was December and the weather had settled into its winter blanket. Beside her was a large brown paper bag.

"Mom? What in the world are you doing sitting out here in the cold?" Helen said as she gingerly began ascending the stone steps. "And why didn't you come to the hospital?"

"Helen, you know I don't go to hospitals. Don't believe in them."

"But I was there. You could have visited."

"It don't make sense to believe in something if you don't pay attention to it. I swore after your daddy passed I wouldn't ever go into another hospital as long as I lived. Now you just have to forgive me, but that's the way I feel. Anyway, that's why I came out here to meet you. I've just been sitting here waiting to see my granddaughter. I may not be the first visitor but I'm the most important." Lena slowly got up from the chair.

Ben held Makeba like a bag of groceries he was afraid would spill out. He could barely see the steps as he trailed Helen. "Hi, Mrs. Brown."

"How are you, Ben? Is that my granddaughter you got there?"

"Yes ma'am. This is Makeba."

Helen waited at the forest-green front door for Ben, who had the keys. She kissed her mother. For the first time, including the sunny May day when they were married, he saw Lena's teeth flashing. She was obviously very happy.

Helen was barely inside the house before she headed for the

couch. "I am really glad to be home. Bring my little girl over here. Sit down beside me, Grandma." Helen patted the cushion next to her. She watched Lena bring the bag over to the couch with her. "What's in the bag, Mom?"

"Nothing much. Just some things I brought with me."

"For who?" Helen was preoccupied with getting comfortable.

"Don't you worry about it. It's not for you. I didn't know anything when you were born. But now . . ."

"Now what, Mom? What are you talking about?"

"I told you, Helen, you just hand me that little girl. Let me take a good look at my grandbaby."

Lena took off her coat and eased herself into the soft brocade couch. Ben ran back outside to get Helen's bag. By the time he had brought everything inside and taken off his coat, Lena and Helen were both transfixed with Makeba.

He sat in a chair across from them and watched an animated Lena make baby sounds. He felt his heart beating rapidly. He could have dismissed it as the result of running out to the car and back, but he knew better. Helen and now Makeba were the objects of his love. That was what caused the fast-beating heart.

He marveled at Makeba's tiny brown hands, her twinkling eyes, her soft, two-toned feet which were now in the world because he loved her mother. And now, he loved *her*. He imagined a series of poems about them. Odes to mother and daughter. And then he looked at Lena. At this moment there was nothing frightening about her. She almost looked young, playing with Makeba's fingers. Perhaps there would be a grandmother poem too.

Ben sat, quiet, deep in thought, as the afternoon light dimmed the room.

Lena noticed Helen's eyes drooping. "Having a baby is hard work, ain't it?"

"All of a sudden I'm really tired."

Ben jumped up from his chair. "Maybe we should get you upstairs to bed. You could take a short nap."

"Maybe I should."

Lena smiled gently. "Sure you should, Helen. You got a lot of time to be worn out. This here girl is gonna keep you hopping from now on. Now, you go get yourself some rest. I just want to sit here and hold her for a while."

Helen looked at Ben, who shrugged his shoulders. "C'mon, sweetheart. I'll help you upstairs. Then, after your mom leaves I'll bring Makeba up."

Helen turned back to kiss her new daughter. "You're so pretty, so pretty. Mommy's just going to lie down for a little while." Then she kissed her mother and began her ascent up the steps.

With Ben by her side, they walked into the bedroom. "You know, I think your mother's going to be a pretty good grandma."

"Of course she is. I told you. She's really a sweet woman. Now remember, as soon as she leaves, you bring Makeba up, okay?" Ben nodded as Helen lay back on a stack of pillows and closed her eyes.

When Ben came back downstairs, Makeba was asleep in Lena's arms. Lena was humming a soft, unidentifiable song.

Regardless of Helen's assurances or his own attempt to quell his fear of Lena, he didn't like being in the room alone with her. He watched her sitting on the couch rocking gently. He tried to engage her in a conversation, but she responded tersely, as if she didn't want to be interrupted.

Even in his own house Ben didn't feel comfortable. He got up from his chair and headed toward the kitchen. "Would you like some herb tea, Mrs. Brown? I have some peppermint and some chamomile."

Lena didn't lift her head from Makeba, but asked, "Do you have any sassafras?"

"No," Ben called back. Ben's mother was also fond of sassafras tea. It was the tea that black folks from the South drank. His mother thought it could cure anything from a stomachache to asthma.

"Too bad." He heard Lena's voice. "Sassafras would be good right now. But that's okay. You just make whatever you like. I'll try some."

Ben smiled. Perhaps there was hope. He had felt a familiarity in her voice that penetrated the tension between them. Maybe, if he was especially nice to her, they could eventually become friends.

In the living room Lena reached down and opened the bag that sat at her feet. She retrieved from it another brown paper bag. It was smaller, an old, intensely wrinkled lunch bag. As she carefully balanced Makeba in her lap, Lena slowly pulled out three small leather pouches. Both paper bags were now back on the floor.

She opened the first pouch and the room was instantly awash in the strong scent of rose. With her thumb and forefinger she produced a pinch of deep crimson powder. "This, my child, is the rose and pomegranate's powder. A touch on your sweet baby skin will make you beautiful and let you live forever. " Lena placed a powder-caked finger on the bottom of Makeba's tan foot. A dot of redness remained after Lena removed her finger.

The whistle of the boiling water startled Ben, who had been standing at the stove staring into space. He poured the tea and headed toward the living room. But just as he passed across the threshold of the kitchen, he heard Lena's voice. He stopped still.

"And this, sugar, that I put on your eyes is the feather of an owl." Ben tried to say something. He wanted to ask what she was doing. But he couldn't move.

He heard Makeba gurgle, an unfolding shriek bouncing around in her small throat. "And last, Makeba, to protect you, the hair of a dog." Ben was stapled to the maple floors. He heard the rustling of paper as Lena continued talking to Makeba.

"There's just a bunch of stuff I'm going to teach you, girl. You are going to grow up and be the best and strongest. I promise you that. I didn't know nothing when I had your mother. But you don't have to worry."

Ben made his legs work and entered the room. He sat the tea on the coffee table and quickly moved to Makeba, sweeping her out of Lena's hands. "How's my little girl? You're tired, aren't you? Yes." And then, to Lena, he said, "I'm going to take her upstairs now."

"Ben," Lena said softly, "don't worry. I'm not going to hurt her. Or you."

Ben couldn't hold himself back. "What were you doing out here?" Makeba started to whimper.

"I was making sure that this little girl survives all the ugliness she has to face in this world. I want to make sure that she stays beautiful, and happy and safe."

"But that's our job. Helen and me. We can do that." Ben felt a sense of rootless desperation.

"It's bigger than the both of you. You have no idea how hard it is. But don't you worry, Ben. Everything is going to work out fine. I just know it."

Ben forced a weak smile and turned to carry Makeba upstairs. As he started up the stairs, Lena called strongly, "Wait, there's one more thing I have here for my granddaughter." Ben stopped and turned around. He watched as Lena pulled a small stuffed animal from her bag. It was a golden-brown lion. She held it out to Ben. "I want her to have this."

Ben reached out his hand to take it.

"Would you just do me one little favor? Would you let her touch it first?" Ben was weary of Lena. He held Makeba's tiny body out to Lena.

"This is yours, sweetheart," Lena said as she put the lion next to Makeba's skin. "See, his legs move around like this." The lion's legs were fitted to its body in such a way that each leg could rotate in position. Lena demonstrated the way the legs moved. Then she pulled the front legs up over the lion's head, so it looked like it was standing straight up with arms outstretched.

"She must never part with this. It's hers. I got it especially for her. Its name is Ka."

"Whatever you say," Ben said flatly, as he turned and walked up the wooden stairs. As he laid Makeba in her bassinet next to Helen, who was already asleep, he heard Lena gather up her paper bags and coat and leave.

Makeba's Journal

You know, the thing I said about children should be wished for and not discovered is still going around and around in my head. I don't think I'm going to have children. It doesn't make any sense.

Nana told me about what she did when I was a baby (the powder and stuff). I love her very much. You got her right though, she does know magic. I've seen her do it. And I think if it wasn't for her I wouldn't have made it. Lord knows Mom is not the strongest woman in the world.

When we were in North Carolina I can remember laying in bed, listening to her cry, thinking that I would never ever be in that position. Never.

And Nana just made it worse. Every day she would make sure she talked about you. She wouldn't do it in front of me, but I could hear her anyway. She ragged you out. And when she started getting on you Mom would start whimpering, but Nana wouldn't stop, she'd just keep on, all day long, until Mom was bawling like she was a little baby. It went on for weeks. We were staying in North Carolina at one of Nana's sisters.

But Nana still didn't stop. Even on the days when Mom was like stone and nothing seemed to bother her, Nana kept on. She'd say stuff like: You had gone crazy in college. And college kills black men. She said you were probably somewhere acting like you weren't even black anymore. Probably with some other woman. Probably saying the same things to some other woman that you said to Mom. Stuff like that. I mean to tell you, Nana can completely go off on you. One day she even told Mom that you were evil and that she had fallen under your spell.

Anyway, one day Nana said something about you, I don't remember exactly what it was, but it was totally wild. Something like, "Helen, that boy is the real devil walking the streets." Something completely crazy like that and Mom just burst into laughter and said, "Mom, you ought to go on with that stuff. Ain't no man on the face of the earth as bad as you make that Ben out to be. You ought to just hush up." And that was the end of it. Well, nearly the end. Nana's pretty sick right now, but she can still find something bad to say about you.

Eleven

When Lena produced Ka, Mates stopped laughing. Mates wasn't exactly afraid of the toy lion but it worried him. He wasn't sure what Lena was capable of. But the way she was going about spooking Ben made it clear that she wasn't to be taken lightly.

In the days that followed, Ben found his heart thoroughly opened by his love for Makeba. Lena's words thumped in his brain. He too wanted Makeba to be safe. He plunged himself into her child life. He wanted to do everything. He wanted to change her. To feed her. He was aware of how black men were portrayed. He wanted to be a model. His father had done it.

The days passed, just as they did for his father, and he began to learn more and more about himself. He discovered that as long as he was writing, he could be silent about his fears. He never talked to Helen about them. Indeed, as time passed they seemed the perfect family.

Slowly a sigh, a rolling sense of relief enfolded him. He was a father, a husband.

Sometimes as he came home from work, tired and hungry, he faced Helen with a heart full of love and admiration. He could almost hear the music in the background. They could have been on television. Makeba was the daughter of two people who expected success. And she grew that way, loved, even pampered, self-aware and confident.

As a baby Makeba knew Ben's hands and face just as much as Helen's. Helen tended to go to sleep early, leaving Ben up, staring into an open space of the empty page. When Makeba was young, still breaking the night, still with demands for milk, for dryness, it was Ben who materialized over her.

And most of the time he embraced the interruption. He had a hard time writing at home. He spent a lot of time in his den trying, but there was something about the house, the air. He always felt Helen over his shoulder.

At school it was a little different. He was taking a poetry class and there were a lot of in-class assignments. He liked that because it forced him to write and he got immediate feedback. His classmates and the professor loved his sensitivity, his boldness. For some reason nearly all of his poems in class were about sex. They were erotic and often graphic. The first time it happened, the class was stunned and nervous, but they liked it. And he wasn't ready to throw the political stuff at them. So he hid behind sex. Besides, his classmates were much more open to expressions of love than of anger.

At home there was no such inspiration. Most nights he gazed at his typewriter as if it was supposed to talk to him. So he welcomed Makeba's interruptions. And he didn't mind changing and feeding her. Ben's early years as a father were successive waves of revelation, frustration, fatigue and recommitment.

Every day he came home to a growing little girl who met him with youthful anticipation. He could almost hear her as he got off the bus, her soft footsteps caressing the concrete. She came gloriously, running to him, her arms outstretched with one hand clutching her Ka.

Time ran too. He watched Makeba unfurl like a morning glory in a blushing sun. They all felt the special light of a fledging family.

Every night, after dark, deep moving shadows rose up in the old house and became a part of the family. They had names. They had distinct personalities. Like the shadow on the wall that faced the bathroom door or the shadows that lurked in the living room or the upstairs hallway. And given the way her clothes were strewn or the way her toys were positioned, the shadows continuously changed shape. Makeba had a room with shadows of her own. And of course there was Ka, always near her. It was her favorite toy.

They re-created Sage Street. Turned it from a sleepy block of white college professors and post-hippies into a running discussion of African American community.

Six months after Makeba's fourth birthday another African American family, Rita and Scoby Rollins, moved across the street from them. Three months later, Hannibal, a tall, gleaming young man, moved into the upper duplex next door to the Rollinses.

As Makeba got older, Ben spent increasing amounts of time alone with her. He read to her. Told stories. Talked. He would often bundle her up and take off for long drives, leaving Helen smiling in the doorway.

Helen liked the idea that he would spend so much time with Makeba without her. She reveled in the image that Ben tried so hard to create.

When Makeba was five he began to make up stories about the shadows.

"On dark nights when you're tired and you want to sleep good, you just tell the shadows to put you to sleep. They'll take care of you." Ben's voice dropped to a whisper. "And if you wake up in the middle of the night and you've had a bad dream or something, don't worry. The shadows will take care of you. Nothing gets into this room that doesn't love you."

"Not the boogie man neither, huh Daddy?" Makeba asked in total seriousness.

"Not the boogie man or no other kind of man or woman. The only people that can come in here are people who love you."

"And what about Ka, Daddy? He wouldn't let anything bad happen to me either, would he? That's what Nana says."

"That's what she says."

Makeba just smiled. She loved her father and felt completely safe when he was around. She liked the sound of his voice and his laughing eyes. She knew nothing bad about him. She only loved him absolutely.

For a while there was so much laughter in the Crestfield house that Ben accepted his stuttered growth as a writer. Forgot that there was a world outside the world which dominated him. He was home by choice. He was a father by choice.

Within their world there was constant celebration. Every new phrase Makeba learned. Every new food. Every circus, zoo, animated film. Everything new was celebrated. He thought it would go on forever.

Makeba's Journal

This must be the fiction part. I don't know. Maybe you did used to tell me stories. Maybe it was happy. I just don't remember. And I've never heard Mom or Nana talk about anything that was good. All I've heard about are the arguments and confusion and all that. I've actually tried to think of the times when I had fun with you. Because whenever somebody asked me about you I wanted to have something to say. But I never came up with anything. I knew that you liked to write. That was all I knew for sure.

By the way, you have no idea what it's like when one of my friends asks me a question about you. Hardly anybody even knows that my stepdad isn't really my father, but I have told a couple of people. Almost as soon as I tell somebody, I regret it. Because then they want to know stuff that I don't know. Is he nice? Why don't you communicate with him? Where does he live?

Do you know how it makes me feel? Can you imagine?

Anyway, I know there must have been *some* good times because I still love you. But I don't know why. So now that I'm reading this I'm really confused. It's hard for me to remember specific details. I just don't know whether to believe you or not.

Twelve

Lena was proving to be a force in Makeba's life. She did indeed have a connection to a knowledge that neither Helen nor Ben was even aware of. She *was* strong.

Lena had found Makeba's Ka in a toy store and transformed it, using an art known only to her, into the child's twin and protector. Lena knew that the ka was a great ancient power. The ka was better than a shadow because it could actually challenge one's enemies. It was an aggressive guard, able to see what its double was unaware of.

She had learned this from a book which had picture after picture of Egyptian deities with their kas, miniature doubles of themselves, at their heels. And she knew instantly that that was what Makeba needed most. Someone to watch over her. Someone who could see what she couldn't.

Every child could use a ka. Parents have to make money and live out their own lives. Children become the victims. They are the helpless, innocent by-products of life's complexity.

And children need everything. They are brought to this festering world with nothing. They are completely at the mercy of mostly unqualified people who do not yet know much about themselves or their place in the world.

Makeba's Journal

I'm reading this and I'm thinking yeah, that's right. Children do need everything. That's something incredible. You know this and yet . . .

I don't know how to talk about being your daughter. I know we have a history. But I don't know what it is, or how to talk about it. I know we did things together. I know we ate together every day. Went to the park. Visited relatives. I know we went to Rehoboth Beach together, we saw movies and you read to me. I know that we played together a lot. I remember all of that. But those memories feel empty. It's like that's all I can do— remember them. I don't feel very much about them. Maybe I once did. But to tell you the truth, this is what I really think happened. I think that I couldn't stand to think about you. That I couldn't stand feeling the way I felt when I thought about you. Do you understand? So I understand the idea that you are my father. But in reality, I guess I have to say that Dwight is more of a real father than you are. Even though living with him was hard.

If I was already quiet, he made me stop talking completely. I was always afraid of him. He had a terrible temper. Just saying that makes me tremble. Why am I telling you this? I don't know. But I've never told anyone what I'm telling you now. This is why I like to write. Because I can communicate without speaking. And if I decide not to give this journal to you, you'll never know what I'm thinking. That's how I am. It's all inside.

Anyway I don't want to talk about Dwight. But I guess since I started I'll just say that yes, he did beat me. It was probably for talking back to him or saying something I shouldn't have. He only had to do it once or twice for me to see how crazy he really was. I can see his face, contorted in rage, ripping off his belt, coming after me. After that I just kept my mouth shut, or I said what I knew they wanted me to say. For most of my life I have been the perfect daughter. He loves me. I know he does. I love him too. But I also know he loves his son, Kwame, more than me. Ever since Kwame was born, I've known the difference between living with a man who is your father and a man who loves you like his own.

So, I just wanted to say that there is one memory I have of you that makes me smile when I think of it. It is the one memory of you that, I think, makes me think of you as my father. Remember when you took me to see your friend Harold in North Philly? I don't know how old I was, I must have been really young. But I knew my telephone number. That was one of the games we played. Remember? If I said our phone number right, you'd pick me up so that my stomach would be on your head and you'd twirl me around. I used to love that. Anyway, we were at your friend's and he had a little boy—his name was Troy I think—and we went outside to play. I don't know what you were doing. So we were running up and down the street. I remember it was very hot and there were a lot of people on the streets. Then, Troy went in the house and got some money and we went to the store.

We went to this dark little corner store on a street full of people. In the store, Troy was first and after he bought something he went outside. He had given me some money and I was buying a strip of button candy. Then when I walked out of the store, I didn't see him anywhere. I had no idea where I was. I stood there for a long time and then I just started walking, thinking I could find my way. I don't know what I was thinking actually, because I was in a completely unfamiliar place. And there were so many people walking around and all the houses and streets looked the same. After a while I just started running.

Have you ever been lost? I'll never forget that. I was running up and down those streets. Everything around me was like streamers of color. I only remember seeing colors of things passing me by. I know people were probably wondering where this little girl was going, running and crying. And it was getting darker and darker. At some point I started screaming for my mom. I remember screaming "Mommy, Mommy." That was when somebody stopped me and took me into a different store. I just kept saying I was lost. Finally somebody asked me if I knew my telephone number. They called my mother and she called you.

When I saw you come through the doorway of that store I burst into tears. So did you. You scooped me up in your arms and hugged me so hard. I'll never forget that or the look in your eyes. I knew then I was important to you. I knew it that day.

I didn't know you knew so much about Ka. I still have her. Probably always will. That's right, her. Ka is not a man. All lions are not men. She's really the one who convinced me to confront you. She's always liked you. Ka told me that you would never forget. I wasn't sure, but Ka has never lied. When I told Nana that Ka had told me not to forget you, she said that I probably didn't understand what Ka was saying. When it comes to you, Nana even disagrees with her own creations.

I took Ka's advice.

P.S. You'll probably think I'm nuts or something to still believe in Ka.

Thirteen

Children are not miracles. Just little people who give off a blinding, directionless light. It shines into the eyes and asks important questions like, "Will you show me how?" Parents gaze into the light, become enraptured and scream back, "Yes. I will show you."

But the child does not know the better question to ask and the light it throws off confuses. Instead, the newborn breath of life might ask, "*What* will you show me?" It is the "what" of life that sets the course.

And it was the "what" that Ben confronted at college. He was slowly being sucked into a world which filled his head with ideas, information and dreams. Suddenly after six years as a part-time student his professors and fellow students began to recognize his talent.

When Ben was on campus, he lost all contact with Makeba and Helen. He was known as a budding writer. He wore a fatigue jacket, jeans and combat boots as his uniform. He hung around a group of younger black students who were also fascinated with the celebration of culture. They believed that the culture of a people defined its political viability. They believed the battle was over ideas and self-identity. African Americans had to know their history, had to believe in their own beauty before white America could be forced to reckon with them.

Of course, except for the Black Writers Workshop, he was usually one of only two or three blacks in his classes. In those classes, he was considered to be a fiery, sensual, edgy writer. Ben could be depended on to say "fuck" in a poem that *wasn't* a diatribe against the system. His professors weren't always so impressed with his work. In his poetry class he was constantly encouraged to find a form, iambic pentameter for example, to channel his thoughts.

And in the short story class, his professor, Molly Berner, told him, "Mr. Crestfield, I think you have an ability to make us feel, but I can't *see* the places you're writing about. I can't *see* this house. I don't know this neighborhood. I want to *see* it."

"What difference does it make where the action takes place?" Ben knew what she was talking about. He just disagreed.

"Making love is different in Beverly Hills than it is in North Philly."

Ben opened his eyes wide and hardened his jaw. "You must be kidding. Right? You don't believe that bullshit, do you?"

Molly Berner, in her mid-forties, a published novelist who had been teaching for five years, rushed to protect herself. "Are you saying that two people who have all the money they could possibly need, who are having sex, is the same as two people with absolutely nothing who are making love in the ghetto? When they don't know how they're going to eat when they're finished screwing? It's not the same, Ben. Place is everything."

"Place ain't shit. When a man and woman come together it don't matter where they are. What I think is that white people need black writers to describe these squalid situations just to make them happy. It satisfies some weird need to minimize or even exoticize the idea of black love. Shit, of black life in general. It all happens in the goddamn ghetto. Anybody can fuck anybody in the ghetto. That's what you people think."

"I resent that, Ben. That's not what I was saying at all." She wasn't sure where this conversation was going and it worried her.

"What I'm saying is if you can describe the 'squalor,' as you put it, and then show me the beauty in it, then it's more powerful."

"That's bullshit. What about Camus and Sartre? All those existentialist white boys who could do anything they damned well pleased and everybody just accepted it. You can't name me one black existentialist. Why? I'll tell you why, because everybody wants us to tell the same damn story."

Molly didn't know much about black literature and was feeling very uncomfortable. "Okay, okay. I'm just trying to tell you what I think will make you a better writer. You have to follow your own beliefs. You have to discover what works for you."

Ben appreciated her surrender. He wasn't sure how much further he could push his argument. He wasn't even sure he was right. It was just what he felt. He knew there were black existentialists. He had even been influenced by them. And he had correctly guessed that the good professor would know less than him.

That conversation, as well as others with other professors, made it all the more surprising when one of his short stories and five poems were selected for the annual English department literary journal.

When he saw the list and the announcement of the reading in which he was predominantly featured, in the hallway outside the department office, he almost flew home on a wave of images and colors that flowed like jet streams right from his stories.

"Helen, Helen!" He was barely within the house before he was screaming her name.

She and Makeba were in the backyard. Helen was turning the brown soil in anticipation of planting her annual garden and Makeba was playing with Ka in the sandbox by the fence near the alley.

Ben felt the breeze rolling through the house and moved in that direction. It was like magic, the way he could always sense where Helen was. If he came in and she was upstairs, he would instinctively know it. If she was downstairs washing clothes, he would know it. He had internalized her.

Ben passed through the house like the breeze itself, through the kitchen and to the back door, where he stood facing the afternoon sun.

Helen was bent over, her face focused on the earth. Makeba was absorbed in a game with Ka. The toy lion looked just a bit weathered over the years but still smiled on the child. Ben stood there inhaling the image of the two of them for a moment before speaking. When he spoke, he startled both Helen and Makeba.

"Hi there, sweet stuff." And in the same breath he called to Makeba, "How's my African princess?"

Helen jerked her head up at the sound of his voice. She dropped the garden fork. "How long have you been standing there?" Makeba jumped up and ran to him with her arms open.

"Long enough to see a fine woman digging in dirt." He was dying to tell her the news. He had driven home in a fog of surging hopes. He was very excited and yet he felt like he had to control it. He couldn't appear too much so. For some reason he almost felt guilty about his good news.

Helen had steadily gained weight since Makeba's birth. Ben couldn't help but notice the roundness of her stomach which marked the place that Makeba had been.

Helen smiled and demurred. "What's wrong with you?"

"What do you mean?" Ben grinned as he released Makeba.

"Anytime you start talking like that I know something is going on. Most of the time you walk around here with a frown on your face."

"C'mon, that's not true. Anyway, there *is* something. I've got incredible news."

"What, Daddy?" Makeba looked up at him. Ben looked into her eyes. He felt the late April sun on his face. He felt Helen's presence just on the edge of his field of vision. He took it all in.

"Well, sugar, your father is going to have a whole bunch of his writing in a magazine and then, when it comes out, I'm going to stand up in front of a lot of people and read the poems and the story to them."

"Oh." Makeba's response was quick and flat. Ben let his hand rest on her head. He knew she had no idea how important it was to him.

"Your own work? That's great. That's really terrific. At least now I know you're doing something when you're up late trying to write." Helen stood up and hugged him. "That's fantastic. How? Where?" He felt her arms pull him close. He smelled the sweetness of her perfume diluted by the sun and light glaze of perspiration over her skin.

"Well, it's an English department thing. Really shocked me. I thought they thought my shit was lame. Anyway, most of this stuff I wrote at school. Like I said, they're going to publish it and then there will be a reading." Ben tried to contain his excitement. He didn't feel comfortable screaming or jumping up and down but that was how he felt.

"Wow. I'm really happy for you." He heard her words but there was something buried in the sound of them. Some reservation, a hesitation. Helen stood back; he watched the news sink into her. Slowly a smile, an understanding flicker of a smile flashed. "Am I married to a famous writer? Are you going to be a black Shakespeare or something?"

"More like Langston Hughes." He hated comparisons to white writers. He was constantly fighting his colleagues and instructors in school on the same point. They wanted him to pick a mentor, someone who *they* thought was good. But they had no idea of the influences pulsing inside him. None of his instructors knew about the Black Arts Movement, the young artists in New York and in the South who were defining a new aesthetic.

"Anyway, it's a beginning. My first publication."

"Well, I'm proud of you. This calls for a celebration, doesn't it, Kayba?" Helen grabbed Makeba's hand. "Daddy's going to be a famous man one day."

"For your poems, Daddy?"

"Maybe, sugar. We'll see." Suddenly he felt nervous. Was he going to be famous? Could he be? How could the artistic expression of an African American man penetrate the same culture that enslaved him? How? And how could it ever come to mean as much to them as it did to him? And why did he care?

"You know what?"

"What, Daddy?"

"If you grow up and think that my poems are great, then I'll be happy." That was what mattered. That she would see what his art was. That she would see what art could be.

"Who knows, Ben. Maybe she'll become a writer too." Helen kissed him on the cheek.

Ben felt her lips burn the side of his face. That kiss was an unconscious message. Helen didn't know it but her kiss was a question. "How?" How was he supposed to be a writer? They were barely making it now. How would he ever pull it off?

And yet, the kiss also gave him a sense of security. She would be there. Makeba would be there. Every empty space he had felt when he first met Helen was full. He wasn't sure if it was Helen or Makeba or what was happening with his work in school, but suddenly he wasn't lonely anymore. Maybe he would never feel lonely again.

As they walked into the house Helen asked Ben to show her the work that had been chosen. "You never let me see what you're doing." She watched Makeba run ahead, and up the steps, cradling Ka like a baby.

"That's not true, Helen. I've read you poetry. You know how I write."

"I know that. But that was a long time ago. Most of those poems you had written before I even met you. When you were in the Navy or even before. But you haven't shown me any of your new stuff. I have no idea what you've been doing in school."

"Well . . ." Ben had purposely not shown Helen his work. "I guess I just wasn't sure I was ready to let you see them."

"Why?"

"I don't know. I guess I'm a little worried you won't like them." He knew she wouldn't like them. He knew that once she found out that he was primarily writing about women, about sex, she'd freak out. Particularly since they weren't about her.

Helen turned to face him. "Now I honestly don't understand why you would say that. When have I ever said anything bad about your writing?"

"I didn't say you did. I just said—"

"I know what you said. Now why don't you just go and get some of that stuff so I can see what my baby is going to be famous for."

They were standing in the living room. The sun flowed in the front window, exposing the airborne dust around them. Ben shuffled his feet. He was trying to determine how much he would say. Finally, realizing his silence was going nowhere, he said, "Most of my work is at school. But I do have a couple of poems in my bag." He lied. All of his work was in his schoolbag. He never went anywhere without all of his manuscripts with him. That was one of his idiosyncrasies. He needed his work with him. He couldn't imagine being separated from it.

"Well, get it. I don't understand you, man. Why are you acting so strange?" She watched as Ben fished through his bag.

"Here it is." Ben pulled the two tattered sheets of paper free. He handed them to her.

Helen took the poems and sat down on the couch. She patted the cushion next to her. "Sit down. Now, let me see what you're being so mysterious about." She was about to look at the paper when she looked back at Ben as he sat down. "This is fun. I finally get a chance to see what you're writing now."

Her smile seized as she finished the first poem. She opened her mouth to speak but nothing came out.

"Helen, listen, it's no big thing. I just write what I see."

Helen was trying to gather her thoughts. She knew that the woman who was the subject of the poem couldn't have been her.

"Who is this? It's not me. That's for sure." She tried not to sound frantic, but she felt that way. "Who is this?"

"What difference does that make? She's just someone I saw on campus. A student. No big deal."

"Oh, I see. That's what goes on when you're at school? You spend your time trying to find young girls with hips like 'rock butts' to write poems about?"

"No. That's not it at all. Anyway that's 'like a butte of rock.'

Butte, not butt. But why would I try to explain it to you? I'm a poet and a writer, I should be able to write what I want to. There's nothing going on here."

"I told you once before that I'm not stupid. I know this woman isn't me and I wonder why you had to write a poem about some other woman." Helen looked at the other page. Why was he writing this stuff? She began reading aloud: " 'There is nothing dangerous between her legs/nothing warlike as a penis fully armed/only the promise of peace/the complete understanding of life/and the stream of truth.' What kind of poetry is this? You're always talking about the black man this and the black man that. What's this got to do with being a black man?"

"I don't know. I'm trying to figure that out myself. But right now this is what I'm writing. That's why I haven't been showing them to you. It's hard enough doing the work, that I have to justify it to you. And I knew that if you saw them you wouldn't understand."

Helen had heard enough. "You're damn right I don't understand. Why do you have to write about sex and other women?"

"Because there's something there I'm trying to figure out. There's so much connected to sex that we don't understand. It rules us and yet we don't understand it."

"Yeah, right." Helen dropped the papers on the couch. They fluttered briefly before coming to rest. She stood up. "I know you want to be a writer. And that's okay. If you have to write about women and all this, I'll live with that too, but I don't have to like it." She walked into the kitchen.

"I guess you don't." Ben picked the poems up and put them back into the portfolio. He was confused. He'd known all along how she would react, and yet he was unprepared. How was he supposed to do what he wanted and what Helen wanted him to do at the same time?

He followed her into the kitchen. "Come on, baby, it's not that big a deal. I'm not interested in the women I write about. Except that I have the same feelings all men have. I'm just trying to put it in context. Sometimes I just try to shock people. You know. In a way, what I'm doing has nothing to do with sex."

Helen, now standing at the sink, wheeled around. "I told you, if this is what your writing is all about, fine. I'm not going to stand in your way. Write away. Or write on, I guess I should say. I don't care."

Ben could feel the dirt flying in his face as she dug the trench between them. The next part wouldn't be any easier. "Okay. Okay. Well, will you come with me to the reading?" At this moment, he wasn't sure he wanted her to come. But he knew he was *supposed* to want the woman who loved him to accompany him to one of the most important nights of his life.

Helen turned her back to him. "Do you really want me to?"

Ben sighed. "I wouldn't ask you if I didn't."

"Then I'll go. I don't want you to think that I don't care about what you're doing, because I do. I just want you to be honest with me."

The weight that had been gathering in Ben's body lightened. "I will be honest, Helen. It should be a fun night."

The reading was two weeks later. He had decided to read the beginning two pages of his story and two poems. He practiced every night as the event approached.

On that day, Ben worked a short shift at the cab company and came home with a racing heart. Helen met him at the door.

"Makeba's sick."

His stomach turned instantly sour. "What's wrong?"

"She woke up this morning with a fever and wheezing. I finally had to take her to the doctor's. She's got some kind of flu. She's got to stay in bed. He gave me a prescription."

"Oh no. How's she doing now?" Ben was struck by how fast things changed. He always kissed Makeba before he left for school. He remembered now that she had been sweating in her sleep. When his lips touched her she had started mumbling something about Ka.

"She's sleeping now. I know you really want me to go with you tonight, but I think I should stay here with Makeba."

"But I thought Lena was going to come over."

"She is, Ben, but Jesus, Makeba could be really sick."

"I know, but you've seen a doctor. She's got medicine. Your mother's going to be with her. Everything's going to be fine." In the days leading up to the reading, Ben had gotten accustomed to the idea that Helen was going with him. Now he really wanted her to go. It wasn't that he wanted her on his arm for decoration, he wanted her to see his classmates and friends. And he wanted her to see how they reacted to his work. *They* wouldn't be embarrassed by it. He wanted her to see the world he wanted to be a part of.

He went up to Makeba's room. The shadows were thick there. Makeba was curled up with Ka, in a deep sleep and breathing heavily. He sat down on her bed. He placed his hand on her forehead. "How's my baby? You're going to be just fine, sweetheart. Daddy loves you." He kissed her lips. "Daddy loves you very much."

Helen's shadow joined the others. "I'm worried," she said in a whisper.

Ben was now up and standing beside Helen. They both stood there looking at their daughter, her little chest heaving fitfully. "I know. But I think she's going to be okay. Now, why don't you get dressed. Everything will be fine. Besides, Lena can always get in touch with us if she needs to."

"All right. If you think it's okay."

"I do."

Helen slipped into their bedroom to get ready.

An hour later Ben sat downstairs waiting for Helen. He was dressed in a black cotton cavalry shirt and black Levi's. He planned to wear a black cowboy hat he had bought while he was in the Navy. The perfect costume for a writer's coming out.

He had changed his mind three or four times. One idea was to dress in one of his dashikis and lots of African beads. At the last minute he decided against it because on this night he wanted to make a different impression. He was a renegade, a modern-day cowboy, demanding respect for his work.

Helen wore a blue pants suit. As she came down the steps, Ben couldn't help but feel a little disappointed. He had wanted her to wear something more exciting, more bizarre, something people would remember. But that wouldn't have been Helen. He swallowed and got up from the couch.

"Black? Are you wearing that?" Helen was shocked.

"What's wrong with what I'm wearing?"

"I don't think you look good in that much black. I mean, it's so dark. I think you look better in colors. Are you sure you want to wear black?"

"Yes, I know how I want to look. Now, if you've finished giving me a critique, can we get ready to go? Where's Lena?"

"Don't worry, we won't be late. Mom's on her way."

Lena arrived and assumed residence among the shadows in Makeba's room. Ben and Helen left for the university.

As they walked into the room, Ben felt the tension rise in Helen's body. This was not her territory. The room was full of chairs. The dark mahogany wood which spoke of the years of contemplation. Contemplation about words and life, about good and evil. And in this room were the bright eyes of those struggling to take their time in the same space.

Ben spotted two seats in the second row near the middle of the small wooden stage on which a chipped but newly varnished lectern sat. He tugged at Helen and began moving toward them, but was stopped by a young woman, a classmate named Monica. She was tall with straight black hair that ended abruptly at her shoulder. She wore a black-and-white checked sweater and black toreador pants. Ben sat next to her in a number of his classes. She was a rebellious preppie from Connecticut, but he thought she was blessed with an incredible wild energy that exploded in her writing. Monica slid her head through the air and kissed Ben on the cheek.

"I saw your stuff in the ragmag, Mr. B." Ben couldn't help smiling. She had never called him that before. "Spread out big as day. It's all the hush, you know. It's magnificent. It's the hit of the magazine." She stepped back and looked Ben up and down. "Urban cowboy. Heaviness. Right on." As she finished speaking she turned her head to Helen and stuck her hand out.

"Helen, this is Monica."

Helen put her hand into Monica's. She was conscious of not shaking Monica's hand, but of having hers shaken. She smiled.

Monica returned the smile and switched her attention immediately to Ben. "This is gonna make you, Ben. I swear. This is it."

Ben turned to Helen and said, "Monica's short story is in the magazine too. You'll like it, she's totally wild."

"I don't believe this. You're calling me wild? I think not. You're the one with the line, how does it go?" Monica shook her hair gently and flipped opened the *Touchstone Review*. "Ah, here it is, and I quote, 'as a penis fully armed.' No, my black brother, you're the one who's wild."

As she talked, Ben tried to keep his smile. He thought Monica was cute with her stark, angled face. She was obviously interested in being his friend. But he could also see the shock and anger rising in Helen's face. He didn't know what to do. He hoped the story would end soon. He had made a mistake in introducing Monica that way. He should have known better. Monica had no sense of control, no sense of consequence. She was so full of Monica she was oblivious to Helen. Ben couldn't tell whether it was deliberate or not. But he knew that Helen thought it was. She was starting to narrow her eyes in a way that made Ben immediately nervous. If Helen "went off" on Monica it would be nuclear.

Luckily, as she ended her monologue, Monica caught the eye of another student across the room. She waved at him and turned to face Ben. "Give 'em hell out there, my black brother. I'm really proud of you."

"You too." Ben felt a surge of relief sweep over him. While Monica was standing with them, the tension had thickened the air around them. For a moment he felt it subside. And then he looked at Helen.

Ben smiled an awkward discomforted smile. He knew Helen had had enough. He felt her pushing him quickly to their chairs. Almost running from any other interruption. He watched as other students would catch a glimpse of him, start in his direction only to flash on Helen's face and change directions. When she smiled, rooms lost their walls and were awash in light. When she frowned, she was a protective amulet, a force field.

He brought his eyes back to Helen. "Are you okay?"

"Okay? Why yes, Mr. B, my black brother, I'm doing just fine. My beautiful black brother."

"Come on. She didn't mean anything."

"Since when do you let some white bitch call you a black brother?" Helen's voice was held in the air by the thinnest of threads. It sounded on the brink of breaking away.

"I don't know. When I first met her I got into this really heated argument about race. Ever since then she's been calling me that. It's no big thing. She's okay."

"Yeah, uh-huh, I'm quite sure she's okay. Long as she can be up in your face."

"She wasn't up in my face, Helen." Ben was trying to act like they were talking about the stories and the poems in the magazine, or the impact of the hostage crisis on the election or anything important.

"Well, she damn sure wasn't in mine. For all she could care, I was your goddamned breeding whore or something." Helen was crumbling inside. The entire time that Monica hovered in front of Ben she had chewed the inside of her bottom lip. How dare she? How dare he?

Ben would have done anything to change the subject. "I've got to go up there and find out when I'm reading."

"Go. Am I asking you to sit here with me? You know, Ben, that really hurt me. You didn't even say I was your wife. What was that about?"

"It's not about anything. I just didn't think of it, that's all."

"Right. Go ahead, I know you'd rather be over there with them anyway. I think I'm going to find a telephone somewhere and check on Makeba."

"There's no need to do that. Can't you just sit here for a few minutes. It's just about to start." Ben was half out of his chair. He wanted to go but he wanted to know that Helen was okay.

"Will you just go. I'll be right back."

Ben made his way to the group of young writers standing at the front of the stage. Most of them he didn't know, but there were two others besides Monica he had talked with. One was Derek, the only other African American who was a part of the program. And Derek was whisper-quiet. He hardly spoke at all. They nodded to each other. Both recognizing the significance of the event.

"Is that your wife? She's pretty." Monica was at his side.

"Ah, yeah, thanks." Ben quickly looked to Helen's empty chair and again breathed relief. He gathered himself, put on his aspiring writer's face. "So what's the order, who's the first to get executed?"

Monica's hazel eyes gleamed. "You are, my black brother. You are the first to be sacrificed."

Ben looked at Derek. "Where does it say that the black man has to be the first up there?" Derek hunched his shoulders.

"They wanted to hit them hard, right from the beginning." Monica smiled.

They were signaled by Molly Berner to take their seats. Ben stood at the steps of the stage waiting for Berner to introduce him. He kept looking back to Helen's chair, but she hadn't returned yet.

He was introduced. He walked up to the podium and lost his physical body. From the moment he began speaking, he was transformed to a flow of words. His body disappeared under him. He read a selection from his story "Fast Feet on Cement" first. It was about an old man who sat outside a North Philadelphia candy store and his fantasy about a young woman who walked by each day. The audience laughed at the right time and were deadly silent as he finished. He knew he had them. And they erupted in applause. Helen was still not in her chair.

And then, he began to read his poems. He was just beginning the second one when he saw Helen creating a shadow in the doorway. His poetry always made people uncomfortable. He liked it that way.

> *As she turned to face me*
> *my eyes became shutters open*
> *for natural light*
> *and she posed, her hip*
> *like a butte of rock*
> *teasing climbers into*
> *adventure.*

When he stopped, there was a brief moment of indecision and then the audience complied and clapped again. As he turned to walk off the stage, he was once again conscious of his body. Of his legs and his feet hitting the floor. He sat down in the first chair that was empty. Ben sat there, nearly numb, unhearing of the other readers until Monica took the podium. He summoned his attention back and listened to her read. Her voice was soft and almost broke at times as she read an intense story about a nightclub on South Street.

There was an intermission after she finished. He quickly rose and started to make his way to Helen. Suddenly, he wanted to be with her in the worst way. But it was difficult. People were all around him. Telling him how good the story was. How much they appreciated his writing.

When he finally got to Helen she was standing by her chair. Her face was softer now. She was smiling. Helen had realized, for the first time, as she watched Ben read the end of the second poem, how important it was to him. She had never been to a poetry reading. She had never been on a college campus. The whole thing was intimidating to her and she wasn't sure what she was supposed to do. But she was happy for Ben. She could see how much it meant to him.

They nearly fell into each other's arms. "Congratulations, you were great."

"You only heard the last bit. I saw when you came back in."

"I'm sorry, I just had to talk to Mom. I had a funny feeling."

"It could have waited." Ben wasn't angry, but he couldn't stop himself. He wanted her to know that he had missed her and she should have been there.

"I told you, I had a funny feeling. Aren't you even going to ask about Makeba?"

"I was just about to. How is she?"

"She was coughing a lot but she finally got back to sleep. I think we should go home."

"Go home? I can't go home now. I've got to stay long enough to hear the others. And there's a party after that."

"Except for yours, this other stuff is boring. Makeba could write better than that. *I* could even write better than that. I was almost falling asleep."

"Are you kidding? There was some good work being read up there."

"I couldn't even figure out what the hell they were talking about. And that little Miss Thing over there almost drove me crazy with that stupid voice of hers."

"Come on." Ben was completely deflated. The lights flickered.

"Ben, please. I need to go. I don't want to be away from Makeba. I would think you'd feel the same way."

"I don't. I need to stay. I need this." Ben waved his hands like a magician. "I need this. This is important too."

Helen stared at him. He could see the hurt deep in her eyes. He had never turned her back this way. Never directly challenged her. He didn't want it to be a choice. This wasn't about choosing Makeba or writing. Was it? Makeba was in good hands. This was Helen's discomfort. This was her problem. If she had something else in her life besides Makeba and her family, maybe she would understand. But as he looked at her, he knew there wasn't a chance that he could get through.

"Suppose I take you home and come back? Would that be okay with you?"

"Sure. If that's what you want to do. That's fine. You can come back and be with your stuck-up writer friends." Helen was breathing heavily. She couldn't understand why he didn't see what they were supposed to do. They were supposed to go home to their sick child.

A form of panic fluttered in his body. He knew she was angry, but so was he. He hated the way he couldn't be right. There was no way that he could be right. To Helen, it *was* about making a choice, and he had made it.

They made their way to the door. He waved to Monica and the others, calling over his shoulder, "I'll be right back."

Ben could only think of the sound of his voice reading his story as he drove home. Helen was perfectly silent. She didn't want to believe that he could just drop her off like a package at the front door.

When the car stopped in front of their house, Helen was out like a rabbit jetting to freedom. She wasn't going to talk about it. Ben watched her run up the steps into the house. He knew she was crying, he heard her disintegrating even as she opened the car door. By the time she was at the front door, he could tell that the tears blurred her vision because she dropped her keys and in a fit of exploding frustration, she stomped her foot. Lena appeared at the door.

He slowly let the car roll down the street. When he reached the corner, he gunned the engine and raced back to the university. On this night, that was where happiness was.

Makeba's Journal

THIRTEENTH ENTRY

I wish I could have seen you read your writing. I wish I could have known more about what you were trying to do. It might have made a difference. I understand the struggle of black men. I know it's not easy. And I think that Mom understands too. She's hung in there with my stepdad ever since you left. She's stood by him through all kinds of bad stuff.

Mom never mentioned the reading to me. If it happened the way you say it did I guess you felt pretty bad. But look what happened. In the past six months I've been secretly clipping articles about you and this book. You finally are a writer. And it all started on that night. And I was home sick. I don't even remember hearing Mom come back in that night. There's so much I don't remember. Anyway, from the articles I have learned more about you than I ever did from Mom. I know how hard you had to work to get where you are. You probably figured if it was going to be that hard, you should just be by yourself. I read in one story that you had a nervous breakdown. That you were in an institution for a while. Was that because of us? I can't imagine being out of control.

By the way, I wasn't going to tell you this, but since you wrote about that girl Monica, I will. The one thing that Nana used to say that would make Mom go nuts is that you left her to be with a white girl. She'd go nuclear when she heard that. And Nana would say it all the time.

Fourteen

There was a tear in the fabric that connected Ben and Helen. Helen wasn't enthralled with literature and writing. She wasn't interested in the same people he was. And at times Ben's desire to be a writer overshadowed everything. At those times it was clear that he didn't care as much about family as she did. It was happening right in front of them, and yet, life seemed to just keep going.

It was Makeba who would feel the brunt of this tragedy. It was her heart full of hope that would eventually be ruptured. It was her idea of future that was in jeopardy. She was defenseless. Immersed in a love for her mother and father that defied qualification. She was a child.

Mates began to spend more time with Ben.

It was the unqualified, unquestioning quality of her love that scared Ben. "I tell you, man, that little girl is so goddamned pretty sometimes when I look at her I almost start crying." He was sitting in a downtown bar with his friend Ramsey. He had left school early and decided to play hooky from work.

He had first met the plump, plum-colored Ramsey in Naples, Italy, in the Hole in the Wall bar. It was a favorite of the black sailors that were in port. Over tequilas they had discovered they were both from Philadelphia. Ramsey, a welder, was a crew member of the U.S.S. *Forrestal,* an aircraft carrier, and Ben was stationed aboard the U.S.S. *Kenosha,* an oiler.

In their first conversation they discovered that the night before, they had unknowingly been connected by rubber hoses which pumped black oil from one ship to the other in the deep pitch of the wavering, ever shifting swell of the Mediterranean Sea. It had been just after midnight that the *Kenosha* had steamed alongside the hulking aircraft carrier to give it oil and jet fuel.

At-sea refueling, especially at night, conjured a different reality. The deep darkness of the ocean. The flickering deck and running lights of the ships. The sound of men working, screaming, singing. People who lived a life separate from those who make the choices of war. Time was suspended. The hoses of the oiler were slowly pulled across the churning alley of white water that sprinted between the two ships. Two ships that pursued completely parallel courses at precisely the same speed.

When the hoses were connected, the *Kenosha* would give its liquid cargo over to the larger ship. And all this in the middle of the night. While nearly everyone else slept. In the vacuum of the vast desert of water.

Both ships had arrived in Naples the following afternoon. And Ben had chosen a seat at the white-walled grottolike bar of the Hole in the Wall right next to Ramsey's. From that day their friendship began a blooming life. The two ships were often in the same ports and when back in the States, both ships docked in Norfolk, Virginia.

Now, nearly eight years later, there was a deep affection between them. Ramsey picked his drink up, held it up to the red lights that glowed from behind the bar. They had been drinking shots of tequila for two and half hours. Ben's head was reeling. Ramsey's eyes were like marbles, round and glazed, and his grin seemed set in brown concrete. "You're a lucky man. You've got a wife and a kid. I keep thinking that one day I'm gonna find me a woman I can settle down with." Ramsey had continued to gain weight and was bordering on being fat.

"Yeah, Rams, just be patient man. You'll find one."

"I guess I should've gone to that party with you. I always think about that night. That night you met Helen? How come I wasn't with you?" Ramsey took a sip of his drink and put it back on the table. "I still don't know how I missed that jam. We *were* out together that night, wasn't we?"

Ben smiled. He had been deflecting Ramsey's inquiries about that party for six years. "Yeah, you know good and goddamned well we were hanging out that night."

"Then why the fuck didn't I go to the party? You never said a goddamned word about it. Next thing I know, you're getting god-damned married."

"Maybe you should have come." Ben laughed.

"You're laughing, my brother, but I still don't know why you didn't tell me about it."

"I guess I just forgot. We were doing some heavy drinking, remember?"

"All I remember is you leaving me at the Thirteen saying you had to go home. You were bullshitting me, man. You wanted to go to that jam by yourself."

Ben stared down at the table and in a barely audible voice said, "That's the way it happens, man. You go to a party and bam, next thing you know, you're out looking for a crib."

"Thought you was into the family thing."

"I am, man. That's just it. You know how it is. I'm a father. I'm supposed to do the right thing. I'm the one who talks shit in my classes. You know—'Black men have to take care of their families,' and all that stuff. I mean, I'm supposed to make it so Makeba can deal in this white man's world."

"Yeah, I've heard this before, so what's the problem?"

"I'm not sure, man. I sit in my classes and write my poems and stories and I realize the kind of commitment it takes to be a writer and the way most writers have to live, nearly starving all the time, and I can't see how I'm going to make it."

Ramsey ordered another drink. The bar was nearly empty in the late afternoon. The after-work crowd hadn't started arriving yet. He turned to Ben. "Man, you better forget that poetry shit. Your ass is a motherfuckin' family man now. That poetry shit is history, man. If you want my advice you'd do better to drop it and get with something useful like accounting or computers or some shit like that."

"Ramsey, my brother, you are a good friend and if this was about a prizefight or a football game or something like that I'd be all ears, but to be honest with you, I don't need your advice about my career."

Ramsey pulled the glass away from his mouth. "You need somebody's fucking advice. Let me tell you. Somebody needs to straighten your black ass out right now."

Ben leaned back in his chair. The Budweiser light behind the bar competed with the waning sunlight to throw a faint glow against the charcoal interior. The air was slow, woven with stale beer and cigarette smoke. The carpet beneath them held memories which murmured in indistinct odors.

"I guess you're the one who's gonna straighten me out?" Ben smiled and looked into Ramsey's eyes.

"I just want to see you make your mortgage payments being a poet after your fucking G.I. Bill runs out. That's when I'll believe this shit. You're fucking up big-time. Here you are, getting money from the government to go to school. Not like me. You're in goddamned school and here you are talking about being a goddamned poet? Who the hell is hiring poets? I hear about computer programmers and advertising executives and shit like that, but I never heard nobody rushing in to hire poets. In fact, I ain't never seen no ad for poets in the paper." He paused to take another swig. "You're fucking up, Ben. That's what I say."

"Ramsey, you've known me for eight years and you know I have never listened to a goddamned thing you had to say." Ben was chuckling. "Shit, if I had, I'd have been court-martialed at least three times. I just want you to know that I have this thing . . . ah . . . I don't understand it. Sometimes I wish I could be a fucking insurance salesman or something like that. Sometimes I wish I could. But there's something going on in here." Ben tapped his chest. "Something's pushing me, man. Talking shit to me. You know?"

Ramsey looked into Ben's clouding eyes. He studied them. He

saw the fear that danced in his pupils like water drops on a thin layer of hot oil. He stared at Ben. He had a feeling that Ben wanted him to soften up, to open up, so that Ben could tell him something. He felt that whatever Ben wanted to say was big, important. And yet, he didn't really want to hear it. What Ramsey wanted to hear from Ben was that being a father and a husband and having a good job were the important things. Nothing else.

And in spite of his feelings, or perhaps because of them, he broke into a broad smile. "No, motherfucka, I *don't* know. What I know is that you better be getting yourself together so you can get yourself a job. Get your ass out of the taxicab-driving business and get behind a desk. Dumb motherfuckas like me, who can't get into college, barely even finished high school, well, we ain't got a chance. But you, you can make it, man. This is your time."

Ben looked away. "I don't think I can do it that way."

A woman came in the bar. She was followed by a man who quickly put his arm around her and guided her into a booth. Ramsey watched the couple as he said, "You're in deep shit, brother."

"I know, man. It's starting to feel that way to me too."

"Let me try to get this shit straight. Okay. Now, do you love Helen?"

"Of course. Yes. I love her. I mean, it ain't like I thought it was going to be, but yeah, I love her."

Ramsey nodded. "And you love your daughter?"

Ben feigned a menacing grimace and brought his fist into the air.

"Okay, okay, be cool, my brother. Just be cool." Ramsey smiled and relaxed his body. He seemed to grow into the chair, filling all of its empty spaces. "So, let's see here. You love your family. You're doing okay in school. Just about to graduate after all these god-damned years part-time. You're using the fucking G.I. Bill, so you've got some change in your pockets. The future looks bright and all that good shit. What the fuck are you complaining about?"

The bar was filling with the after-work crowd. Ben's blurred vision locked on a black woman in tight jeans. She wore a leather jacket that outlined a head-turning figure. Which is what happened. Heads swung in her direction as she came in the door. She didn't look like one of the refugees from the office buildings in the area. She maneuvered her way to a table directly across from Ben and Ramsey.

Ramsey hadn't seen her, but Ben had followed her all the way in. He nodded in her direction. "Now *there's* a woman."

"Boy, what has gotten into you? One minute you're crying the blues about being married and the next you're slobbering over some other woman." Ramsey's smile was still strong as he shook his head.

"I'm not interested in her, Rams, not like what you might think. I was just admiring, that's all." Ramsey looked in her direction.

He quickly turned back to Ben. "Wow, man. You wasn't lying about that." In the same instant, he was moving toward her. Ben could hear him say, "Hey momma, my name's Ramsey, what's yours?"

"Vicki," she said flatly, as she found a cigarette. Her skin was like ermine. Her hair fell alongside her face, creating flattering shadows in the dim light of the bar.

"Well, hey Vicki, why don't you join us over here? Let me buy you a drink."

Ben tried not to act interested. But he was. His heart was moving a little faster. He wondered if she'd respond.

"No, thank you, I'm waiting for someone."

Ramsey accepted his rebuff and faced Ben again. "I tried. Woman like that ain't interested in me no way." Ben smiled back. They ordered another round and another after that. Ramsey had forgotten their previous line of discussion but Ben hadn't. In between the lines of his spinning head, he thought about Helen. Where were they going?

He thought about telling Ramsey about Monica. It wasn't just Helen's imagination. Monica had made it quite clear she was interested in him. But Ben had decided then not to open up to her. He was curious, but he didn't want to risk his relationship with Helen. Besides, this was Philadelphia with its East Coast tightness and he wasn't ready for an interracial relationship in a city where a hysterical mayor, Frank Rizzo, had the city in the grip of a palpable racism. And finally, he knew that it would really hurt Helen. Not just the infidelity, but the race thing. She would never be able to get over that.

He had seen the growing number of interracial couples on the streets of downtown Philadelphia. And on campus, there were a number of interracial liaisons happening under the protection of the safe university environment. He had also heard the not-so-quiet rumblings from black women who took it as a personal affront. Helen was one them. She would set fire to his pants while he was in them if she ever caught him with a white woman.

In the throes of this contemplation, Ben missed it when the man Vicki was waiting for arrived. At some point Ben looked over at her and saw she was talking to someone. But she caught Ben looking and winked her eye at him. She painted a faint smile in the smoky air. Ramsey was now talking about the Philadelphia 76ers and Dr. J. Ben could barely make out what he was saying. He turned his head away from Vicki just long enough not to appear to be staring at her.

Ramsey kept talking and Ben drank and nodded his head and played eye games with Vicki. She was sitting so that he could see her without having to cross eyes with the man she was with. Music was now all around them. He had slipped into a cocoon of music, smoke, noise, basketball talk and Vicki. Somewhere in the folds of his reverie he heard Ramsey say he was going to the bathroom. He heard the chair slide back and Ramsey's presence dissipate. But he was fixed in his dream.

Now, maybe he *was* staring at her. Even when she wasn't looking at him. At first her open eyes had drawn him in. He had traced the delicate contour of her cheeks, the fullness of her lips. He watched her as her pink tongue formed a lisp at the back of her teeth when she talked. But it was also like a hypnosis. He was lulled through her and into a different place. Suddenly he wasn't looking at Vicki anymore but at a picture of himself standing in front of a new house. There was his station wagon in the driveway. There was Helen in the window. Makeba was tooling toward him on a bicycle augmented with training wheels. She was moving at full speed. He realized she wasn't going to stop. The bicycle began to get larger and larger, its wheels growing into tank treads. Her legs became huge pistons which pushed the vehicle at increasing speed. She was bearing down right on him. In an instant he felt panic deep in his stomach. He was just about to scream when everything became blue. He blinked his eyes.

Ramsey was still gone. But now, standing in front of him, was the man from Vicki's table. He was even larger than Ramsey. Except he wasn't fat. He was a hulking mountain of weathered dark skin. Ben's eyes reached up in confusion.

"What the fuck were you looking at?"

"What do you mean?" Ben couldn't think of anything else to say.

"Just what I said. I'm tired of you staring at my woman. I don't play that shit."

It was then that Ben realized that the man was angry. That he had committed a cardinal sin. It was dangerous to let your eyes linger too long on a woman who was with another man, even accidentally. If the stare held there too long, war was certain. Ben's stomach jumped again.

"Is there some reason why you got to be checking her out so tough?"

Ben's throat was suddenly dry. "Naw, man. I was just day-dreaming, that's all. I didn't mean no harm."

The man bent down and set his face an inch away from Ben's. "I'm gonna tell you something. I don't like you. I don't like nobody staring at me or her like that. You understand?"

"Yeah." Ben's voice was a cloud. "I understand."

" 'Cause I'll kick your motherfuckin' ass. Clean this whole god-damn bar with your skinny behind. You hear me?"

Ben was trying to swallow but he couldn't. He was frozen. The man seemed already out of control. All kinds of warning bells were going off in Ben's head but he didn't know what to do. Vicki's voice rose from behind the man's body. "He didn't mean no harm, Donnie. It's cool."

But the man grabbed Ben's right hand and held it tightly. The touch of skin was startling at first. The connection between them. And then he felt the pain. The man closed his fist tighter and tighter, as if Ben's hand was made of clay and would give.

"You need this?"

"I need my hand, man. I need my hand," Ben said, tears forming in his eyes.

"What you need it for? You gonna hit me with it?" The man's breath was in Ben's nostrils. His sweat was there too.

"No, I don't want to hit you. I'm sorry, man. I didn't mean no harm. I was just thinking. Just daydreaming."

But he wouldn't loosen his grip. It had stopped getting tighter but there was no blood moving in Ben's fingers. His hand felt like a dishcloth that was being wrung dry. Time seemed to stop. His mind flashed on an unfinished poem sitting in his typewriter in his den. It was a poem about a woman and her daughter sitting on a stoop in front of a house on Diamond Street in Philadelphia. He was going to call it "Safe." But could he write with one hand? That was what he was thinking when Ramsey came back.

Ramsey was drunk; his voice instantly found the right edge for a barroom confrontation. "What's the problem, brother?"

"I ain't your fucking brother. Dig it?" And then to Ben: "I think you should apologize to me and my lady."

"Sure man, I told you I was sorry. I didn't mean to bother you."

"Let his hand go." Ramsey was surging now, Ben could sense he was about to get into it.

"It's okay, Rams. Just a misunderstanding, right? I mean, I didn't mean no harm."

Ben felt the pressure release from his hand and a swift wave of pain shot through it. Ramsey stood staring as the man turned back to his girlfriend. But now she was up and walking toward the door. He grabbed his coat and followed her.

Ramsey eye's followed them. "That motherfucka is crazy. What the fuck did you do?"

"I didn't do a goddamned thing. I was just thinking, man. He thought I was making eyes at his girl. I mean, I was for a minute, but shit, man, he fucking crushed my goddamned hand." Ben felt like crying.

Ramsey collapsed into his chair. Ben got up from his seat; his right arm felt as if it stopped at his wrist and all the blood was dripping onto the floor. He had no feeling in his hand at all.

"Rams?"

"Yeah?"

"I think he did smash my goddamned hand, man. I think he really did. I can't feel shit. I think I'm going to have to get to a hospital. I got to have my hand. I can't write without it." Ben was afraid of the words that came out of his mouth. He shuddered at the idea of utter silence.

"Write? Is that what you're worried about? Let's get your ass to a hospital. You should have kicked him in the nuts or let me smash his fucking head in. Motherfuckas walking around thinking they can do whatever they fucking want to. And you're talking about writing. Shit. Let's go, Ben. We better take care of that hand of yours. I'm telling you, brother, like I was saying, you're gonna have to get your shit together."

Makeba's Journal

My love scared you? My love scared you? Maybe I should put this book down. Maybe I don't need to read this. I definitely don't appreciate knowing that because I loved you as my father, you would take that love as a threat. As something to be feared.

The story about Ramsey and that man is interesting I guess, but even now, just a minute after I finished reading this chapter, the only thing I can remember is that it was my love that made you afraid. I didn't choose you. I didn't choose this life. You're damned right I felt the "brunt," whatever the hell you mean by that. If you mean did I have to figure out why you left? If you mean that I had to get used to some other man who wanted, insisted that I call him Daddy? If you mean that I had to try to act like you never existed? If that's what brunt means, then hell yes, I felt the god-damned brunt.

Fifteen

Mates could feel himself becoming stronger, his senses more acute. He looked at Ben and his poor little hand. What irony. Mates wondered how in the world Ben would be able to write those wonderful stories and poems he expected to write.

Tragedy comes to people in more convoluted ways than one might think. Ben's hand could have been crushed and he could have lost the ability to write forever and that would have been that. Perhaps such a disability would have ended the anguish. But it doesn't happen that way. His hand suffered only a bad bruise and in time he was back at the typewriter. If only he could write a new life. If only he could write himself a way to live up to the image he promised.

It was June 1982. Ben had finally graduated from the University of Pennsylvania with a degree in English with a creative writing concentration. That spring he had applied to the Iowa Writers Workshop. He'd sent them a short story as a writing sample and immediately started praying every night before he went to bed. "God, please, please let them accept me." That was his prayer. "Please."

But Ben was sure that God would see through the lie. Writing had become his religion. He felt called, as a minister would be called. But called to what? To continue the effort of African griots and scribes to capture the full stroke of black humanity? To tell lies in the search for truth? To talk shit on paper with the bluster of Superfly on the hustle? It was all that. Ben was developing in a new breed of African American writers. Having felt the energy of the revolutionaries of the generation just before him, he was driven to define the contemporary black man. And it wasn't all fight and fire. The activist writers of the sixties and seventies had burned out. They had screamed and scratched and fought until there was nothing left. Only a handful of black writers survived the revolution. From this Ben knew he had to control his rage so that it would not destroy him.

Still, as he approached the end of his undergraduate life, he was worried about money. How would he make enough money? In a fit of anxiety, he had taken to scouring the want ads, and actually sending his résumé out.

He told himself that he would leave it up to fate. If he was accepted into Iowa and was not offered a job, it would be a sign. If he got a job but couldn't get into school, that too would provide direction. He made it as hard as he could. He applied to only one school and was very selective about where he sent his résumés.

He actually didn't expect to be accepted into graduate school. There was something about the way he wrote that began to turn his classmates and his professors against him. He'd finally lost his appetite for the shock and the erotic. Now he was trying to deconstruct the lives of African American people to reveal the interior. Not the perceived stereotype of drugs and violence and welfare, but the inner life. He wanted to go beyond the superficial effects of slavery. He wanted to go deeper. To explore the detail of complexity. Now, suddenly he was obsessed with the spirit. The essence. The humanity.

But he'd noticed a distinct change in the way his classmates responded to his latest work. When he dropped the clever sexual references and began talking about the strength of his father, the quiet exuberance of his mother, the beauty of Makeba, they weren't interested. When he started to write about the way black people lived with such dignity in an unbroken struggle against the system, the excitement about his work disappeared. Even Monica had said something about his need to "find that edge that was in your other work." He couldn't get Baraka's words out of his mind. If you really told white people what you were thinking they'd have to kill you.

So when he put the application to Iowa in the mail, he was sure he would not be selected. And when a personnel manager at Benson Glendale, a young public relations firm, called and asked him to come in for an interview, he did.

He actually went out and bought a suit at Krass Brothers down on South Street. He tied a tie around his neck and walked into the company one day. The next day he was offered a job as copywriter.

And on this same day, when he opened his mail he was stunned with the news that he had been accepted at Iowa. He had hoped the choice would be made for him but suddenly it was harder than before. He had to choose.

Helen tried to be supportive. After the episode at the reading, she had shied away from talking about writing at all. And then, when he talked about considering going to work or back to school, she had tried not to reveal her desire that he pursue a career in business. She was convinced that he could never make a decent living as a writer.

And yet, when he told her about the two offers he again tried to make it clear that he was the one who had to make the decision.

"We can make it," she said. "I know how badly you want to write. I don't want you to feel like me or Makeba are going to keep you from doing that."

"But how will we make money? I would do it if I could figure out a way, but I can't," Ben said softly. It was clanging in his head. His own expectations of himself. It was his job to provide for them.

It wasn't Helen screaming at him all the time to get a better job, even though he knew that's what she wanted. It wasn't that she didn't contribute money to the household budget or that she wasn't even working. It wasn't anything Helen was or wasn't doing. It was him. Something inside *Ben* made him want to take full responsibility for *his* family. Even though their marriage was already slipping, Ben clung to the image of himself as a stereotype buster. Someone everyone could point to as an exception to the rule of black men.

Helen stared at him. She was thinking too. She remembered

Geri's warning about Ben being a writer at the Valentine's Day party where they met. Then, it had been a joke. But now it wasn't amusing. Ben was much less concerned with the details of their lives than she thought he should be. Doing the things he should have been doing around the house, keeping the family tight and strong—she felt as if he left all of that up to her. He worked hard, that was true, but he also came home and closed himself up in his den. She knew he had an enormous sense of responsibility for her and Makeba, but she wanted more from him than money.

And yet she realized how serious writing had become to him. And now, faced with this choice, she wasn't sure what to say. He was right. There was no way they could survive if he didn't get a full-time job. Without the G.I. Bill, the cab-driving job wasn't close to bringing in enough money.

Helen wanted to be home with Makeba. What she saw on the evening news only strengthened her conviction that a mother, a father, someone, had to be home to raise a child. A parent had to know where their child was, and what they were doing. The way she saw it, anytime a young person was killed, or in a gang, or taking drugs, it was the parent who was at fault. In her way of thinking, there was no choice except for one of them to be home with Makeba. That was why, after Makeba was older, she wanted to start her own day-care center. She knew what was needed. It was love.

Ben knew how to read her silence. He knew that she didn't want to say out loud what both of them were thinking: that he had to take the job.

"It's okay, Helen. I think I'm going to take that job at Benson Glendale anyway. I was talking to one of my instructors and she thought that I wouldn't learn that much more about writing anyway. Her advice was to 'live.' She said, 'Live and then write.' So that's what I'm going to do. I'm not exactly the next Richard Wright or James Baldwin. They're not ready for my shit anyway."

Helen remained silent. There was nothing she could say. She agreed with him on all counts. She didn't want to acknowledge the pain that she heard on the inside of his voice.

Makeba's Journal

I can't help but be suspicious about all of this. I don't get enough of what
Mom was thinking. You thought you knew her so well, but I don't think
you did. Yes, she is really traditional but she is also very smart. She reads a
lot. And she's very sensitive. If she wasn't so wrapped up in the church
there's no telling what she would be. And even at that she's accomplished
a lot. I don't feel like you know her.

Besides I don't know why you never did what you wanted to do. If
you just wanted to sleep with her, why did you marry her? If you didn't
want me, then why weren't you more careful? If you didn't want to take
the job, why did you?

In spite of myself, I was very proud when I read those articles about
you, but now, I don't know. The problem is that I don't understand what
this is I'm reading. I remember when you got the job, but I thought it was
a happy time. You and Mom had champagne and we had this great
dinner. Do you remember that? I do. I even remember how you gave this
toast to us, me and Mom, and said how happy and excited you were to
finally get a chance to make a lot of money. I remember that. How come
you didn't write about that?

Sixteen

He took the job. And with that decision Ben had chosen a direction. He wormed himself into a young company where the only thing as dark as him were the desktops and the suits his colleagues wore. He was the only one who had known the blue lights of basement parties. The only one who had run from pursuing street gangs. Out of twenty he was the only one.

From the beginning everyone at Benson Glendale smiled a lot. Ben did too. It was a new world. He worked in a department with two other copywriters. Benson Glendale, though a young company, wasn't the typical laid-back advertising/public relations firm. In fact it was quite conservative. Ben was expected to wear a tie, to be in the office all day and to be involved in the life of the company. He was expected to become a part of the Benson Glendale family.

Ben's history was work. His father had always worked hard, as had his mother. His experience in the Navy had solidified this legacy and now he applied himself at Benson Glendale.

Almost immediately he began to feel the way he had felt in the Navy. Used, manipulated. His superiors were always surprised that he was articulate, that he was well-read, that he was smart.

In the Navy, *he* was the one the captain would usually ask to compose official letters and messages. He was the one the captain asked for private advice. But when promotions and special privileges were being handed out, Ben never got any. At Benson Glendale it was working out the same way. People were surprised at his ability, impressed even, but they expected him to completely assimilate himself. To prove he was one of them.

In the early days at Benson Glendale, Ben tried to do that. He worked the long hours. Volunteered. Socialized. And when he came home he tried to write. But he was often weary by the time he made it to his den.

At night his hand still ached from his altercation in the bar. Even though no bones had been broken, pain would unexpectedly erupt. He still found it hard sometimes to make a sudden movement. To hit the *o* or the *i* keys on the typewriter. It made the fight to write more real, more immediate.

Still, every so often he became totally deflated. Empty of all energy. Then he would collapse on the living room couch and open himself up to the mindlessness of television.

This was such a time. He was flopped on the couch, waiting for an early-season Phillies game to come on television. Just the night before, he had been up late trying finish a short story. On weekends and holidays, he tried to throw himself into his writing. After which he always felt sluggish, almost sleepwalking on the fringe of the family life. But he was committed to not letting his dream of being a writer slip completely away.

Helen was sitting next to him, reading *Tar Baby,* a book by Toni Morrison. After a while Helen put the book down.

"I don't know why Mom has to get Makeba so much. It's like she's trying to be her mother or something."

From the time Makeba was six months old, Lena had insisted on spending time alone with her. Every other Saturday she would drive up from New Jersey to pick up her granddaughter. Most of the time Makeba's outings with Lena were welcomed by Helen and Ben. But there were some Saturdays when Helen didn't want to let Makeba go.

"Oh really, I didn't know you cared. I've been saying that since

Makeba was born. She's always taking that child somewhere." Ben was surprised by Helen's statement. She had never before questioned the amount of time Lena spent with Makeba.

"I really don't mind. A girl needs to know her grandmother. They should spend time together. It's just that on some of these Saturdays I'd like to spend some quiet time with my daughter. The week is so hectic I hardly have enough time with her."

"You're not working. You could do things during the week if that's how you feel." Ben couldn't help wanting Helen to go back to work. He didn't buy her argument that Makeba needed her at home full-time. Besides, if Helen went back to work, maybe he could eventually plan to go back to school.

"I know I'm not working. Don't throw that up in my face. You know as well as I do that even if I was working, day care and transportation would eat up all the extra money I would make. It's cheaper for me to stay home and take care of Makeba."

Ben decided to let the conversation, one which they had periodically, fade. "I wouldn't worry too much about your mother. I guess all grandmothers are like that. That's one of the benefits. They get to spoil their grandchildren." The truth was that Ben had never figured out how to handle Lena or even how to talk about her to Helen. If he tried to voice his apprehension, Helen immediately came to her defense. But when Helen complained, he knew he had to be careful. If he agreed too strongly, she would turn the tables on him.

Helen had succeeded in convincing Ben that Lena wasn't capable of doing anything mean. So now, as he thought about Lena's influence on Makeba, he tried to be more accepting. It was ironic that it was Helen who was suddenly asking questions about it.

"I know. It's just that she never spent that much time with me. I can't remember a time when just she and I went out together. Or even just sat around the house alone. She hardly ever talked to me. Except to tell me to clean something, or to criticize something I did."

Ben got up from the couch and walked to the television. The game was coming on. He could feel Helen wanting to talk. He decided not to turn it on. Instead he faced her.

"Do you want to tell her to maybe only make it once a month?" As he listened to Helen talk about her mother, he realized that there was something fundamental missing in her relationship with Lena.

"No. I don't think so."

Against his instinct, Ben asked, "Do you think maybe you're a little jealous?" It was the best way for him to say what he was thinking.

"Jealous? Of what, Ben?"

"Of how much attention your mother gives to Makeba?" He watched her facial muscles knot.

"Do I have to be jealous just to want to spend more time with my child? Do I sound jealous to you?"

Helen's voice had gone cold. When Ben heard it, he realized he was in deep weeds. "I didn't say you sounded jealous. But I never thought I'd hear you complain about how much time Lena spends with Makeba."

"I wasn't complaining. Why do you have to twist everything up? You stand there, detached from everybody and everything around here, and make judgments about me."

"Helen, what are you talking about?"

Helen tried to rein herself in. She tried to get a grip on the life that moved around her like a rope. She didn't want to be angry at Ben, or her mother. But something was happening. She could feel Ben's anxiousness. She knew he didn't really want to work at Benson Glendale. She knew he really wanted to write. She couldn't suppress a feeling, deep inside her, that her life was unraveling.

And her life depended on stability, the continuity of their family. She just wanted to be a woman who read books, took care of her daughter and loved her husband. But everything seemed to be getting more and more complicated.

"Oh, so now you don't know what I'm talking about? You have the nerve to stand there and tell me I'm jealous of my own mother. What do you know?"

Ben retreated further. "Forget it. I'm sorry I brought it up."

"So am I."

He turned the television on and tried to lose himself in the baseball game. Helen went back to her book.

The next morning as Ben still slept, Lena rang the doorbell and walked into the house. Makeba was waiting for her on the couch alongside Helen. It was a gray Saturday morning, a cover of rain clouds hovered.

Helen kissed her mother. "How was your drive?"

"I hate coming into the city, Helen. This place is filthy. I don't know how or why anybody in their right mind would want to live in this mess. It's the middle of the morning and there's gangs of people all over the place, like there ain't nothing better to do than hang out on a corner."

"It's Saturday, Mom. What do you think people should be doing?"

Lena untied the soft baby-blue scarf from around her hair. "They should be finding something to do. It ain't like there's nothing to do in this godforsaken city."

A seven-year-old Makeba hugged Lena's waist. "But Nana, you're supposed to play on Saturday. No school or nothing."

"I'm not talking about you, sugar, I'm talking about those good-for-nothing lazy bums standing around all over the place. Saturdays don't mean nothing to them. You can find them doing the same thing on Mondays that they doing now."

Helen had gone back to the couch. She knew her mother well enough to know that if she didn't respond Lena would eventually change the subject.

"Where are we going this week, Nana?" Makeba wasn't interested in the discussion about people standing around on the streets. She was tall for her age. Her freshly straightened dark brown hair rested just below her ears. She was nearing the end of first grade and seemed to everyone, especially Helen and Ben, older than she was. She had personality.

"I was thinking about a nice June picnic. I know just the place."

"Where's that, Mom?" Helen let out a slow sigh. She had never been on a picnic alone with her mother. There was the annual church picnic and the family reunion in Clinton, North Carolina, but she had never sat with her mother in the grass and looked up at the sky.

"It's a small, beautiful little park in North Philly, Rock Garden."

"Are there lots of rocks there?" Makeba asked.

"Well, in a way. It's like a little mountain in the middle of the city. There are caves and little streams running through it. And they've put in paths so we can walk around up there."

"Really?" Makeba's excitement rushed forward.

"Yes, dear. I just hope those North Philly hooligans haven't ruined it since I was there last."

"So how long was that, Mom?" Helen fiddled with Makeba's hair.

"Hasn't been that long. About a year." Lena opened her eyes to her daughter. She wondered about Helen's tone of voice. She slowly walked to the couch and sat down beside her.

"So, do you go there often?"

"Every year since your father died." Lena leaned back into the soft chair. "You mean you don't know about Rock Garden?"

"No, Mom, I don't know anything about Rock Garden. Why would I know about Rock Garden? Have you ever taken me there?" Helen couldn't control herself. Her anger close to the surface.

Lena felt the chill. She turned to face her daughter. Makeba stepped back from the two of them and stared first at Lena, then her mother and then to Lena again.

"Is there something wrong, Helen?"

"No, Mother. Nothing's wrong. Everything's fine." Helen looked into Makeba's eyes. She could tell that Makeba was uncomfortable.

Makeba was trying to figure out what was going on. She had never heard her mother unveil her sharp-edged voice to her grandmother before.

Lena spoke softly, almost into Helen's ear. Makeba even took a step forward but still couldn't hear.

"You are a woman now. I'm sorry if I wasn't a good mother to you. Maybe I didn't tell you everything you needed to know. But I didn't know myself. I was doing the best I could do. There were so many things I was learning when you was just a little girl."

Makeba tried to see into her mother's eyes. Maybe there she would be able to find the words that she knew were coming out of Lena's mouth. But Helen's head was slowly dropping, a little at a time, and already her eyes were hidden from Makeba.

Lena continued. "But I'm getting old now, and I *should* know more than I did then. Every day I put something together that I didn't realize before. That's what I'm doing these days. I'm reading and studying and putting things together. Trying to make sense out of everything. Especially you. I've been trying to figure out what I could have done better."

Still moving very slowly, Helen lifted her head. "Do you know?"

"I think I do. I taught you how to tie your shoes. I taught you how to wash dishes, how to talk. All that kind of stuff. But I didn't teach you how to feel. How to see through all the mess in front of you so you could find your way. That's what was missing in my life. Probably missing in yours. Unless you learned it somewhere else. I know you couldn't have learned it from me, because I didn't know it myself. But now I know. I can teach it to Makeba. I can show her how to protect herself. To transform the energy of all of us into something strong. Something fierce. Something that will define her and help her turn back all them forces out there that will try to stop her."

Helen closed her eyes and let her head drop back on the couch. Lena fell silent and looked up at Makeba, who was still standing there looking very nervous.

"Come here, Kayba. Come to Nana. Don't you worry about nothing, child." Lena opened her arms and enfolded Makeba in her thin black grasp.

"Mom?" Helen sat up. She had thought about what her mother had said. Inside, her stomach was quivering. "What about me? What's going to happen to me?"

Lena slowly rose out of the chair and brought Makeba with her. "Kayba, get yourself a sweater. It's liable to be chilly later on. Get the red one. And bring Ka too." Makeba, thankful to be dismissed, raced up the stairs.

"I been thinking about that, Helen. I been thinking a lot about that. And I just don't know."

"So you're just gonna pass me by." Helen felt tears on the inside holding themselves there.

"No, girl. What's wrong with you? I ain't planning on passing nobody by. But I'm gonna work with that daughter of yours first. So I know she's taken care of. But I'm still your mother and I ain't gonna let nothing happen to you. I love you." Lena reached over and put her arms around her daughter. Helen made herself small and crawled back into the belly of her mother. She lay there for a second before slowly pulling away.

She took in a deep breath. She felt better. Her mother was probably stronger than she was. Her mother could at least see the future in Makeba. Helen was still stuck on Helen.

Makeba's Journal

Nana took me everywhere. Every week it was something else. We'd go to the Franklin Institute or to the zoo. And she taught me all kinds of things. The most important thing she taught me was how to let all parts of life exist at the same time. That was how Ka came to me.

I know you don't believe it, but one day, after Nana had taken me to this restaurant for lunch and we were driving back home, she asked me to give Ka to her. I thought, for a minute, that she was going to throw her out of the car or something. But she just propped her up between us as we drove through the city.

About a block before we got home, she pulled the car over and turned to me and told me to close my eyes. And then she started talking to Ka. Just like she was a real baby lion. No, like she was me. A girl like me, but older. It was like a prayer. She asked Ka to love me like she did. To soothe me whenever I hurt myself. And then, after this long list of things she wanted Ka to do, Nana asked her: "Will you stay with her, be her living shadow and show her what you have learned?"

And then, believe it or not, I heard Ka's voice, only it sounded like me. And Ka said, "Don't worry. This child will live to discover the truth."

I swear to God. I heard her. With my eyes shut tight I heard Ka's voice. Later, I asked Nana what Ka meant about discovering truth. She said that Ka would let me know when it was time to know. Ka has led me back to you.

Seventeen

Mates was very comfortable in the shadows. He liked the feeling of freedom, of being disconnected from a body, of being present and yet unseen. People often knew he was there, but were unable to explain it. People needed substance. They were helpless to explain those things which couldn't be touched.

Of course, Mates knew there was this widespread belief in God which he understood. The problem was that people thought that their God was supreme. That no other God existed. In his world there was a different god for everything. He was one of them and an emissary for them.

Mates could see now that Ben was the chosen one. So many promises. So many hopes. It was clear that it wouldn't be Helen. She was committed in a way that was unshakable. He knew that Helen would never feel guilt. If their life together fell apart, it would be Ben who would shoulder the weight of guilt.

And if Ben had known better he would have feared Lena more than he did. She held the voice. She was in touch with the other world.

Lena's tutelage of Makeba worried Helen. As a young girl, Helen had been brought into the church by her mother, who was then a devoted Apostolic Baptist. But as the years passed, Lena had become increasingly disaffected with church.

"They don't do enough for me, child," she would say every Sunday after services. "Just a lot of screaming and hollering and shouting and babbling and nothing happening. People don't get stronger, they don't get richer. Ain't nothing changed."

But for Helen the church took on greater significance. At about the time her mother was leaving the church, she joined. And now, every Sunday was her day to spend there among her friends. Ben never went and did his best to keep Makeba home with him. But every Sunday, Helen would try to talk Makeba into going. Sometimes she was successful.

On those Sundays, Makeba would sit uncomfortably next to her mother in the third pew of the small storefront church. Helen could tell that Makeba didn't enjoy it. She wouldn't learn the hymns. She was nervous when people started shouting. Makeba didn't like church.

It made Helen more aware of how dissatisfied she was with the influence both her mother and Ben had on Makeba.

"I'm telling you, Ben. I think this stuff my mother is filling Makeba's head with is not good for her. She shouldn't talk about ghosts and visions and all that stuff in front of my child like that."

Even though Lena still scared the bejesus out of him, Ben wasn't worried about Makeba. He could see how much Lena loved the child. He knew she wouldn't do anything to hurt her.

"I don't think it's such a big deal."

"I wouldn't expect you to. What do you ever think is a big deal? Makeba is too young to believe in all this crazy stuff. I'm going to talk to Mom about it. I can't just let her ruin my child's life."

Ben decided not to respond. The same unresolved issues were always present. Helen seemed to worry about everything. What he wanted was a simpler life, an existence that would lead him back to his writing full-time. He wasn't worried about Lena and Makeba because it wasn't worth the effort. There was no way they were going to stop Lena from saying things to Makeba. Besides, he was convinced there was nothing damaging happening. So instead of plunging deeper into the budding argument, he walked over to her and kissed her on the cheek.

"Oh." Helen was not mollified. "Are you patronizing me? A peck on the jaw. Just be quiet, Helen. Don't make a fuss, Helen. I know what you're doing."

"Come on. I kissed you because I just wanted you to know that I love you." Helen always caught him when he tried to steal her anger. And yet, even though she suspected what he was doing, it worked. A simple kiss and the statement of love touched her. He saw her expression change.

She looked into his eyes and remembered the soft sounds of Smokey Robinson. The blue lights. The love that brought them Makeba. "I'm sorry. I love you too. It's just that my mother is getting to me."

Ben kissed her again, saying, "I know. But you have to relax about it. I just don't think she means any harm." He kept moving into the kitchen. There he found a black cast-iron frying pan and placed it on the stove, poured a ribbon of oil into it and turned the burner on.

Helen walked toward the kitchen, still talking to him. "And I never thought I'd hear you defend her."

"Me either." From the freezer he retrieved a rock-hard patty of ground beef.

"Well, I've got to talk to her. Anyway, I'm on my way over to Geri's. Makeba's upstairs playing some kind of godforsaken game Mom taught her. Keep an eye out."

Ben walked behind Helen as she left the house. He couldn't help but admit to himself that he liked it when she left. He loved Helen and Makeba *and* being at home. But sometimes all together it was too much.

There was a serenity in the house that was only present when she was gone. In the beginning, he had discovered peace when he and Helen were together. Increasingly that was lost. Now he found his quiet fullness more when he was alone, or with Makeba.

It was ironic because he loved the house they rented. It was big enough to give him much of what he needed: privacy, a place to do his work. In fact, Sage Street had become home. The small group of African American families on the otherwise all-white block made it feel familiar. Like the streets they had all known as children.

Hannibal, who lived across the street, was a young banker. Next door to him Rita and Scoby Rollins lived in a lower level of a duplex. Rita had just started teaching elementary school and Scoby was trying to make a go of it in his own pest extermination business. They were all struggling with the idea of success. They were all unfolding believers.

At night they ignored the porches and sat on the steps, as they had when they were young in their respective neighborhoods, and talked about the changing world. They talked about the continued threads of racism that wound their way into every aspect of their lives. They talked about their parents and how they had grown up.

They had high hopes for their children. They sketched their love for them and their future on the asphalt river that flowed at their feet.

But Ben was growing more and more cynical about the outside world. The world of junk bonds, corruption and scandal. He knew it was against *them*. Not far from where they lived, the radical "back to nature" group, MOVE, had taken root. Every day on his way home from work, Ben would pass the MOVE compound, a large house in Powelton Village with a tall wooden fence that nearly closed it off from view. But sometimes, when the gate was open, Ben could see the naked children and animals playing in the yard.

People claimed they were unclean, unhealthy, dangerous. But Ben was fascinated with MOVE. John Africa and his clan, all of whom took the surname of Africa, defied everybody and everything. They ignored health laws, they gathered weapons, they wore dreadlocks. They frightened white people. And later, many African Americans would sigh with uneasy relief when, in a hail of gunfire and even explosives that reminded Ben of televised accounts of Vietnam, the group was horrifically dismantled by the city.

The brothers and sisters of MOVE stood in stark contrast to his effort to live the life that was expected of him. He had given up the idea of being a professional artist. He had started wearing suits and sitting behind a desk. He silently cheered when MOVE stared down the police. When they spit at the rules and proclaimed the law as null and void.

And, along with the growing tension that surrounded MOVE, there was the brutality of the police. They were completely out of control. Even his white co-workers were aware of it. In fact the police had crossed the line and were brutalizing white people. No one felt safe. Indeed, feeling safe had become a concept, a dream. There was, in effect, no true safety. Not from the villains on the street or the villains behind the badges.

Slowly, Ben began to feel like he *couldn't* be happy. The happiness that filled him up when he read his poems to the small campus audience was all but gone. There was so much wrong around him that he couldn't allow himself the luxury of happiness.

He began to think that there was something wrong with the *idea* of happiness itself. That the mere presence of happiness in a person's life could block out the truth of suffering. That it could actually obscure the truth of racism and oppression.

He was beginning to think that he would never actually be what he was supposed to be. Not the writer, the father, or even the righteous black man. And yet, he began each day as a continuation of the quest for success.

In the quiet moments at home with Makeba he allowed himself to get as close to happiness as he ever did. He relinquished himself to her and accepted whatever joy she gave him in return.

He watched Helen close the door behind her. And then instantly, mindlessly he left the kitchen and bounded up the stairs and into Makeba's room. The walls were covered in a deep ocean-blue wallpaper with pictures and stickers tacked all over it. There was a yellow plastic pony in one corner and a pile of clothes in another. Dolls and miniature cooking implements were scattered through the room. On the bed Makeba sat, cross-legged, like a spiritual figure facing the wall. Ben heard her mumbling.

"Hey little girl. Who are you talking to?"

Makeba jumped. She had been completely absorbed in her conversation. "Just Ka, Daddy. I was just playing with Ka."

"Well, do you want to do something this afternoon? How about a story or something?"

"Do you want me to tell you a story?" Makeba was smiling at him. When she smiled like that all the lights in the house would dim, so that she was the only thing visible to him.

"Well, actually I was thinking I might read to you. What do you say?"

"Okay."

Ben began reading a book of African and African American folk tales. She sat with her bony brown knees curled up to her lips. Her hands embossed on her sugar face, which now rippled in intensity. Her hair, straightened, was pulled back and in two ponytails. She was in a red plaid sleeveless dress. He felt her radiating. She was someone he loved. It was proof that there was *something* worth being happy about even if he had to struggle to accept it. Makeba was happiness. He loved her.

After listening to him read for a few minutes, Makeba interrupted.

"Daddy, who wrote that book?"

Ben stopped reading and showed her the cover. "Julius Lester. He's a writer. Just like me."

"Did he see Br'er Rabbit?" Makeba's eyes were like torches in the dim light.

"No, baby, he didn't actually see Br'er Rabbit. He's just writing stories he's heard from other people."

"Who saw the rabbit?"

Ben felt the joy he always felt when she embarked on a journey of discovery. "These stories, all of them, are stories that people have told to their children for hundreds of years. It's been so long since they were first told that nobody even knows if they were true. But they might be. Anyway they're fun, aren't they?"

Makeba stared at him, her little brown face turned up. "Yeah, but is it true or is it made up?"

As Ben thought about the question, a thick acrid aroma seemed to assault his nostrils. "What's that smell?" he asked her.

"I don't know."

Ben sniffed the air. Like a finger snap he realized what was wrong. He had left the burner on. The inside of his mind turned red and yellow. He could see the flames, feel the heat.

He grabbed Makeba under his left arm like a rifle. She was completely silent, almost not breathing. He ran with her to the telephone in his room and dialed 911.

"There's a fire. We've got a fire. I've got to get my daughter out. My house is on fire." He gave the dispassionate dispatcher his name and address, hung up the telephone and ran to the top of the stairway.

"Daddy! Daddy! Ka. Ka. We didn't get Ka."

"Makeba, we've got to get out of here. Ka will be okay." Ben had reached the top step.

Now Makeba burst into tears and fought to free herself. "No, Daddy, no. I have to get Ka." He struggled to hold her.

The air swirled with thin ribbons of smoke. "Okay, okay." He gave in and quickly turned back down the hall to her room. Ka was sitting on the bed where she had left it. Ben grabbed the lion by one of its outstretched arms. Makeba snatched it from him and held it close.

They then quickly descended the stairs and headed for the front door. As he reached the doorway, Ben looked back toward the kitchen. He saw new shadows swimming on the wall, like black lights at a disco. He couldn't see the stove, only the side wall of the kitchen with the new shadows.

"There's a fire back there," he said as he opened the door and stepped onto the porch. He heard sirens in the distance. He saw a few of his neighbors coming to the windows of their safe, non-burning homes.

He looked down at Makeba, and realized how lucky he had been. They were safe. He had been there to save her. To hell with the kitchen, or the house for that matter. His daughter was safe. It was then he thought about his manuscripts lying there in his den, innocent and vulnerable.

The fire engines were on the street now and heavy-walking men pushed their way into his house. As they entered, smoke buffeted at the door.

Ben stood trembling now as the weight of the situation set in. He waited, expecting to hear the shatter of glass breaking and the loud chopping and crashing that usually accompanied urban firefighting.

If you were unlucky enough to have the misfortune of a fire in your house, only prayer could keep the firefighters from destroying what the fire didn't.

But those sounds did not issue forth. Only darker clouds of pungent smoke.

"Daddy, is our house going to burn down?" Makeba looked up with onyx eyes.

"I don't know, baby. I hope not."

"Do you think my room is on fire?"

Ben didn't want to think about the details of a disaster. "The important thing, sweetheart, is that you are safe. We made it out. And your mom's safe. That's the important thing."

Makeba didn't say anything more. She was suddenly fascinated by the blinking, spinning lights that flew whirligig up and down the block. She kept turning around and around, trying to follow the pattern of the fire truck's lights.

Hannibal walked over from across the street. "What's going on, man?"

"My house is on fire. In the kitchen. Shit. I think I left something on the stove." Ben was grateful for an adult companion.

"Don't worry, man. These dudes will take care of it."

"Yeah, I know. That's partly what I'm worried about. But damn. Helen's going to kill me."

At that moment a stout man swimming in his firefighter's coat walked out of the house and up to Ben. "This your house?"

"Yes."

"You the one who called the alarm in?"

"Yes, but how bad is it. Is it bad?" Ben's heart pounded.

"You Mr. Crestfield?"

"Yes. Goddamnit, I said yes. Now what's going on in there?"

"Well, Mr. Crestfield. All we had here was a little grease fire. Just a little frying pan with oil in it that got too hot. That's all. No big damage. Do you have a fire extinguisher?"

"Uh, no." Ben was starting to feel a little embarrassed. There were people standing around him and his daughter was below him and the tone of the big fireman seemed just a bit parental.

"Well, Mr. Crestfield. All you had to do was turn the fire out, put a lid on the pan and open some windows. Or you might have used some baking soda."

"I see. Well, I'm sorry. I didn't know. You see, I was upstairs and I smelled the smoke, and I . . ."

"You called us. I understand. No harm done. In a way, you were lucky. It could've turned nasty if nobody had called us and you weren't home or something. No harm done."

The rest of the firefighters filed out of the house. After the trucks left and the neighbors went back to their houses, Ben and Makeba sat on the steps to wait for Helen. Hannibal had stayed on as well. The kitchen was a mess, the stove a disaster. Ben had decided he would clean it up later. He just wanted to breathe the chilly night air for a while.

The quiet Sage Street night had been stained by the smell of burning oil mixed with that of the firefighters. The people who fight fires smell like all the fires they've fought. Their coats and boots and gloves hold the history of destruction and death. They left that smell on Sage Street.

But Sage Street also had found a new kind of quiet. The kind that came after a sudden burst of clatter. The kind of quiet that was restorative. That was still influenced by the noise just ended.

Ben sat there on his stoop holding a sleeping Makeba in his arms as if she was the most precious thing he had ever known. Hannibal now sat silently beside him. Ben told Hannibal how afraid he had been for Makeba. How panicked he was when he smelled the fire.

Among his friends on Sage Street, Hannibal was the most focused, clear about the direction of his life. He was a pure striver. He was intelligent and strong-willed. A confirmed bachelor. He held himself in the playboy image. He drove a canary-yellow Pontiac Firebird. He dressed like a picture. The women whom he coveted as prize often took the challenge in hope that they could change him. No one ever really did.

And yet, Hannibal watched with learning eyes as Scoby and Ben worked the arid, dusty landscape of fatherhood. He would walk across the street to talk to Helen or to play around with Makeba.

"It's understandable. I mean, this is your family. This sweet little bag of sugar is your daughter. You're supposed to be afraid for her."

"I know. But you don't know how hard it is. You zip around in your 'bird and hang out with all those fine women I see falling out of your crib and yet I always get the impression that you think *I'm* doing something special."

"You are. Sometimes hanging out like I do gets very dumb. Sometimes I wish I had what you have."

"Naw, man, I don't know about that. I'm struggling. Really struggling with it."

"What you need to do, Ben"—Hannibal stretched his long legs over the steps— "is stop worrying so much and learn how to make the best of the situation."

"The best of a bad situation," Ben said into the silky summer-night air.

"It's only as bad as you make it, brother. I mean really, if you get about the business of making some money and move beyond this self-pity bullshit, you might make it." Hannibal had moved to Philadelphia from Washington to attend the University of Pennsylvania. He had attended white private schools all his life.

Ben looked at him. Hannibal was *the* tall, dark and handsome equivalent in black. He liked Hannibal for a lot of reasons, but one of them was that he was unequivocal. He believed. "It isn't that simple, man. Do you really think that if you put all your energy into doing your job at the bank you're going to end up being president of the Girard National Bank?"

"If I wanted to. If I wanted to I could run that motherfucka without any sweat. This money shit is a piece of cake. They try to mystify the whole thing so folks like us won't think we can understand it. But shit, man, making money isn't that hard. You watch me."

Ben smiled. Hannibal believed. "So you're going to make big money, huh?"

"Watch me. You just watch me. But let me tell you. . ." Hannibal's soft voice raised a notch. "I'm not going to be no goddamn bank president. Because I do know I'd have to wait forever to get there. I mean, I know I can get there, but. . ."

Laughter left Ben's mouth. "But what?"

"I don't *want* to be bank president. I'm going to do my own thing. We got to get to the entrepreneurial thing. For a man to make things happen for him nowadays, you have to control your own destiny. You have to have your own thing."

"So what's your thing, Hann?"

Hannibal stood up, came down the steps and stood on the sidewalk facing Ben. "Don't know yet, Ben. I haven't figured that out yet. But I will. I'm not ready anyway. You see, even though I said it wasn't hard, there is a lot of shit you have to know." Hannibal stared into Ben's eyes. This was when Ben liked Hannibal the most. Not when he was talking about manipulating his many women friends, or when he hid his closest, warmest emotions. But when he was engaged.

Hannibal continued. "You want to know something? Something I discovered in college?"

"You're not going to tell me any more of those hot coed stories, are you? Because I don't want to hear none of that shit tonight. Helen's not even at home," Ben joked.

"I found out that the whole study of money is the study of white men. If you know it, you know them. If you master the knowledge of money, you master the white man and therefore you become the master of your own life."

Hannibal stood up, satisfied that he had articulated his philosophy. Ben had listened carefully. Something about the preoccupation with money as the primary vehicle to self-determination seemed wrong. But he was fascinated by what Hannibal had said.

"I don't know, man. . . but the more I work—the more I fall into this stream of people who are trying to prove how capable they are at everything, including making money—the more I think about punching out."

"You can't punch out, brother." Hannibal laughed and pointed to the house where Makeba and Helen slept. "You ain't about to go nowhere."

Ben gave up the seedling of thought. Of course he wasn't going to punch out. He had a life of lives to be there for.

"All I'm saying is that I can't help wondering what I'm doing with my life. I'm not writing very much right now. All I do is go to work. I mean, maybe I should be doing something else."

"Like what?" Hannibal yawned. He was ready to go back home.

"I don't know. Just like you. But when I know, you'll be the second person to know." Ben smiled.

"Yeah, well, I got to get up early tomorrow."

"Me too."

And now, in the barrel of the night, as he waited for Helen with a sleeping child in his arms, he wondered again about his life.

Makeba's Journal

It's eerie to read about me from your point of view. I have to keep trying to remember that you are my father and that the child in the book is me. But it's very hard to trust you. The things you say are basically true. I remember the fire. I know I was very scared. And I remember making you go back to get Ka. But there are little things which don't seem right. The problem is you have to lie to write, don't you? I mean, like the way I remember it, there were no firemen. You put the fire out yourself. The kitchen was a wreck but there weren't fire trucks and all that. And I thought you were in your den writing when the fire started. I don't remember you being in my room.

And then, on top of everything, whenever you mention me or Mom it's always bad. Like we were just dead weight on your career. Is that all I was?

The confusing part is that I wanted to read this book because I wanted to know what you thought. But the more I know, the more I'm not sure I should know it. I also want to know whether or not I can trust you. You left me. You walked away. How can I ever trust you after that? I thought maybe as I learned more about your story I would feel something. Maybe it would let me believe in you again. That's what I want. There are things you should know about me, but I can't tell you until I feel it's right. Too much time has passed and the only clear feeling I have about you is that no matter how much you protest, you couldn't have loved me very much.

Eighteen

An alarm went off within the darkness. The air was thick. The fire was a wake-up call. Mates could feel a gathering of strength surging around him. Ben was walking a thin line and would not be able to keep his balance forever. He was looking for an escape but he wasn't a butterfly. He had no power. He was just a man. Poor man. Poor poor man.

Ben was in a relationship with destiny. His race, his sense of history, his education, were meaningless. Ben wasn't doing what he wanted to do. Mates could see it easily. But Ben was already in too deep—a wife, a child.

From where Mates was, ensconced in the shadows, this was shaping up to be very amusing. He'd seen it before. There were men strewn all over this world who had decided that the only way to reach their dreams was to run from their history.

As hope and promise dissipate, a sound is made. Like an envelope being opened, except the ripping goes on until your ears become accustomed to it. And when that happens it is likely that you will lose something. Promises made and held hopes are adhesives and need at least two things to be attached to. They stand between us.

Helen heard the sound. She knew something was very wrong.

She had taken to spending more and more time with Geri. This happened mostly during the weekdays. Geri was hardly ever available during the weekends. Her life was consumed in men and parties. Helen would sit and listen to the details.

She couldn't help but admire Geri. There was something about her friend's complete lack of interest in having a family that both upset and intrigued her. Geri, on the other hand, was oblivious to the issues that preoccupied Helen.

And yet Helen would look for opportunities to say how unhappy she was becoming. How she was growing more and more afraid that she and Ben were coming apart.

Finally Geri got the point and asked, "Okay Helen. What's the real problem here? Do you think he's seeing somebody? What's going on in the boudoir? Does he still make your hair go back?"

Helen was surprised at the directness of the question. She swallowed. "I . . . We . . . Well, everything's not going super in that department right now." She looked down at the pink faux-marble kitchen tabletop in front of her. And then quickly added, "But I don't think he's involved with anybody else. I don't think so. But he doesn't come straight home from work the way he used to. And he's started spending so much time in his den."

"Well, what's he do in his den?"

"I don't know exactly." Helen picked up her glass of orange juice. Geri was eating a chocolate chip cookie. The brown crumbs were collecting in a pile in front of her. "He won't let me in there anymore. And he won't show me what he's working on. He's just become very quiet. It's not like he talked all the time. But now it's like he hardly says anything to me. He spends most of his time with Makeba or in his room. He's up all night in there."

Geri turned her head to the silent television on the counter, where the soft brown face of Oprah Winfrey stared back. "So where does he go after work?"

"He says he's with Ramsey. I don't think he's lying to me. I just think he doesn't want to be home."

"No, Helen. I don't think he's lying either but you've got to admit that he ain't up on it either. I mean, he's acting kind of weird.

You ain't done nothing but be a do-right woman and here he is throwing shit in your face."

"Maybe it's not that bad. It's pretty hard on him really. He wants to be writing. I'm thinking that I should probably go back to work."

Geri looked at Helen as if she realized for the first time that Helen wasn't working. "Yes indeed, girlfriend. If I was you I'd get myself some employment. You just never know. It don't smell like roses over there on Sage Street. Y'all been together a long time, and the way I see it, nothing don't go on forever."

Helen tried not to look into Geri's eyes. "Why not? I don't understand. I mean, we're just getting started. Makeba's only nine. I was thinking about having another child. I want a family."

"But Helen." Geri hunched her slim shoulders forward, her almond eyes sparkling, her now trimmed Afro glistening. "Look around you. Who the hell is staying together? Nobody. I don't know one damn couple in the entire city of Philadelphia that's been together more than ten years. None. Maybe you do, but I don't. All I see are people breaking up like teacups falling out the cupboard. And everybody is always asking me when I'm getting married. Shit. I wish I would get married. Let some asshole sonofabitch treat me like I ain't nobody. Na-uh, baby. I'm staying single. I'm keeping myself in good shape and I'm taking names and kicking ass. If they want to spend time with me they gonna have to sing a pretty tune."

Helen couldn't help smiling. Geri could talk shit like a corner girl. Which made sense because Geri had indeed been a South Philly corner girl. And now, she was working at the phone company by day and playing the streets by night. And she still had a gang of women friends who nearly worshiped her.

Geri continued. "But if I was you, I wouldn't be thinking about having no more kids. That would be just about the dumbest god-damned thing you ever done."

"I'm not so sure. I remember the way he was when Makeba was born. He wanted to be there all the time. You know how close he is to that girl. If we had another baby, it might make a difference."

Geri played in the cookie crumbs. "Tell me you ain't that dumb? Please, chile, please tell me that you are just bullshitting me."

"I'm serious. You never know."

"I know one thing. Having another baby when you and your man ain't down together is like building a house without a foundation. The goddamn thing is going to fall in one day."

"But it might fall anyway." Helen felt very sad. She hated giving voice to her fears. "It's not Ben. I can live without him."

"Well, thank you, Jesus. You ain't totally ignorant."

"It's the whole idea of our family that I don't want to lose. We can do it. Makeba and Ben are my family."

"Not if he doesn't love you. Not if he doesn't want to be there."

Helen was tired of the discussion. She was ready to head back home. "He doesn't know what he wants. His head is so full of all that white folks' stuff he learned in college and his writing that he don't know whether he's coming or going. So I'm not worried about what he wants. We have a daughter and she deserves a father and a mother and that's the way it's supposed to be."

Geri just stared at her. Soon Helen got up from the table and left for home.

When she got back to Sage Street Makeba was already asleep. Ben was upstairs in his den. Helen thought about knocking on his door but decided instead to go to bed. After having spent the evening laughing with Geri the silence of the house was welcome anyway.

Makeba's Journal

EIGHTEENTH ENTRY

I feel sorry for Mom. She had no idea how bad everything was. You could always count on her to keep going when things got rough. I respect her a lot. But I wish she had been different. Maybe things would have been better between the two of you.

Now I understand what you meant in that *Ebony* magazine article when you said that "most writers will declaim themselves in their work. There is no reason to deny my own story through the creation of fictional characters. My life is fiction." I wrote it down because I didn't understand it. I am not fiction and I am a part of your life. But now I see what you mean. You've made all of us a part of a fiction. And yet, it is our lives. We exist.

Maybe there is hope.

Nineteen

Mates could feel his muscles twitching. That was living. With twitching muscles and a nose that never quit smelling. It was coming soon. He ached for the solidification, the transformation into his fated existence. Mates was a natural predator, he needed only prey.

Ben feared Mates even then. Even when he had no idea that Mates was real, Ben was possessed with the need to exonerate himself for his own selfishness. Ben knew that there would eventually come a time when something would force him to confront himself. But he didn't know it would be Mates, the dog. If he had, things might have been different.

One of the driving energies pushing him into new terrain was that he was unhappy at Benson Glendale. He couldn't believe how superficial the world of business was. How intensely people felt about the finite elements of making money. In the Navy he had grown accustomed to incompetence and pettiness. And now, in the private sector he was confronted with a hypercharged, almost frenetic energy to make money. In this world, even the smallest, most minute of functions was considered, discussed and planned. It drove him crazy.

He was supposed to be there on time. Smile. Be neatly dressed—indeed, to reflect his belief in the system simply by the way he dressed. He was expected to make small talk with people he didn't like and who didn't like him. No one ever asked him about his writing, even though everyone knew that's what he did when he wasn't at work. No one cared about that.

"Why were you late this morning?"

"Why didn't you come to the office party?"

"Why do you always look so angry?"

"What's wrong, Ben, aren't you happy here?"

"Hell no, I'm not happy here. How can I be happy here? You people have no idea what I'm up against here. I'm already mimicking you stupid assholes, trying to act like I believe that you will actually give me something if I do right. I'm already selling the fuck out."

This is what passed through his head every day. He'd sit at his desk and try to write "zippy" copy. That was the phrase around the office. "Peppy," "pithy," "electric." And he wasn't bad at it. But it leached something from his reservoir of creativity to have a job in which he was paid to lie. It hit home when he was asked to write ad copy for a fashionable Society Hill furrier.

"We're giving you this account because you've had so much success writing for the downtown crowd, Ben." That was what John Glendale had said as Ben sat facing him in the vice president's loft office. Ben knew that was a lie. He had had terrific success with their largest client, the department store Strawbridge and Clothier. He thought his real talent was in his ability to reach working-class consumers who were seeking a bargain. But of course, he could only assist on such an account. They would never give such a plum to him.

He knew that the reason he got the furrier was because three of the writers had refused to write copy for them. Ben studied the man who sat behind the desk, trying to decide what he wanted to say. John was only five years older than Ben and was a phenom in the business. He'd started out with a small company and wild ideas and built a very successful advertising and public relations firm.

John faced him with his rounded shoulders, thinning blond hair and horn-rimmed glasses. When he smiled his fading San Juan tan seemed to crack open. His conservative blue pinstripe Brooks Brothers moved with him.

"I'm not sure I want to work for them."

"What do you mean?" There was a tone in John's voice which told Ben there wasn't much room to operate.

"It's just that I don't think we should have a company like that as clients. Nobody wants to work for them."

"Ben, this is a great opportunity for you to show what you've got in terms of account management. You don't want to be a writer all your life, do you? I mean, the money's in the management and the sales. I think maybe you could make it here. But you've got to step up to the plate."

Ben played the last sentence over in his head. "Step up to the plate." What the hell did that mean?

"Well, I'd love to try account management," Ben lied. "I just don't want to be the manager for an animal killer." Ben knew this would anger John. He also knew he hadn't ever thought about animal rights before in his life. He knew almost nothing about it. But he did know that there were three white copywriters who refused to do the work and he didn't want to be seen as different from them. He didn't want to be the Negro who'd do anything to ingratiate himself with his white employer.

"An animal killer, huh?" John stood up abruptly. "Let me tell you something, Mr. Crestfield. I don't appreciate your tone of voice or your choice of words. And you get this straight. You work for me. If I tell you to write for the fuckin' Martians you do it. You got that?"

Ben couldn't believe this white man was getting in his face like that. Granted he was a long way from North Philly, but it was still in him. Deep inside him the instincts began to form into action. He stood up.

"Listen man. I won't let you talk to me like that. *You* got that?" Ben threw John's words back at him. "I'll kick your motherfuckin' ass if you raise your voice to me again." Ben couldn't believe he was saying what he was saying. But something was going on inside him and he couldn't control it.

"Get out of my office. I should have known better. This affirmative action bullshit is just that. You're lucky Benson likes you or you'd be history. But I'm warning you, Ben. This is the beginning of the end. He won't be able to protect you forever."

Ben turned and walked out of the office. He'd learned at least two things. One was that Seth Benson liked him and the other was he didn't give two shits.

Makeba's Journal

NINETEENTH ENTRY

I'm tired. I'm not used to sitting so long. And I'm uncomfortable. What was I to you? Sometimes I feel like you never saw me as a person.

I hate feeling uncomfortable. When your skin feels creepy and your stomach quivers. I hate that. Okay, you have to know something. I wasn't sure I was going to tell you but suddenly I feel like it's a part of the reason I'm writing this at all. About five months ago I was at this coffee shop downtown. I like to come into the city every now and then. Sometimes I meet friends, other times I just go to a movie. Well, I stopped in this place where I always get a sweet roll or a croissant and a cup of coffee.

Well, this guy comes in and sits at my table. I didn't mind that too much. Actually he seemed pretty interesting. He had the prettiest wavy black hair I have ever seen on a black man. He said his name was Ricky. So anyway, we started talking and he told me he was in college at Drexel studying to be an electrical engineer. I told him about me. At the time I was thinking about taking a course in computer repair.

I met him a few more times over the next week. Then he asked to take me to the movies. I said yes. I really liked him. Ka warned me. But Ka has never liked any boy I liked. She and Mom never approved of anybody who was interested in me. I always left Ka home when I went out with Ricky. That was stupid.

Well, after the movie he drives me to Fairmount Park and cuts the car off. We kissed. I knew what he wanted but I wasn't sure about him. He acted kind of strange sometimes. Like one time we were buying some ice cream and the guy who was serving us was real nasty. He didn't look up at Ricky or me or nothing. So when Ricky gets the ice cream and the man sticks his hand out for the money, Ricky turns the ice cream upside down in his open hand. Both cones. And Ricky says, "This is for your funky vanilla self and the ice cream too." And we walked out. So I knew he could be weird. I understand that. Almost every black man I know is like that. Like a balloon, full of anger just waiting for a pin. If I couldn't love a man who was angry then I could never love a black man.

Anyway, so Ricky starts trying to feel my breasts. I pushed his hands away and he shoved me up against the car door. At the same time his hands were already under my dress. I couldn't believe it. He wasn't saying anything. Not "I love you" or "I need you" or anything. I just remember his heavy breath and the feeling that his hands were penetrating my skin.

He got his black ugly fingers all the way up my dress, pushed under my panties and into me. I was screaming. I screamed so loud. And I started kicking him. I had on heels so it didn't take long before he backed off of me and slid back under the steering wheel. He started crying and apologized. He said that sometimes he couldn't control himself. And then he started talking about all his problems. *His* problems. He reminded me of Mike Tyson and that Kennedy guy. He had practically raped me. And he had the nerve to sit there, while I'm stinging from his brutality, and talk about his problems. But I was scared. I didn't have anything that I could use to defend myself. Ka was not with me. I was in his car. In the park. In the dark. I was at his mercy.

It was at that moment that I thought about you. That was when I realized I had to talk to you. That no matter how mad I was at you, how disappointed that you left us, I had to talk to you. I promised myself that if I lived through that moment I would come to you. That was before I even knew this book existed. I also made one other promise. That if Ricky didn't kill me that night, right then, in that car, I would kill him. I have been possessed by this thought ever since. I will never be defenseless again.

Twenty

At night, in his room, Ben traveled further and further into the made-up world of his stories. His hands danced in some spiritual harmony with his mind as they struck the keys of his electric typewriter. They seemed to take on a life of their own. He often stared at them. Particularly the backs of them. Sometimes, while he typed, it was the back of his hands that he focused on. He loved the way they moved. The way his skin, like an incredibly detailed brown map, stretched to accommodate their every movement. The pronounced crisscrossing of veins. He often reminded himself how close he had come to losing the fluid grace of his right hand. In one instant, his hand could have been crushed by a rageful stranger in a dark bar. Even now, after he was finished writing, his hand ached. It was a deep, stabbing pain which could not be reached. A pain that seemed buried in the bone.

And yet he was suddenly possessed by his work. Consumed in his need to translate what had become an increasing turmoil into art. Ben's current subject was Makeba. He was trying to write a series of poems to her. Makeba's face was now ever present wavering in front of him like a hologram. Her eyes following his every action.

He couldn't tell her, or Helen for that matter, that he was writing so much about Makeba. They would want to know why. And he wasn't sure about that. They would want to know why the poems and short stories all ended with Makeba in deep sadness. He couldn't help feeling that there was some great tragedy lurking in her life.

Ben didn't want to hear the questions because he didn't know the answers to them. He only knew that he was trying to transform his purest feelings about Makeba, his unexpressed love, his hope for her future, into a poetic language. He wanted to write something that would be like a blanket for her. And he wanted to discover what being a father meant.

Ben was beginning to realize that his presence in her life was tenuous. More and more he could see himself living somewhere else, surrounded by paper. Living a life on the outside of the walls that were presently around him.

But he was not in control of the images that grew on the paper in front of him. He would struggle home from work, eat dinner, play with Makeba and make his way up to his second-floor den. Once there, he would sit in an old, chipped wooden secretary's chair under candlelight and stare at the typewriter until the night opened up. The flicker of the flame from the candle would create hypnotic shapes that shimmied across the walls. Eventually he would begin to mark the paper with little black marks. Clack clack clack clack. His hands would begin a journey of love and adventure.

But increasingly the words were more desperate. There was a growing cynicism about Makeba's future. Or rather it was a cynicism about Ben's future with Makeba.

On an impulse, he jumped up from his desk and walked into Makeba's room. She was carefully folded into her bed, lightly snoring. He looked at her face. Her innocence was so powerful. He moved close to her bed and found himself whispering, blowing flowers of pain into her ear.

"What am I supposed to do, Makeba? How can I do this? I want you to be strong. To feel safe.

"But I didn't exactly plan to be a father. It just happened. Suddenly you were coming and I wanted everything to be okay. I wanted your mother to feel safe. I needed her. And then, I started needing you.

"People say that I've got a special responsibility for you. I made you. If it wasn't for me, you wouldn't be here. And God, how incredible that is. You exist because I do. Okay, maybe I do. I want to take that responsibility on too. Makeba, you probably won't believe it, but I really want to do the right thing. People will say the right thing is obvious. That I belong here, with you and your mother. People will say there is no excuse, no reason strong enough to justify walking away from your family.

"Makeba, please forgive me. I want to be more than a faceless spot in the black crowd. At this moment, I can't think of one black man who has been the father of a family and created great art. That scares me.

"It's really hard to say that I love you and that I love your mother and yet I'm afraid that I'm going to die. That if I don't find a way out of here I'm not going to make it. We need so much. We need black men to be fathers. We need black men to be artists. We need them to make a statement, a final, summary statement to the world that what we see and feel might hold the key to our existence. Might save everybody. I believe that. And yet I don't think I can do it all: be a husband, a father and me.

"So listen, sweetheart, this is what I want to know. Do you understand? Can you forgive me? I mean, if you knew that I was fighting for identity, a chance to concentrate on my gift, would you understand? Would you insist I be with you even if it meant I would never write again? If you were certain that no matter how much I loved you, if I stayed here I would be unhappy, would you still want me to stay?"

Ben stood silent for a long time, staring at the image of his daughter frozen in front of him. Her body pulling in air, holding it, letting it go.

"Makeba, listen. If I ever leave, I won't be leaving you. This thing I'm fighting is not against you. No matter what, we will never disconnect. I will always be your father. We won't be separated so easily.

But I may not be able to live this out the way we first thought. Things may have to change."

Ben heard something just behind him; he whirled around, to face Helen. "What are you doing? I woke up and thought I heard someone talking in here. What were you saying?" Helen's voice merged a hushed whisper with anger and suspicion. She wore a summer-weight blue nightgown. Her hair was wrapped in a silk scarf. She looked at a sleeping Makeba to emphasize the questions she was asking.

"Nothing. I was just checking on Makeba. Sometimes I just like to watch her sleep," he lied.

"Really? I didn't know that." Helen was suspicious. She had clearly heard him whispering. "Did I hear you say something about leaving? That's not what I heard, was it?" She was getting very tired of his lethargic, tortured posture. "Stand up, damn it. Just stand up." She wanted to scream at him.

"I guess I was thinking out loud. I'm sorry if I disturbed you." Ben walked past her and into their bedroom. He bounced himself onto the bed with a heavy sigh. He knew there would be no peace until they talked.

"I don't get it. What's the matter? What's wrong with you?" Helen was still in the hallway when she began talking. And she was speaking clearly now. Not in a whisper. Her voice rose as she passed through the bedroom threshold.

"I don't know." Ben lay back. "But this is really hard."

"What is? Being a father? Being a husband?" Helen paused. She was holding herself together as well as she could. But there was a limit. She was ready to let it out. "I'm tired of you complaining all the damn time. All you have to do is act like a man. Is your life so awful? Are we so awful?"

Ben turned away from her. This would be the perfect time to say what he needed to say. This was it. He exhaled. "My life . . . Helen . . . my life is pretty awful."

Helen looked through him. She was very sleepy all of a sudden. And yet, she summoned more energy. Ben was confused and falling apart and he needed her to help him find his way. She didn't want to hear any more about his life. She didn't want to know how hard he thought it was. She just wanted him to live up to his promise. They had to make it.

She sat down on the bed and gently but firmly turned Ben's head back toward her. "Listen, we can work this out. I know we can. We have the beginning of a great family and I don't want to lose it. I'm not letting this whole thing just fall apart because it's difficult."

Ben put his arms around her. Her body was still warm from sleep. "Why is it that what I want to be seems so far away from here?"

"It's because, Ben, you don't know how close you are to where you really belong. But I'll help you. Together, we'll make it. I know we will."

And with that, she curled up beside him. They held each other and slipped into dream.

The next morning, a Saturday, Helen and Makeba were up and out of the house early. Ben was still lying under the covers. It was midday and the sun fractured the settling dust in the room. He slowly opened his eyes. He knew that Helen and Makeba were at Geri's. That afternoon he was supposed to get together with Ramsey and Hannibal for drinks.

But something wasn't right. As he lay in bed he thought he heard footsteps downstairs. There was someone else in the house. He knew it. There were little movements that disturbed the general stillness. Ben knew he wasn't the only living thing there.

He rolled out of bed and pulled on his sweatpants. Then, shirtless, he walked through the hallway and stood at the top of the stairs. He listened. He was certain there was someone downstairs.

"Hello. Helen? Makeba?" he called as he started slowly down the steps. He grew increasingly uneasy. Now the sound was in the kitchen. "Helen? Are you in there?" he almost screamed.

"You don't have to holler. I was coming out here." Lena, dressed in a peanut-green polyester pants suit, her thin body rattling inside it, came out of the kitchen. "I was just trying to find some tea or something."

"Lena, what . . . ah . . . How are you? Is everything okay?" To his recollection, Lena had never been in the house when Helen wasn't there. "What are you doing here?"

"Well, I just thought it was about time we had a talk."

"You and me?" Ben stood there staring at her.

"Yes. Now you go put on a shirt and come on down here and sit down. I'll make you some coffee. There's some things I want to say."

"Lena, what is this all about?" Even as he asked her the question he was beginning to head back upstairs for his shirt.

"It's about your family. It's about all of us."

Ben took his time as he walked back up the steps and found a shirt to put on. He went into the bathroom, where he carefully washed his face and put his shirt on. Did she know things weren't working out? He headed back downstairs.

Lena was already sitting on the couch in the living room, sipping her tea. On the coffee table was a cup of coffee for him. He bent over and picked up the coffee. "Thanks. This is very good."

"You're welcome. Now, sit down." He did. Suddenly he felt sheepish, like a little boy. "I talked to Helen early this morning. She was pretty upset."

Ben took a deep breath. She knew. "What did she say?"

"She's worried. And that makes me worry. I don't want my daughter to be worried like she is. You know what I mean?"

Ben nodded. He was listening but he was also trying to formulate some kind of response.

"I mean, it just seems that you two have got to get it together. Life's hard. I know that. But I don't know what you must be thinking. You got a beautiful daughter. Helen's wonderful. What's the matter with you, boy?"

"Why do you think something's the matter with me?"

"Well, my daughter is all worked up thinking you're gonna leave her. Now, that's what she told me. You sayin' that ain't true? 'Cause if it is true, then I'd say something was mighty wrong with you."

"I didn't say I was leaving. The only thing I've said is that things don't seem to be working out. That's all." It was hard enough trying to talk to Helen. With Lena it was impossible.

"Well, what do you mean by that? What's not working out?"

Ben just sat there looking into the midmorning. He couldn't say anything.

What Lena saw was a man whose face had hardened into wood. She could perceive his sense of paralysis. She knew he couldn't tell her what he felt. But she could tell him. She leaned forward and pointed herself at him.

"I wasn't in favor of this thing from the beginning. And I told you then I wasn't gonna have no messing around with my daughter. You made a promise and you had better keep it. This ain't nothing to play with. If you're aiming to hurt my daughter or my granddaughter, you had better think twice. Because I'm just not gonna let you walk away from here like that."

Ben pooled his energy and forced himself to speak. "I know you mean well. But don't you think Helen and I should deal with this?"

"No," Lena snapped. "No I don't. If I don't get involved in this ain't no telling what will happen. Just because you think you're so smart and can write all this godforsaken junk you write. You think you brought the world into being when you stepped on the earth. And you think you can decide what is right and wrong. But you can't. This is my business too. My daughter is my business. Now, I'm trying to talk to you nicely about this. But I don't think you have put yourself into this family strong enough. They need more from you. You're going to have to find a way to do that for them. You just are. I know you don't want to hurt them.

"But I want you to know this: I'm not kidding. If you do hurt them, I swear to you, you will have to search the earth to find a way to forget it."

Ben now held his head up. He was on fire with anger. She had no right to intrude into his life this way. He wanted to attack her. He wanted to ask why Helen was so afraid of a future without him? Why hadn't Lena raised her daughter to know her own strength, disconnected from a man? Why did he feel as if Helen had been waiting for him? Waiting to become a wife and mother instead of creating something special for herself, like his writing was for him. But instead, he smothered his thoughts.

"Are you finished? I appreciate your concern," Ben said through clenched teeth. "But I want you to know that this is between Helen and me. It's got nothing to do with you. You have no idea who I am or what I think and I'm not going to waste my time trying to explain anything to you. Now, I've got to go. Are you going to stay here and wait for Helen to come back or are you leaving? By the way, how did you get in?"

"Helen left the door unlocked for me. I just wanted you to know how I felt. And I did that. Now I'm ready to go. So, you tell Helen I asked about her and kiss Makeba for me."

Ben watched Lena gather her things and leave. He leaned back in the chair as she closed the door.

Makeba's Journal

TWENTIETH ENTRY

I know what happens from here on. I know how this turns out. I don't really need to read any more. You got mad one night and left. I remember that much. The argument. The shouting. I remember that. I wonder how you'll write that.

How was I supposed to answer you? What father would ask his daughter to make a choice?

Ricky's face just flashed in my mind. I haven't talked to him since that night. I bought a gun. It's laying on my bed right now. I was really going to kill him. I still might. I promised myself I would.

Twenty-one

Love is a slow walk to madness. To being haunted. And when it wears thin, love knows only desperation. Some of it swims into Mates's body like blood as a clutching, grabbing kind of energy that seeks to prove its own existence. It breathes life into his limbs.

The rest of it escapes and maintains residence in all the spaces where it was expressed. It remains deep in the crevices of the wood or in the small cracks of the mortar, forever. You can go back to a spot where you held hands with a former lover and feel the same intensity, the same emotion. It may make you sick or make you swoon. You may want to flee. But you know it is there just the same.

Things between Ben and Helen had slowed to a crawl. Ben turned further inside, into his writing, into the seclusion of his den. He and Helen now spent little time together.

Every day, Helen became more and more anxious. She had taken to a daily harangue to draw Ben out. She complained about the things he did. What he talked about. Some days her sole objective was to instigate some confrontation between them. She could tell she was losing him. That they were disintegrating. And his inability to talk about it infuriated her.

Sometimes she was sure that he was losing his mind.

At night, after Makeba had gone to bed, after the kitchen was cleaned, after the nightly news, she'd watch him sit in his bent-wood rocker in the living room, ignoring the television, staring into space. Sometimes he would sit there for hours. And then suddenly he'd jump up and run upstairs to his room.

But as Helen watched him sit there, night after night, she wondered if he would ever wake up and see her waiting for him to return as her lover. She hoped he would eventually snap himself into sync with her.

Ben knew what she was doing. He watched stoically as Helen tried to pry open a part of him that had closed. Every time he told Helen he loved her, he felt stupid. He felt incompetent to put his exact feelings into words. He wanted Helen to see that even though he loved her, it wasn't enough.

He was there with her. But it wasn't an honest life. He began feeling guilty and he didn't want Helen to think it was her fault. He didn't want her to believe that their love had already died. He didn't want her to think that he was backing out on any of the promises he had made.

But he was. He felt himself slipping deeper and deeper into a place where she could not reach him. He hoped she would not see how, like evaporating water, he was leaving her all along.

But Helen knew. She felt it, saw it. She couldn't believe it but there it was. When he was home he was usually with Makeba. He rarely came barreling up the steps just for her. He had stopped pulling her out of sleep to crawl into her body.

And yet, while she knew this, she was not willing to accept it, to let it undermine her hopes for the future. If it took her will to hold things together, then her will was strong enough. She expected Ben to emerge from the abyss any day. Every day. She waited.

And so she kept thinking up things for them to do. Trips to the zoo, bowling, miniature golf, romantic dinners out. But one day as she waited for Ben to come home from work, she got an idea.

She was flipping through the classifieds when she came upon the Houses for Sale section. Suddenly she knew what it would take to get

Ben to understand where his priorities should be. They had been renting the house they were living in and if she could get Ben excited about buying a house maybe it would reenergize his interest.

Besides, she reasoned, they needed a house. They needed a place that was theirs. That had a lawn and a garage. A house on a tree-lined street with other black families. Out of the city. The picture was incomplete the way it was. How could she expect Ben to focus on his family life if they had no long-term financial commitments? No long-term commitment to be in a place together? They had to make a change. It was the logical next step.

Later that evening, after Ben came home and they had dinner, she went to their bedroom and changed into her favorite nightgown, a sheer pink peignoir. It fastened up high, near her neck, and draped her tall body. Its flowing chiffon, in two layers, reached the floor. She lit three candles on her dresser, reclined on the bed and called Ben.

When he walked into the bedroom, she looked into his eyes and saw the strain of the mere act of walking up the steps.

"Come here and sit down," she said.

"Helen, please. I don't feel like it tonight." Ben didn't even want to play the game. He was tired of forcing his physical self into action. "I'm tired and I just don't want to make love right now."

"You could at least sit down with me."

Ben looked at her lying there. He hated that nightgown. He knew she thought it was sexy, but he thought it was old-fashioned, conservative. If she wanted to excite him, that wasn't the thing to wear. Still, he forced a smile. "I know you didn't put that on just to get me to sit with you."

"Ben?" Ben recognized the inflection of her voice. This was the voice of incredible hope. This was the voice of excitement.

Helen shifted her body so that she nearly faced him. "Well, I've been thinking that maybe we should move."

"Move? Why?" Ben had never thought about leaving Sage Street with Helen. He *had* begun to contemplate leaving. But not with her. Why would they move anyway?

"Because I think Makeba should grow up in a different environment. You know what I mean? I mean, what if we decide to have another child? Of course Sage is fine but, you know, every year when the school year changes there's all these new people moving in. It's not the kind of place you want to have your children spend their whole lives."

Ben's heart paused. "Children? What do you mean *children?*"

"You never know." Helen broke a sweet, obviously teasing smile. "We might have another child."

"Another child? No, Helen. Not another child. I don't want another child and we can't afford to buy a house." They had battled the bills since the first week of their marriage.

"I didn't say we should have a baby now, but maybe . . ." Helen almost whispered.

"No. I'm not talking about another baby. Don't start that."

Helen sat up, reached her hand over and grabbed his face, turning it to her. "I think we can afford a house. We have to. It's something everybody else does."

"But we're barely making it now." When she called him upstairs, Ben had been thinking about going to his room. He had come into the bedroom on his way there. This was an ambush. He wasn't prepared for it.

"Don't think about the negative part. Just listen to me. Suppose we had a smaller, newer house on a beautiful street in Chestnut Hill or somewhere like that. And Makeba had friends. And we had families, just like us, all around. We could have a front lawn. And a garage. A big brick barbecue pit, you know." She paused, breaking into a big smile. "And you could put up a basketball hoop." She nudged Ben's side with her elbow.

He fought a smile. She was so strong and able to penetrate his first line of defense. She knew him well. He had always wanted a basketball hoop. But in North Philadelphia no one had garages. You put the hoop on a tree or a telephone pole.

"I mean, just think about it. It could be just the thing we need. Just the thing that . . ."

"That what?"

"That might make us all very happy. Happy as a bunch of little piggies in mud." She tried to keep from laughing at her inability to use the right word in the old saying.

"Pigs in shit, Helen. It's pigs in shit."

"Who cares? We can be happy. We've been happy." Helen knew how to fight the negative energy that rose from his body like puffs of smoke.

Ben wanted to change the subject. He didn't know how to respond. He knew he didn't want to dig the hole deeper. He knew that. Still, unprepared to tell her the complete truth, he said, "Okay. If you want to look into it, go ahead. I just know one thing."

"What's that?" Helen slid back down on the bed, satisfied that they were on the verge of a new beginning.

"I want you to be happy." Ben looked into her eyes and tried to make her believe him. And it was true. He really did.

Helen reached up and pulled him down on her. She kissed his lips. "Then we got this thing under control, baby. Trust me. We'll make it."

Ben returned her kiss and at the same time began pushing himself up. "I've got work to do, Helen." As he walked down the hall toward his studio, Ben hoped that their lives would soon find new light.

Makeba's Journal

TWENTY-FIRST ENTRY

Have you ever held a gun? I bet you haven't. They're heavier than you think they'd be. I've never fired it. I just hold it a lot. But do you know what? The longer you have a gun that you haven't fired, the harder it is to not pull the trigger. Actually I can't wait to shoot it. Every day I imagine Ricky standing over me thinking he can do whatever he wants and then I pull out the gun and he knows it's all over. I can see his soft brown eyes wide open, gleaming, frightened out of his stupid mind. His body trembling. Maybe he'd be begging me to let him go. I know just what he'd say too, he'd say something lame like, "I didn't mean it. I'm sorry. I didn't mean to hurt you." And then I'd smile at him and pull the trigger. Fuck him. He doesn't deserve a break. I don't care whether he deserves it or not. He wouldn't get one from me.

Does it surprise you that I have a gun? Your little girl a gun-toting hoodlum. Well, it's treacherous out there. It's not even safe out in the suburbs where we live, much less in the city. But I didn't buy it because I'm afraid of the knuckleheads in the streets. I can pretty much handle them. Nobody messes with me too much. It's just that after Ricky tried to pull a number on me I had to have a way to take care of myself. I don't want to go out that way. At the hand of somebody I actually know. I'm not having it.

Okay, I'm finished venting about Ricky. But I wanted you to know. To be honest I don't really want the gun. It has a sort of personality to it. Sometimes I find myself standing in my bedroom touching it, stroking it like it was Ka or a pet or something. And you know how Bilbo Baggins in *The Hobbit* finds the ring that Gollum lost? Well, remember how hard it was for Bilbo to let the ring go even though the longer he kept it, the more dangerous it was to him? How its power of invisibility was actually driving him crazy? Well, that's how this gun is. It's getting to the point that I should either shoot it or give it away.

Mom should have realized it was hopeless.

Twenty-two

Two weeks later they sat on the porch waiting for the realtor to pick them up. Ben couldn't sit still. "There are so many things I could be doing. Why are we doing this?"

Helen was resolute. She hoped that Ben would get excited about buying a house—about starting over. "You know why we're doing this." She was relieved when she saw the white LeBaron pull up to the curb.

The agent, Sam Moser, was a white man who specialized in selling houses to upward blacks. He knew just the right neighborhoods where his clients would find what they were looking for and be welcomed at the same time.

Ben and Helen climbed in the car. Ben sat in the back seat as Helen, with paper and pen in hand, sat next to Sam. She had already spent an hour in Sam's office the week before, discussing price range and general areas of interest.

"To tell you the truth, folks, I don't think this is going to take a long time. I've got a couple of beauties that I have a feeling you're going to like."

Helen, riding the moment, gushed, "I hope so. We don't want to waste a whole lot of time looking at houses we don't want. We want to find the right place as soon as we can."

Ben felt like he was being chauffeured by two people who didn't care where they were going. He heard them talk about the weather and the crime rate. He heard them talk about schools and block clubs. But he was hopelessly disconnected from them. He was missing a day of work for which he'd have to atone. He was already missing the house on Sage Street. Even if he didn't own it.

Finally they stopped in front of a house that looked a lot like his parents' house. It looked a lot like all the rest of the houses on the block. And the houses in the neighborhood. He heard words flying by him. Two-car garage. Lawn. Quarry kitchen. Finished rec room.

He heard the words fall like water balloons splattering all around him. Helen was now not touching the ground. She glided through the house. The kitchen brought yelps. The master bedroom a sigh. The living room, with a dramatic fireplace, a scary silence. She looked in every closet. Opened every cabinet.

But Ben took only two steps through the door. He stood like a tree in the clay-toned foyer. He listened as the agent led her from feature to feature. Sam talked incessantly. The price was right. The terms were right. He thought they could qualify. After all Ben had the G.I. Bill, right?

Ben felt his roots digging into the shag carpeting, searching for some sort of nourishment. But there was none and the foundation on which he stood could never support his weight. If trees could scream he would have screamed. He would have opened a knothole in his trunk and let out the loudest, fiercest scream he could muster. "No! Helen, stop this madness right now!"

"Is this perfect or what?" Sam said simply and triumphantly as they reached the front door again. "Everything you want. Ready to move in. What's more to ask for?"

Sam was looking at him. Helen was looking at him. He saw the questions in her eyes. Ben's body began to unravel. Suddenly he realized that this was a life or death situation. He had seen the sheaf of commitments he would have to make brimming forth from the portfolio that Sam carried. He felt tight, stuffed, full. The house was now very small. He was swelled with panic. He could have said it then. He should have. He wanted to but he couldn't. He forced another smile.

"What do you think, Ben?" Helen looked at him, this time incapable of reading his thoughts.

"I like it." It didn't matter what he thought about the house. He wasn't buying a house. From what he could see the house was fine. It was like all the other houses. He just didn't care. "I think we should talk about it some more at home."

His words breezed by Helen. "Yes, Mr. Moser. We love this house. This is perfect. Suppose we look at the others you have too though, just to be sure?"

"Of course." Sam led them back to the car. "By the end of this afternoon, your head's gonna be swimming in beautiful homes." Then Sam turned around and spoke over his shoulder to Ben. He knew that if there was a barrier to making this deal it would be Ben. Real estate agents have a way of sensing where the resistance will come from. "And don't worry, Mr. Crestfield, everybody feels the same way the first time. I can tell you're a bit nervous. Everybody is. It's a big decision."

Helen stared ahead, beaming.

Ben rode the afternoon out in the back seat. Followed Helen through houses he didn't like. Smiled approvingly when he was supposed to and breathed joy when it was over.

He was silent during the ride back. He had told her he was wasted, burnt out from the house search. He just wanted to go home and lie down.

Ben found a way to avoid the subject for the next two days. He managed to be out of the house during dinnertime each night, claiming work held him. But Helen was growing more and more anxious.

On the third night, as he used his briefcase to push the door open, she met him there already deep into the discussion. She was beside herself with frustration. There were applications to file. Money to get together. In her hands was a yellow notepad, and two pencils. The first sheet of the pad was full of numbers and lists. As she talked she tapped the pencils on the paper like it was a drum.

"Ben, what the hell is going on? Why haven't you at least talked to me about the house? Huh? You haven't said one single word. Nothing. Not 'I liked them' or 'I didn't.' Not 'We have to keep looking,' or anything," she said as he passed her in the door.

Ben knew he had to face her. Had to deal with everything. Not just the house. But he was afraid. It could also be the end of everything.

He slowly put his briefcase and newspaper down. "Why do we have to buy a house now?"

"Because it's time. We should give Makeba a better environment to grow up in."

"There's nothing wrong with where we live. This is just fine for me. I don't see why we've got to go deeper in debt right now. I just don't think we can do it."

Helen drew a deep breath. She wanted to penetrate him. Go beyond the surface and insert herself into him. To make his mind work for her. "What are we waiting for? For you to get a promotion? Publish your poems? What? Listen, if it's your job, I know that you hate your job. But you can change jobs. You've been there almost three years. If you hate it so much why not just get a new job? And let's face it, your writing isn't going to get us anywhere. You've said yourself that it's almost impossible for a black man to publish a book. I just want to know what are we waiting for?"

Ben stared at her. What did she know about his work? She never tried to understand what he was about. She didn't understand that whatever it was that was pushing him to write had to do with something greater than his connection to her. He wanted what Langston wanted. What Hurston wanted. What Baldwin wanted. He wanted to be free enough to tell the truth.

He couldn't imagine taking such a journey while in the grip of the pressures of mortgage payments and the middle-class life Helen wanted to lead. Ben was afraid that her dream realized would be his deferred. And he knew, and flinched whenever he thought it, that Helen's dream was Makeba's future. And here he became speechless. Speechless but not thoughtless. Ben realized that he could not let Makeba suffer. That couldn't be the cost of following his heart. He was becoming more and more clear that he didn't want the life that Helen wanted. His challenge was to separate Makeba from the gravity of Helen's control. It was Helen he was falling out of love with, not Makeba.

He knew he couldn't buy a house.

"I know you're not going to like this, but I can't do it. I just can't. In a way, I want to. I mean, I want you to be happy, but I don't think I can make myself do it."

Helen planted her feet firmly to stem the rush of energy flowing over and through her. She wanted to uncoil all of her anger and fling it at him. "You can't do what?" She flung the pencils and pad across the living room. Ben shuffled his feet. "You can't do what, Ben?" This time her voice was bottom-heavy with feeling.

"We can't buy a house. It's not the right time."

Helen lost her sight. The room shaded into early pre-evening shadows. Not the familiar ones but some others she had never seen before. These shadows formed the shapes of animals.

She screamed, "There is no right time for you. You're being ridiculous. This is our chance at a new start. Isn't that what you want? Don't you want us to make it? This is it."

As the shadows gathered in the corners of the room he saw Helen's face change. Suddenly he could tell that she had finally realized that they had already peaked. That they were somewhere on the downslide. He just stood there and prepared for the storm he knew was coming.

"And I guess you don't care. You don't give a shit. Not you. Not selfish Ben. What the hell do you care if Makeba only has half a father? What do you care if we just go through the goddamn motions? Always talking some shit about African American men and how great you are. You ain't shit, Ben. You understand that? You ain't shit. Can't be a goddamned husband. Can't be a father. What can you be? Huh? What can you be?"

Helen's eyes were red. Ben was still. The air skipped with yelps. The passing wind. The shadows completing their transformation. His life was being judged. Everything had come to this.

Helen wanted to hit him. To nail her disappointment to his face.

But instead she abruptly began walking toward the stairway. She walked through Ben, reducing him to painted air, and ascended the steps.

Ben was left to a pack of shadows, their eyes holding Helen's anger.

Makeba's Journal

When you went to look at houses I remember talking to Grandma Crestfield about the kind of house I wanted. I even drew her a picture. I imagined that when you and Mom came back, I'd get in the car and we'd drive to our new house and live happily ever after. All of the things that scared you were the things I dreamed of. A lawn. A garage. All that stuff. It wasn't just Mom.

And I remember when the two of you came back, you were so quiet. I knew something was wrong. I just thought you were disappointed that you didn't see a house you liked.

I didn't know that that was almost the end. I didn't know. It's too bad that when you're young you don't even know things are just about over. I guess I shouldn't feel too bad. Mom didn't know either. I know she was pissed, but I think that she never believed for one minute, up to the absolute end, that you and her would ever not be married. She believes in love in the purest sense. No matter what was actually going on between the two of you, I *know* that she always romanticized your relationship. And she thought it would go on forever. So did I. What was I supposed to do? How could I have known you were so unhappy? What a mess it turned out to be.

Twenty-three

Finally Helen's growing anger had bloomed and Mates became immediately stronger. It would be only a matter of time before he breathed Ben's air.

Mates's blood, transformed from anger (which itself was transformed from love), now flowed. Even as a shadow, he had a heartbeat. And he could hear the crying. It cascaded inside Helen's body.

In the end there is always a scream of anguish, of abject pain, of being lost, cut loose, set adrift in a mysterious sea. Suddenly you can't remember the beginning. The time when everything was new and magical. You don't know why you are where you are. How could you have given yourself, your heart and soul to such a magnificent emptiness? And yet, when all the things connected to love have gone, the emptiness is immediately filled with mournful silence.

Helen's grip on her own future began to slip. Ben was resolute in his refusal to sign his name to a mortgage. She cried and pleaded, but it was clear that he wouldn't change his mind. Slowly, over time, the house receded to dream.

And by 1985, ten years after they were married, life had spoiled. The unraveling had ended in a pile of thread. Everything hoped for was now unmoored and ambient.

The end came one dark, cold March night. A night before the brisk winds brought spring. Makeba was upstairs, trying to be invisible and formless, like a breath of air in a warm house.

Her childhood world had deteriorated into a cavern of dread. What Makeba now heard pass between her mother and father was not love. Indeed, it was the raw nerve of disconnection.

She listened.

Makeba looked down the dimly lit stairway. The white-yellow light from the outside brought life to the shadows. There was nothing present to soften the harsh, unthinking words that came from below, except her Ka, who still smiled at her. Nothing protected her.

And when the voices below rose like smoke, up the stairs and into her room, she began an involuntary tremble. She clutched Ka tightly. His soft golden body gave in to her hug. Ka had remained remarkably well kept during the years. Makeba had kept him scrupulously clean. If he fell in the mud or had cereal spilled on him, Makeba would stop whatever she was doing and wipe her beloved Ka clean.

She confided everything in Ka. Ka *was* good for her. He was the perfect balance. When Makeba was sad, he could make her smile. When she was giddy, he would sit quietly until she calmed down. Now she held on to him. The muscles in her face knotted. Her nine-year-old mind flexed as she tried to measure the severity of the storm below her.

From the bedroom, Makeba could only hear the aura of the anguished exchanges through the filter of the shadows, the night light and the tall stairwell. The words were indistinct but the sentiment made her anxious. She was loath to move. Actually she wanted to be somewhere completely different. She wished she could just leave by the window. And she would have if she had money or clothes or somewhere else to go. But this was her home. Makeba heard the resonance of her father's voice ripple through the air.

Downstairs, Ben and Helen Crestfield were engaged in a battle of futures; theirs and Makeba's teetered on the rim. Weeks of border skirmishes had finally yielded full-fledged war. Ben had finally struck the match to the keg.

"Helen, I don't see how we can go on with this." His future had suddenly become very dark.

He wanted to say something different. He wanted to say he loved her. That he thought she was a wonderful woman, a terrific mother. That he had always wanted them to be television's Dr. Heathcliff Huxtable and his lawyer wife, Clair. He and Helen had always had at least as much passion as they did.

Ben wanted her to know that he didn't want to hurt her. He needed space. Everything smoldered like burning trash and the smoke hung over his head in a thick cloud. He just needed to be out of the relationship.

He couldn't believe how hard it was to say. He knew she would not understand. Helen had so much invested. For a second as he watched her standing in the kitchen doorway, he prayed she'd make it easy. He wanted her to smile calmly at him and say, "Yes, Ben. I understand how things can change. I understand that sometimes a person can fall in love with someone and love them deeply for a certain period of time and then after a while, when it wanes, feel lonely and unsatisfied. I understand. I'll make sure you get all the time with Makeba you need. I know you'll be a good father to her." He wanted her to say that. If he could write the words that formed on the inside of her brain that's what he would have written. But that's not the way it went down.

"You can't go on with this?" Helen repeated. "What does that mean?" She had emerged from the kitchen, her caramel skin sparkling with beads of sweat. She had a queasy feeling in her body. She stood there silent. She wanted Ben to drop it. Simply to stop talking. She hoped he wouldn't take the subject any further. She didn't know what happiness was either. But Helen did know that she felt full and wonderful when she gazed into Makeba's eyes or when they were all gathered together in their darkened living room, in front of the television on a Sunday night.

"I'm not happy. Are you happy?" Ben asked in his softest voice. As if its gentleness would let it pass.

"Am I happy? That's kind of stupid, isn't it? I thought you didn't want to be happy." Helen felt steam rising inside her. She deflected the question by asking one of her own. She felt little sympathy for him. Life was hard. But in the hardness a person could still find happiness. They had their family. They had their health.

Ben knew she'd turn the question back at him. He didn't have a good answer. He had changed. Once, being happy hadn't been important. But now . . .

"I've changed. We can't go on living together like this."

"Like what?" She challenged him. "I thought you loved me." Helen slid into a chair at the table, where drying spaghetti sauce stared back at her. She tried not to get up to find a dishcloth to wipe up the spill. Instead she began picking at it with her candy-red fingernails. Sometimes when she looked at Ben she would feel liquid from the intense emotions that coursed through her. And sometimes, like now, those same emotions made her want to strike out at him.

"I do love you. But life is flashing by us. Like a slide show we can only watch. It's not about us. We aren't living. We're being parents, Helen. We're working and we're taking care of Makeba." He looked her in the eye.

"If you wanted to, you could do more. We could go to a marriage counselor or we could talk to my minister. We could do a lot of things. You could spend more time with us. You used to. Remember how we used to drive out to the country? We don't do things like that anymore."

Ben hadn't broken his stare. She was right. There was no way he could blame his boredom, his lack of enthusiasm, on anyone but himself. But that didn't stop him from trying.

"It just always seems like too much work."

"Too much work? What the hell does that mean?" She hated to hear him complain. That's all he did. Her anger was forged into a point.

"I'm an artist. I don't want to think about bills and buying houses. I don't want stocks and mutual funds. Sometimes I don't even want to be Makeba's father. She deserves better than me."

"Yeah, so?" Now, armed and willing to fight, she connected her eyes to his. Ben could see the pain etched into her forehead. He could see the beginning of a tear form. He knew he had turned a corner. He had never expressed any regret regarding Makeba. And then, what he had said wasn't true. He knew it wasn't Makeba. It was Helen. Their relationship was paste now and he wanted more, or less. But between them now was Makeba and the connection seemed unbreakable.

"It's too hard." There were no words in him, only rocks in the bottom of his stomach, rolling around. There was nothing he could say that would help.

"Too hard! I do all the damn work. All you do is complain about how hard everything is." She was tired. Weeks of trying to anticipate Ben's moods, trying to understand why he wasn't as excited about everything as he once was.

"That's part of the problem." He picked up the classified section of the newspaper that sat on the table in front of him. He didn't look at it, dropped it back on the table. There was no painless way to do it. He knew Helen would not let go easily.

"You bastard. How dare you? Ten years. Ten years of this shit and you want to just leave? I've worked like a slave around here and you have the gall to tell me it's *too hard*." Her scream broke off into a chuckle. He watched her compose herself. "You have a responsibility to your family." He knew that was coming. That was it. It was the formula for the survival of a people.

"This is your family. You have to make it work."

"I'm sorry."

"Sorry?" Helen was enraged. There was no turning back.

"Sorry?" she repeated. "It really doesn't matter to you, does it? Ten goddamned years. You're a selfish, egotistical ass who's tired of playing and wants to take his toys and go home. Well, this ain't no game. You can't be a part-time husband or father. This is some lame shit, Ben. What is wrong with you? You don't understand a goddamn thing about being a man, do you?"

She paused to catch her breath, then she changed her tone. "I'm not just worried about me, you know. What about Makeba?"

"This is not about Makeba. It's you. I just don't love you the way I used to."

Helen's eyes widened. She jumped up from the table. For an instant he wondered what she was going to do. She started toward the kitchen but stopped, turned around to face him. She leaned forward on the table opposite where he sat; Tina Turner whispered in her ear, "What the hell does love have to do with it? We need you, Ben," she said quietly, her emotions transformed to water.

Helen turned her back on him, trying to gird herself. She grappled with the fleeing energy inside her trembling body. She loved him. Loved her daughter. She wanted everything to work out. She softened her voice even more. Reached inside herself to find the thin thread of their life together. Perhaps she could give more. Do more. Still with her back to him she said, "Is it me? I mean, is there something I can do . . ."

Ben felt her in his head. "Helen, please try to understand. I don't want to hurt you."

Again she wheeled around to him. "You don't want to hurt me? What do you think you've been doing for the last five years? This whole marriage has been a string of hurts. You're never home and when you are, you're upstairs in that stupid room writing stuff nobody wants to read."

"It's depressing being here." Ben realized immediately, and really for the first time, how difficult it would be to separate the life of his child from hers. He didn't mean that Makeba depressed him. It was Helen. But in a way, Helen *was* Makeba. At that moment, he couldn't tell where Helen ended and Makeba began.

Helen didn't hesitate, didn't flinch this time. "Then leave. I don't care anymore. If you want to go, you can get your things and get the hell out of here. You can just get the fuck out of my life. I'm not going to spend the rest of my life trying to convince you that you belong here with me and Makeba." The terror in her voice scared him.

"Listen babe." She turned away from him at the word. She wasn't his "babe" any more. That was for sure. And she didn't want him to confuse the issue. But Ben couldn't help it. He still cared about her. They still had a history. She was the mother of his daughter. "I've stayed here, tried my best, *for* the family."

"Well, don't do us any favors, okay? Just get the hell out of here."

"Helen, please, don't make this—" Ben never got a chance to

finish his sentence. There was a stack of dishes on the breakfront in the dining room. Helen had slowly walked over to them and in a flurry of motions flung them to the floor. The pieces of blue-trimmed white china crashed into themselves and threw a chilled air throughout the house.

Along with the crescendo of breaking dishes, there was a smothered yelp from Makeba's bedroom upstairs. Ben heard her jump up and run into the bathroom.

He had almost forgotten about her. But she was there, upstairs, listening.

Makeba sat on the toilet and faced the closed bathroom door. She still held fast to Ka. "They're cursing," she said to the lion. There was a long pause as the sound of two people arguing rolled up the steps.

Like a tornado, anger swirled everywhere throughout the house. Every now and then a car would pass in the street and break the arrangement of the other shadows but they would quickly resume their places and their smiles.

With a sigh, she said again to Ka, "I don't believe it. I'm afraid." The smiling shadows held their pose. Even among smiles there was sadness. Makeba had lived through many fights between Helen and Ben but there was no preparation for this moment. Everyone in the solid, middle-class stone house was unhappy at this moment.

Makeba thought about going downstairs for a glass of milk. Maybe it would change the atmosphere. Sometimes her presence was enough to soften the air between them. She tried to move but found herself stuck to the toilet. And instead of really caring about what was going on, she abruptly turned to face the wall behind her. She found her free hand at the wall picking at the blue wallpaper. There was greater distance now between her and the spoken words that originated below.

Makeba repeated everything she heard to Ka. And as she did she pulled small sections of the wallpaper away from the bathroom wall. "She's gonna make him leave if he don't start changing. She's saying she's gonna make him go. And he don't care, he will go if he has to but he don't love her anymore and he's tired of trying to act like he does just because they got me." At the last word Makeba's mouth froze like a jammed sewing machine. What was going on?

"He's really mad now. He's calling her names again. Saying she don't know how to love him. And . . . and . . . and she's saying how can she love somebody like him?"

Makeba closed her eyes. It almost sounded funny. She felt a smile creep across her face. But before the smile became a laugh the humor was gone entirely. It evaporated into the deepening darkness.

Soon she heard a clear, scream from her mother's body. "Get the hell out of here. I don't need this. Get out."

She could tell that her mother meant business. Her scream lacked terror. It was solid and backed by a leaded emotion.

Helen had finally let go. All of the energy she had used to hold on to Ben for the last two years had now reversed itself. She wanted to erase his existence. To purge his image. To relieve herself. "No. You want it this way? You want your freedom? Leave. Why wait? Why keep trying? Why not just get the hell out right now?" Her pretty face was tortured. Ben couldn't keep from crying. They both cried.

Eventually he got up from the table and walked to the hallway closet to get his jacket. He left Helen crying. The early spring chill was like a spirit swimming through the house. As he got to the closet he looked upstairs. He turned and began the climb. He had been thinking about this for a while. Yes, he would leave, but he would be back for Makeba. He would do whatever he had to to convince Helen to let him have her. He would not let his separation from Helen mean separation from his daughter.

And he didn't want to have to visit on weekends and play that game. He wanted her with him. Maybe they could work something out. He had gone to school. Maybe Helen would want to do that while he raised Makeba. Something. There had to be some way he could stay with his daughter.

The maple steps creaked under his weight. Ben moved slowly up. At the landing he turned toward Makeba's room.

"Kayba? Are you asleep?"

Makeba sat in the bathroom, Ka's face buried in the space between her cheek and shoulder. She was fighting her own tears. She knew what was happening. She had friends who had described the ending of marriage to her. When it started rolling up the stairs, she recognized it immediately.

In this, Ka was no protection for her.

"Kayba?" Ben peeked into her bedroom. He flung the bed-clothes off, thinking Makeba was hiding.

Makeba heard him. She tried to say something but the sound never made it past her throat.

Ben was now in the hallway in front of the bathroom. He saw the light glowing from inside. He knocked softly.

"Yes?" Makeba's voice was weak.

"It's Daddy, sweetheart. Can I come in?"

"Yes." Makeba saw her father fill up the darkened doorway. She saw his contorted face, smudged with the mud that tears make.

"You know I love you, don't you?"

"Yes."

"Do you know what's happening? I mean, what's going on between your mom and me?" Ben couldn't stand still. He bounced inside the door frame from side to side.

"I think so," Makeba said flatly. Ka was now on her lap, the lion's expression unchanged since the day it arrived. The only thing Ka could do was absorb some of her pain. But there was so much of it in that small blue room. "You're leaving us."

"I have to, baby. I have to. I can't stay here anymore."

"Why?"

Ben exhaled, nearly losing all of his remaining strength. "You've seen how we are. All we do is argue. I just don't want to live with her anymore."

"But what about me?"

Once again, he was crying. What a question. He knew it had to come. The question that never dissipates, never goes away. The question that is never completely answered. The question that perhaps cannot be answered. But at least he was prepared to try. He bent down and put his arm around her.

"How would you like to come live with me?"

"You mean without Mom?"

"Yes, just you and me. We could make it."

Makeba fidgeted. She stared first at her father and then at Ka. "Where would we live?"

"I don't know right now, Kayba, but we could find a nice place somewhere."

"But how come Mom can't be with us?"

"Because we're not happy together anymore."

"But I don't want to leave her."

"I know. I know you don't, baby." Ben hugged her and stood up again. "Listen Kayba, I want you to think about it, okay? I'll come to see you on Saturday, maybe we'll go to the skating rink or something. And you can tell me what you think about it then. All right?"

Makeba nodded her head.

"I love you. I want you to believe that. I love you now and I always will, no matter what happens. You remember that. Okay?"

Makeba nodded again.

"I'm leaving now. I've got to go. But I'll see you on Saturday. And sweetheart, don't worry. Okay? Everything's going to turn out fine."

He turned to leave, paused at the door to look back at her sitting there, holding back tears and stroking Ka's back. He walked into his den, where he closed the cover on his Smith-Corona and gathered his poems and the first pages of a novel he had started.

Helen had turned off every light downstairs, so Ben came down the steps in complete darkness. Everyone and everything was being left behind.

Makeba's Journal

TWENTY-THIRD ENTRY

No. I don't believe you. You had no intention of coming back. You left. You ran out of the door. You never meant to come back. This is a lie. Mom would have told me. I would have known. Okay, so it sounds good. I remember the argument. I remember you coming upstairs. And I remember when you asked me if I'd come live with you. I thought about it all weekend. I thought and I thought. How could I leave Mom? I didn't think I could do it at first. But I couldn't stop thinking about it. She was a basket case. All she did was cry. I was in my room almost the entire week. I know I didn't go to school. We were both really scared.

After you left she came into my room and told me that you were leaving but that she didn't think you'd be gone too long. She tried to make it sound like you were going to the barbershop or on a vacation or something. I think she really thought you just needed some time out. But I can see now that you were dying to get away from her. It just wasn't the right mix. You weren't right for each other.

Anyway I talked to Ka about it and I dreamed about it and finally I realized that I didn't want to be away from you. That's right. In my sleep I decided that I would ask Mom if I could go with you. I woke up the next day even more afraid. You were gone, she was crying, Nana was just sitting on the couch, sucking her teeth and shaking her head. I didn't know how I was going to tell them. I wasn't sure I could at all.

At dinner that night I tried to say something about you. Nana almost screamed at me. She said it was best not to mention your name in the house for a while. I think I said something like, "Do you really think he'll be gone for a long time?" And then, even after Nana tried to shut me up, I finally said what I really wanted to say.

"Well, if Daddy's not going to be gone that long, then maybe I can stay with him sometimes."

Nana put her hand up as if to tell me to shut up, but Mom said, "You mean visit your father? Of course, sweetheart."

I remember that I was instantly excited. There was a moment there when I understood what was going on. And then I went too far: "And do you think I could live with him for a while? I mean—" Mom's eyes lit up and I knew I had said something wrong.

"Did he say something to you about that?"

I didn't know what to say so I told her that you had asked me if I would want to. She looked at me and then at Nana and got up from the table.

But you never came. And you never called. And like magic we were suddenly in North Carolina. I had chosen you and you never even came back to get me. What am I supposed to do with that?

Ka has always said that this story wasn't over. I didn't know what she meant, but I guess I'm beginning to.

How much of this is true? I can't keep it all straight anymore. I just know that I've always thought you walked out and never came back.

Twenty-four

Mates could feel the tightness of his body coming together. The shadows around him had congealed into a solid blackness. At the same time he felt a strong force pulling him away from the darkness. He was being separated and moved toward Ben. He floated like a kite just behind Ben. Inside Mates's stomach was an urge to lunge at Ben. But the terror was still not real. There remained only the call to bring him forth.

Ben checked into a hotel near the university campus. He was struck by the silence that immediately invaded his life. There was no wondering Helen to evade, no needing Makeba to tend to. Exile gripped his heart.

Ben sat in silence, staring at the thin white walls of the small room. From the first moment he began to miss Makeba. Miss her intensely. He cried for her. He wondered how he could face the pain of missing his daughter.

He didn't turn his television on. He didn't read. He didn't try to write. His eyes couldn't focus on small images. He could only see the wavering reality as it trembled under the veil of his tears.

On the second night Ben began to hear Makeba's voice. Her voice invaded his silence. When he ate, took a shower or sat in the gray armchair, Ben was likely to hear her soft voice. He couldn't tell what she was saying. But he sensed she was talking about him.

Ben was stuck there in that room, listening to her voice, imagining her thin body, feeling her hurt. He wallowed in it. He didn't call anyone, not even Ramsey. He wanted to face this life alone. But he knew it was to be a journey. And that it was just beginning.

At night, Makeba's eyes sparkled like tiny torches. Disappointment flickered. Her eyes were nighthawks in the bluedark sky, free-flying and sorrowful.

Ben couldn't conceive of living his life without her. Visiting her on weekends. Buying toys that he wouldn't get a chance to see her play with. Maybe he had moved too hastily. How could he write? How could he survive being disconnected from Makeba? Helen was his problem. Their relationship was over. Right or wrong he saw her as the symbol of the barriers he had to overcome to be a writer. But Makeba? Makeba was an innocent. Even more, he needed Makeba. She was his blood. His inspiration.

How could a man leave his child? How could he make a decision that would take him away from her? Break the bond that is special and unique between a father and daughter?

Could the cost for identity, for freedom be so high that he would have to let go of the one person in his life who belonged? He had already chosen a path. He was living in a hotel away from his wife and his daughter. He had broken the connection between him and Helen.

And yet, in his new freedom, he felt immediately paralyzed. With one breath, he looked forward to visiting Makeba. With the next he dreaded facing Helen. All of the feeling that had been love was now something else, something which made him want to run, to escape its lingering power. Ben knew it was shame. He was profoundly saddened by the shame that swam through his body. He had destroyed all of Helen's dreams in an attempt to keep his alive.

But he could save Makeba. He could go back and get her. He could show her that he wasn't deserting her. Maybe she would want to live with him. When he went back on Saturday to get his things, he would ask.

And then Saturday became the only day of the week. Ben

planned his speech to Makeba. He wanted to relieve any fears she had that he was leaving *her*. She could choose to live with him.

Friday night he dreamed he was on trial. The judge was a black woman, not Helen, but someone who could have known Helen. Someone who had felt the crush of a family being torn apart. Perhaps she was the daughter of a divorce. Perhaps . . . Ben sat in the witness box terrified.

His defense was presented by Ramsey:

"This man is a good man. This man has climbed out of the shadow of slavery and formed himself into something strong, full of potential. He is an educated man. Not a 'trained' man, mind you. Not like those which society 'trains' to do its dirty work. He is not an accountant, a lawyer, a teacher or a bus driver. He is an artist. A thinking man. A dreaming man. And you would want him to reduce himself. To limit his potential simply to follow through on a commitment to his wife."

The judge stared down at Ben, all but ignoring what Ramsey was saying. "You know of course, Mr. Crestfield, that you are guilty. There is no defense in a situation like this. You had your obligations and responsibilities clearly outlined for you. Indeed, you created them yourself, in a partnership. Besides, you are not separate from your people. You are only an 'educated' man because your parents stayed together to give you a proper life. How could you want any less for your child? You are guilty. There is no defense."

Ben woke up before he found out his punishment. He had made his decision. His only chance at redemption would be to persuade both Helen and Makeba that he could provide a decent home for his child. That he didn't need Helen to do that.

In the morning, when he approached his house on Sage Street, it was like he had never been there before. The sun blasted the street in light. And it was quiet. Eerily quiet. After five days in a hotel room, he was disheveled, tired. His body ached. Parts of him felt like they might simply fall off.

For a second he thought about stopping off to see Hannibal before he faced Helen, but he didn't see Hannibal's yellow Firebird. For some people Friday night could extend into the next week.

He walked up the steps, passed through the porch. There was an empty, crumpled brown paper shopping bag sitting by the door. In the window of the door was an envelope with his name on it.

Ben reached for the envelope and as he grabbed it the door swung slowly open. He began to tremble as he snatched the letter open. But he kept moving into the house.

There were no lights on inside. The house was empty. He strained his ears. No. There wasn't even the hum of electricity. There was no energy, electric or human, flowing within the house at all. It was perfectly still. Instinctively he ran up the steps to Makeba's bedroom. It was empty there too. To the closet. Empty. Hangers lined up like functionless sculpture. Barren.

There were no sheets on Makeba's bed. No clothes in the dresser. No toys, no dolls, no books, no jacks. Makeba and her Ka were gone. Her paintings from school were the only things left. Foremost among these was a picture she had drawn of the house when she was in the third grade. It was a simple, crooked drawing of an A-frame house. In it Makeba had placed Helen, Ka and Ben. In jagged writing underneath: "I love my house."

Ben stumbled into the bathroom and sat down on the toilet as his body dispersed into the air. It was then he unfolded the letter. His stomach dropped into the still toilet-bowl water. His head began unraveling like a ball of string. The tears started, one at a time, until unchecked, he was breathing them out like air. He read the letter.

Dear Ben,

I know this letter will come as a shock to you. I know that it will hurt you. But you did this to yourself. I didn't begin the last ten years knowing that at this point I would be doing what I'm doing. I have no choice. You've made your mind up about what you're going to do, and now, I've made up mine. Your decision hurt me deeply.

I love you, Ben. I truly do. I wish things were different between us.

But like I said, you created this whole mess. My mother taught me wrong. She always told me to find a man that is closest to the ideal and then stick by him no matter what. She never taught me how to let go.

Anyway, I'm not about to let you talk me into giving Makeba up. After you left she asked me about living with you. Do you think I'm crazy? You have no idea who I am if you think I'm going to let you take Makeba away from me. I can hear you now, telling me how it will be for my benefit. All the things I could do if I was free to do what I wanted.

You can forget that. I'm sitting in your den writing this letter. At your desk. In your house. I know you'll hate me for this. I've already accepted that. They say love is really very close to hate. Well, I'm prepared for your hate now, just as I once was open to your love.

I am Makeba's mother. I brought her here. And I'm not leaving her.

Actually I'm feeling very calm and peaceful. I know what has to be done. It's taken me a little while. I guess I knew it was over long ago. I should have done something. But I didn't. Neither did you.

So, by the time you read this letter I will be gone. Makeba will be gone. I'm sorry. I don't want to deprive you of your relationship with her forever, I'm not cruel. But for a while, I think it will be best if you don't know where we are. I'll get in touch with you later.

I'm doing this for me and Makeba. Be happy if you can. And don't hurt too much.

Helen

Ben's head was swimming. He had made a huge mistake. If he had had any idea that Helen would leave, he would've stayed there. He didn't really want to leave the house. Just her.

He sat there for a long time. Most of the afternoon. He had stopped crying. Stopped reading the letter. Stopped thinking. He was like stone. Like the house, empty. Finally Ben regained consciousness and left the bathroom. He was in no mood to move his things. He wasn't sure what he was supposed to do. Helen had become the enemy. And now she was gone. With no one to fight, he was purposeless.

He dragged his body down the steps, into a shadow-drenched living room. Without thinking he walked toward the front door. But he was struck stiff by a movement in the vestibule. Someone was standing there.

His heart fluttered but he found no escape. His body was stuck. He tried to speak. He moved his mouth. His brain was screaming. Inside him was a swirl of noise. It wanted release. His head was spinning under the stress. Had Helen come back? Was it Makeba standing there? If he had known terror before, then this was worse. More powerful.

He tried to grab the words that were flying around him. "Helen?" came weakly from him. "Helen?"

"It's not Helen. Helen is gone." Lena stepped into the house. "I wanted to see you. I was here earlier but I guess you hadn't got here yet."

"Where's Helen?"

"She's gone, Ben. You drove her away."

"I didn't drive her away. I left. I've only been gone five days. This is ridiculous."

"You've been driving her away from you since you met her. What did you think? That you would be the one to decide everything? When you got married. When you broke up. Who was going to have Makeba. That's what you thought, isn't it, Ben? That it was all up to you?"

"Lena, ever since I met you, you've been all in our business. You've been more destructive than I could have ever been. Now, tell me, where's my baby?"

Lena's thin body railed back in laughter. "Me? You're blaming me? You're incredible. You blame my daughter. You blame your daughter. Now you want to blame me. You're less of a man than I thought. You're nothing." Lena paused, shutting her laughter down like a powerful engine. Then she was ice. "If I could have I would have made Helen leave you years ago. You always talked a good game but you never did a damn thing. Typical good-for-nothing nigger of a man is what you are. College-educated. Ha. You're nothing. And now you have nothing."

Ben's skin felt suddenly warm, like he was oozing blood. A wet sticky warmth. This was a war. And he was losing it. Perhaps it was already lost. Lena stood in front of him, shielded by the shadows, and continued the pummeling.

"I can't cry anymore. And I don't know what to do with my anger. Please. Can't you tell me where they are?" Ben's voice bounced around the empty room.

"Why? Why should I tell you anything? You're just going to make their lives miserable."

"You're talking about my wife and my daughter. What is wrong with you? I just want to know where they are." He took two steps in her direction and stooped over so that his face was close to hers.

But Lena didn't flinch. "Ben, the only reason I'm here is to tell you to leave them alone. You hurt my daughter. I warned you. I told you to take care, but I guess you didn't take me seriously."

Ben felt himself slipping away. He couldn't intimidate her. He wheeled away from her, his control crumbling. "What the hell do you know? You're some crazy-ass old woman who thinks she can scare people by walking around in the dark and carrying weird shit around in bags." He turned back to her. "You're as responsible as I am. If you knew how to be a mother instead of a fucking witch or some shit, things might be different. Maybe Helen wouldn't be so afraid of her own life and she wouldn't focus so much on me if you had raised her better."

Ben reached out and grabbed Lena by her wrists. He brought them up into his face. "Where are they?" he screamed at her.

Again Lena smiled. "They will always be behind you. At your heels. In your shadow. Forever, Ben. You will know them when you can't sleep. When you are tired and unable to rest. You have created ghosts. Your dreams have created your own haint. And if I have any-thing to say about it, you will never be free."

Ben threw Lena hard to the floor. She made no sound. Her eyes shot fire up at him. He stood over her with his hand raised. He wanted to beat her into the floor. Banish her from his life. Instead he turned and walked out the door.

And Mates took his first real breath. He was there, waiting just behind Lena. When she hit the floor, there was an explosion inside him, which, instead of breaking him apart, pulled him together. The truth was that Mates had been waiting there for ten years, following them around, watching. And now, he *was* them: Lena, Helen, Makeba and Ka. Everything they held inside, their hope and their frustration, was his blood. Their anger, his heartbeat.

Mates stepped over Lena as he followed Ben out the door.

Outside, Ben was frantic. His skin crawled, his stomach hurt. Sage Street seemed alien. Hannibal was on the porch across the street. He called to Ben but Ben ignored him. He thought the car coming down the street was being driven by Ramsey and that Geri was a passenger. He started trotting. Going he didn't know where—just going.

Ben ran out of Sage, out of concrete. He ran across asphalt, over grass. He ran through alleys, across front yards. And Mates was right behind him. At first, like so many times before, Ben didn't know Mates was there, ten paces on his trail. But when Ben turned to look behind him, for the first time he could see Mates, panting, galloping behind like a hound. His thick coat glistening in the afternoon sun. Mates saw the recognition in Ben's eyes. Ben knew then that Mates was pursuing him.

A low growl groaned from the black dog. Ben heard it as a voice. Mates knew by the look in Ben's face that he could hear him. That Ben would twist the sounds that flowed from his new body into words. "Ben, it has finally happened, you have disappointed everyone. Only Ka has the faintest faith in you and that's only because Ka will hope to the end for Makeba's sake. Not me, Ben. I already know the truth. You are mine."

Ben was stricken. He turned a lighter shade of brown. There was a dog, a huge, bounding, frightening black dog, just strides behind him. And it had spoken to him.

As his breath shortened until there was barely space in his chest for any air at all, he tried to reassert some semblance of internal control. He was running to madness. He felt it. Everything he had tried to fashion for himself was shredded. He had nothing, no one—except Mates. And what was Mates? What was happening to him?

Then Ben did a curious thing. He slowed down. Mates could have pounced on him then, but he didn't. Ben came to a full stop and turned around to face the dog.

Mates pulled up quickly. He bared his teeth and let his fiercest growl rise out of his chest. Mates stood up on his hind legs and swung at Ben with his right front paw. Ben jumped back, just out of reach.

"Mates wants you now."

"What's going on? What the hell is happening?"

"You watched each piece fall into place. You know all there is to know."

"My daughter?"

"She is Mates."

"My wife?"

"She is Mates too. And Lena. And everyone who cares about them." Mates lunged again.

Ben turned away and began running. He was unhinged. This was the way Mates wanted him. Running through the city terrorized. Afraid to stop. Afraid to do anything but try to elude the demon just behind him.

And do you know what? He would never be able to do that.

Makeba's Journal

TWENTY-FOURTH ENTRY

I remember being awakened early that Thursday morning by Mom and Nana. We got dressed and packed everything up and went to the airport. My mind was swimming. I didn't know what was going on. I kept asking Mom if you were coming. And she just told me to not ask her any more questions. She said that everything would turn out fine.

We flew that day to Clinton, North Carolina, where we stayed for about six months. I kept asking Mom if you were coming or if you were going to call or what. She would say that when you were ready you would call. That you knew where we were. I know that Mom wrote you a letter. She told me that. And she said that she had also told Nana to tell you where we were. And I heard Nana tell Mom that she had given all of the information to you.

So I waited. Every day when I came home from school, I'd ask if you'd called or written. Nothing.

And now you're trying to say that Mom and Nana never told you where we were? I can't believe it. It doesn't make any sense. Why would they do that? They knew I loved you. They had to know how much it would hurt me. They had to.

And you. All of these years. Through all this time . . . if you had wanted, you could have found me. Even if they never told you anything, it's been a long time. You could have done something.

Ka always said that you had not lost your love for me. She told me not to forget you. And I haven't. And recently, Ka has encouraged me. She told me to find you. I guess to learn what I've learned about you. I just wish you could have made contact with me. I've needed you.

The thing is, regardless of how long it's been, I can't get you out of my mind. I still remember you and I guess I still love you. Maybe this whole story is just a lie. Maybe it didn't happen like this at all. It really doesn't matter. I feel like I've gotten to know you again. I hope that we can find a way to talk.

I've also decided to get rid of this gun. I can't actually use it. I think if it gets to the point you have to use a gun, you've already lost control. And like I've been telling you, that won't happen again.

Yours, Makeba

Twenty-five

Ben ran all afternoon. He ran through West Philadelphia like it was scenery scrolling by. He ran through the streets of University City seeing only the speckled pastiche of cement sliding under his feet. He couldn't think. Couldn't see. Only run. He felt Mates behind him. He heard Mates occasionally screaming at him. Growling. Sometimes he could even feel the dog's sweet hot breath encircle his head, then fade away. He ran until he passed into darkness.

Suddenly the moonlight was in the trees. It illuminated the leaves, which were full of speech as the torrent of movement passed below them. Ben Crestfield was running and splashing and reaching for something which would save him. He was frantically trying to outrun Mates. But the dog was not impatient. It pursued Ben in a measured pace. It seemed content to follow, staying just a step or two behind him.

Inside Ben's head was a swirl of colors and lights. Exhausted, he realized he had run into the park, except that now it seemed thick and dense. There was only the narrow path on which his feet barely touched as he pressed forward. The trees were wide and dark and leaned together, creating a shroud. He felt the skinny limbs reaching out to scratch him. And then there was a sudden break. There, the narrow path opened into a wide patch of green grass, shimmering like water. It wooed him there. It silently promised safety. And, since safety was something he desperately needed, Ben put everything into his pumping legs.

The air was still very thick among the trees. Whispers died there. Only the laughter of the leaves and Mates's heavy howling breath followed him. Mates was his approaching dread.

But Mates was having fun. For the first time in ten years he was alive. His prey was right in front of him. He could feel Ben's heart thumping. Every beat.

Mates imagined that Ben was probably praying that his heart was strong enough to withstand this terror. Mates wanted to be close enough to Ben so that the man could smell him, feel the strength of his power moving near him.

Mates was in ecstasy. He knew that it was Ben's fear which made him run as if he were made of wind. Mates barked at him. He wanted Ben to see his tongue, long and red, dripping with the taste of the first taste of him. Every now and then Mates lunged even closer and snapped at his churning legs. He toyed with Ben.

Mates was at his best in the chase. He loved the pure freedom of running, the streams of color that passed through the corner of his eyes, the internal combustion which pushed him forward.

But Ben was fast. Strong enough to keep his pace. He broke into the clearing. Mates abruptly stopped and stood still in the dark behind an elm tree, staring at Ben.

Ben had finally stopped running. He had slipped to his knees and was now crawling on the wet grass. Slowly he pulled himself up on a fallen tree.

All was silent. No crickets. No owls. No skittering mice.

Ben tried to bring his eyes into focus. He craned his neck in each direction, straining to see if what he thought he had seen was indeed real. Was there really a dog—a dog who talked—chasing him?

Slowly Ben recaptured some of his composure, caught his breath. He sat still, his breathing becoming lighter. He tried to become invisible. He tried to disappear into the scaling bark of the tree trunk that he was sitting on.

But the more his body returned to its natural state, the more his mind asserted itself. Where was Makeba? Where was she? Why had he let himself stray this far from what he lived for? How long would this thing chase him? How long did he have to run? And then his heart froze again. He saw Mates's eyes peering from behind a tree. It *was* real. What he thought he had seen, he had seen. And at that moment he was willing to give up. He had claimed to be a father. He had created a child. He was incapable of being what she needed him to be. Clearly he was not able to do it. He was, in fact, caught in a waking dream. Pursued by something he didn't understand and crumbling inside like sandstone to a rough touch. He was falling apart. It was the last thing he was supposed to do. He was a black shout in a white whisper world. He was supposed to stand up and scream back. He was the bad motherfucker. What terror could frighten him? Ben stared at the silhouette of the animal and suddenly couldn't control his voice.

"Come on, then. If you want me, come and get me. I'm tired of running. I can't get away anyway. Come out into the open and let me see you."

"I want to. I want to put myself in front of you. Force you to flee again into the forest where I can dominate you . . ." Mates's speech broke into a howling. It was a mix of feelings. He wanted to continue his patient wait for Ben to get up and continue running, and yet there he was, just sitting there taunting. Asking for him.

"Ben, you know what I am. You know why I am chasing you. It is a common story really. I have pursued many before you and there will be others.

"The disappointment and pain you have caused is not a fleeting memory. I am here to remind you that there is a place for those who destroy the dreams of children.

"I want you to contemplate being torn apart by me. Being ripped apart, your fingers snatched from your hands, one by one, as appetizer. The blood a sauce, the bones toothpicks. We are meat, all of us.

We all have our predators, the things that would eat us as we do others."

The darkness of the woods around the clearing made the voice seem to come from everywhere. "What do you want? What are you?" Ben tried to sound strong. He waited for Mates to respond. "You heard me. I asked you a question."

Mates considered what to say back to him. But he didn't want to give Ben any comfort. His silence was as strong as his teeth. Mates sat back on his haunches.

Ben stood up and began walking toward Mates.

"That's right. That's right. You come to me."

"I can't run anymore. I'm tired. I've dodged and ducked and lied and slithered long enough. I'm tired."

"Yes, I know." Mates's whole body quivered. Now *he* was drooling. His jaws muscles spasmed. "I want you, Ben."

"What was I supposed to do? What was I supposed to do?" He was crying, he was already beginning to fold up. His knees were buckling. He was moving forward toward Mates, but only barely so.

"There is nothing to do now but give yourself to me. There is no other way out." Ben was just to the edge of the clearing. The shadows of the trees were caressing his face. "Just a little more. Just a little more."

Ben collapsed. He was throwing up and crying and gasping for air. Makeba's face hovered over him, Ka floated next to her. There were tears in the lion's eyes. Lena was laughing. Helen stood back in the darkness, trembling.

Mates took a step forward and bared his teeth, his red gums like neon. Now he was standing over Ben. All Mates wanted now was for Ben to open his eyes. To watch his long white teeth plunge into his chest. Mates couldn't wait any longer. He lowered himself, swiveled back on his haunches in recoil. Mates then let out a scream that was made of all the pain of all the innocent people throughout time.

The scream was a red light in Ben's head. He turned toward Mates and saw the dog two feet away, eyes like candy apples, glistening in the night light. Ben looked into the animal's mouth, was drawn inside as if it were a tunnel with the faint sound of trickling water deep inside it.

Mates threw all of his weight into his leap at Ben. He was in the air like a bird and would land in the middle of Ben's back.

Ben twisted around quickly, raised his hands in a futile attempt to ward Mates off. At the same time, Ben found himself screaming too. "No. No. No. I'm sorry. I didn't know what else to do."

Ben was startled into frenzy when Mates landed on him. There was no pain, no tearing of flesh. Nothing. Mates simply vanished into his skin. And then he felt it. Like spontaneous combustion, his stomach began to quiver uncontrollably, a pounding began in his head, his mouth went dry. He opened his eyes and saw only red; a deep crimson on the edges and nearly pink at the center. And he felt it moving around inside him. Suddenly there was only red running through him.

Epilogue
Part One
1994

For days, Ben wandered the streets of West Philadelphia. He felt like his stomach was slowly being chewed up. He could hear a fierce growling inside of him. There was a buzzing sound in his head. He couldn't stop crying. He no longer had a job. He had no money. He slept in alleys, ate garbage. He was dirty, vagrant. He was on the streets like that for two weeks before Ramsey found him.

"Ben, is that you?" Ramsey had been searching West Philadelphia for Ben. He had been calling every possible place Ben might be. Finally he began driving through the streets of University City, and going in and out of bars. He'd been at it for about six days when he got a notion to head downtown. He instinctively parked his car in the lot behind the Thirteen Bar and as he walked through the alley adjacent to the bar he saw Ben, huddled in a doorway, talking to himself. But it was clear as he approached that Ben was completely disoriented. And when Ramsey grabbed him and hoisted him up, Ben was lifeless, a smelly muttering sack of a man. The only thing Ramsey could think to do was take Ben to the hospital.

As he stood Ben up, Ben opened his eyes and stared at him without a glimmer of recognition. "How can we be fathers in a world that won't let us be men?" He stared at Ramsey like a child. As if Ramsey was his father. At that moment Ramsey felt sad because he was holding something less than a man. He looked into Ben's soft brown eyes, dirt and scratches making a mask of his face, and he thought that maybe Ben should have actually asked his own father that question. Fathers should teach their sons what it means to be men.

"You got to get yourself together, brother. This ain't cool."

"Do we have to choose? Is that it?" It was the last lucid thing Ramsey heard Ben say. He had lapsed into a deep growl that scared Ramsey.

Two days later Ben awoke in a fresh-smelling white bed in the psychiatric ward of Pennsylvania General Hospital. He was on his back and strapped to the bed. He had suddenly erupted from his catatonic stupor into a violent flurry of activity. He had hit two nurses before being subdued.

That was the nadir. But time and a lot of therapy had allowed him to slowly regain his stability, his ability to manage his life. As he recovered he tried a halfhearted search for Helen and Makeba. But Lena's house had been sold and all the telephone numbers he had were disconnected. And almost with a sigh of relief he packed his things and left Philadelphia.

He told himself it was for the best. That his tortured mind was not functional in the small, articulated world of family. He taught himself numbness about his daughter. At least he tried to numb his heart. He knew it was Mates. He knew that Mates had damaged him. The guilt that Mates had buried like bones throughout his body occasionally erupted in a fit of questions.

"Will you face your guilt? Will you fight me?"

"Will you run, be my plaything?"

Ben's first instinct had been to run. Believing that his ability to carry Mates around with him was easier than trying to change history.

He had gradually started writing again. But the only story he had to tell was his own. And after he tried writing everything but the truth, he finally gave in. But Mates was there again. Taunting him.

"Tell it. Tell it. I dare you. You can't survive it. I'll have you all to myself then."

But Ben wrote anyway and found himself embarked on the

hardest task of his life: the telling. And the telling was a painful, healing thing. The telling rendered Mates docile, less destructive.

In a way he had written the story for just this moment.

This moment. This glorious, incredible moment when his daughter, Makeba Crestfield, sat across from him, looking like a lost soul. The overalls, the combat boots, the slumping boyish demeanor, revealed a young woman who was completely out of Ben's range of understanding. Where was his cute little Kayba? Where was his baby? That woman whose face was now just two feet away from his was a reflection distorted by time and distance. He knew he would have to start over.

"I know you think your mother is the hero in this drama. I understand why someone could think that. But I've fought the monster too. I've survived the guilt. I still love you. It may not seem like such a big thing to you. But I still cling to the idea that we can be close. That family with you is possible.

"After everything I still have hope. I know we will be for each other in the end. I know life is strange. That people go their ways, seem totally unconcerned, but that's only how it looks."

At first, Makeba wasn't going to say anything, but something inside put words in her mouth. "But Dwight and Mom both have drilled into my head, it's what you *do* that counts. They were the ones who *did* things for me. Because I was a child and because they loved me. You can't ask me to condemn them."

"I'm not asking for that. I'm asking that you just understand that what seems simple isn't simple. Some people choose to see the complexity in life. I'm like that. There isn't anything simple about life. I know that responsibility and obligation are important. I know that I ran from that. But I would have been a tragedy if I had stayed with your mother."

"So you'd rather I be the tragedy? That's it, isn't it? You sacrificed *me* for you."

"Makeba, I think I would have sacrificed both of us if I had stayed."

"Tough life, eh?" It was out of her before she could stop it. "Well, actually I shouldn't have said 'sacrificed.' My life hasn't really been that bad. If you hadn't written this book, if I hadn't thought about finding you, I would probably have left town about now. I'm not a disaster." She jumped from the bed, walked into the bathroom, where she found tissues. She hadn't known what she would feel when she actually saw him. Heard his voice. But now she was very sad. There had to be a way out. She looked, for just a second, at her tired face in the mirror before rejoining him. "It's just this father stuff. If it wasn't for you I could just go on like children do and have a life."

And then, without realizing it, he was crying again. But this time the tears flowed in streams of complexity. He was happy and sorry. Yes, he had put her behind him. He had had to. How could a man suffer through the loss of a child every day? He wasn't that strong. Yes, he had, at some point, decided he wouldn't call. After he recovered his health, he was afraid even to talk to Helen.

He was embarrassed that his relationship with Helen had destroyed his ability to have a relationship with his daughter. That was what was wrong. The way men relate to children. The way men are taught to make their connection to children through women. That was what had separated them. When the love dies between mother and father, it is the father who catapults away. Anything else was a fight upstream. What else had history demanded?

Throughout the time he had been separated from Makeba, Ben had felt the sting of anonymous criticism from social workers, lawyers, the government and an assortment of other angry voices who all saw him as a criminal. But his own conscience was stronger and more merciless than all of them. He had been a father without a child. And he was ashamed.

Makeba had no tears for him. She felt his anguish. She knew her appearance would unsettle him, but she wasn't sorry. This was the best thing she'd ever done. Even sitting there as she was now, back on the bed, watching him try to keep from completely collapsing, she felt lighter than she could remember. She fondled Ka's remaining strands of fur. Ben pulled his chair close to the bed.

When they'd reached the hotel, Ben had ordered food. She had eaten the hamburger and fries and apple pie à la mode while he read her journal. Occasionally he would hold his head up and look at her. More than once he said, "I love you. I've missed you so much." At those times she'd avert her eyes. Inside she smiled. This was what she needed. What she had wanted for so long. But she wasn't ready to do anything but sit there.

Makeba's nervousness was gone. She had traveled the distance. Had done the thing she set out to do. She felt strong. Able for the first time to think clearly. Her emotions, buried in the journal, in her life, had receded. She felt calm for the first time since he had gone.

After Ben was finished reading, he leaned forward and hugged his daughter. She was stiff in his arms. But he didn't care. She was in his arms.

"What can I say? What can I say to you?"

Makeba looked at her father. She was still getting used to being with him. "I don't know. Maybe nothing right now. We have to start over. But I can't do that right now. I just wanted to see you." She reached into her bag and took out a sheet of paper she had written her telephone number on. "Here is my phone number." She handed him the piece of paper.

Ben was dumbfounded. He wanted Makeba to drop all of her coldness, her aloofness. He wanted her to open her arms wide and accept him back into her life. But he watched as she got up from the bed and put on her coat. He watched her moving deliberately, gracefully. She came back to him and hugged him lightly.

When she reached the door, she turned around and again reached into her black bag. This time she pulled out a stack of pictures held together by a rubber band. "Every year I took a picture of myself for you. So you could see how I grew up. I didn't know if I'd ever give them to you, but I guess now is as good a time as any."

Ben saw the flash of brown on the Polaroid squares. In her hand was missing history, formed images of his imagination over the years. Makeba fondled the pictures, fully aware of the moment. And then she gently tossed them on the bed. "Maybe we can have breakfast tomorrow morning. I'll call you."

Ben watched the flight of the pictures, picking out her little face as it hit the pink bedspread. She was with him now and she would always be there.

He thought she'd simply walk out. But instead of opening the door to leave, she smiled at him and said, "I hear it's pretty cold up there in Minnesota."

"Yeah, it is. Sometimes I wonder why I'm there."

"Why *are* you there?"

"Where else is there to be?"

"I'm headed for California, I think."

"Really? Where in California?"

"San Francisco."

Ben looked at his daughter. She was beautiful. Full of tomorrows. "I've thought about living out there, but . . . I don't know, earthquakes . . ."

"You could live anywhere, couldn't you? I mean it's not like you have a job or something."

Ben chuckled. It was the first time in a long time he'd done that. A laugh caused by the smart mouth of his own daughter. "That's true."

"You could follow me for a change." Makeba didn't know what the hell she was doing. This was delicate china. Rice paper.

"You mean move out to California and live with you?"

The "with you" part brought Makeba back to reality. "I didn't say nothing about living with nobody. I just said you could live out there if you wanted."

"But you would be there too, right?"

"That's where I'm going."

"But you wouldn't want us to live together?"

"Listen, ah . . . I don't know what to call you, but I'm not looking for a father in the way you might want. I just want to feel you. Feel you, you know, like take a deep breath and not have any doubts about anything . . . you know. Like Terry McMillan talks about in *Waiting to Exhale,* I just want to breathe. So if you wanted to live in the same town with me, that might be cool. We could have dinners and get to know each other. Anyway, we can cross that bridge when we get there. Besides, I'm not making any promises about anything. *If* I call you tomorrow and *if* you're still here, we'll go from there."

"I'll wait right here until you call, sweetheart." The door closed and so did Ben's mouth. But not before Mates, once again a shadow, escaped and took position for his new vigil.

Part Two
1995

Ben was on his hands and knees applying a coat of wax on his kitchen floor when the telephone rang. He had his portable clipped to his belt. He unhooked it and pressed the talk button. It was Ramsey, calling from Philadelphia.

"I just called to wish you luck. I know this is going to be hard for you but I think it's right. I mean, it had to happen." Ben could hear in his friend's voice an appreciation for the way events were unfolding. He thought it was actually quite ironic that in the year since Ben had left Philly, Ramsey had met, married and was expecting his first child.

"I'm ready, though. I'm cleaning my apartment from top to bottom. When she gets here I don't want anything to be off, you know?"

"Yeah, I know. Delores told me to tell you to hang in there. She thinks this will be good for you."

Ben had never met Ramsey's new wife, but he knew that the news of Makeba's reentrance into his life had filtered way beyond Ramsey's household. It seemed to be quite the topic of conversation.

"You tell Delores that I don't have a choice. I have to hang in there, if you know what I mean."

"Yeah, well, I just think that you needed this. You can't walk

235

around in this world being a father of a child you don't know. That ain't right. I been telling you this for ten years or more. I'm just glad Makeba made the first move."

And it was true. She had made the first move. How hard was it for a child to do that? If the father wasn't capable of making that contact, then what could be expected from the child?

"Yeah, so am I." Ben thought about all the years between him and Makeba. It was clear that she was still searching for a way to explain his absence. It was the main reason *she* had insisted on only talking on the telephone, even though Ben had tried tirelessly to get her to visit him or allow him to come to Philadelphia to see her. But it took nearly eleven months for her to *want* to come to him. And almost a year of daily telephone conversations before Makeba could actually trust that he was really going to be there for her.

She understood the confusion. The way in which he and Helen split. She understood that Lena, probably with Helen's implicit consent, had sabotaged any chance of Ben gaining custody of her. They had helped to push Ben into oblivion. But why oblivion? Why not just a short absence and then a reconnection? Why had it taken ten years? And then why was she the one who had to make that contact? In a way, she was asking the question: "If I am your daughter and you love me, why am I chasing you down?"

Whenever it came up in their conversations on the telephone, he would answer by saying how ashamed he was. He tried to tell her how the breakup of his marriage to her mother had happened at a time when he just wanted to get away. And the way things had exploded had made it easy. He did get away. And the longer he was away, and the greater the distance between them, the harder it had been to do anything about it. He tried to tell her how difficult it had been to *think* about calling, much less visiting. But even as he tried to say it, he realized how silly it sounded. *No one would understand this—especially Makeba.*

"Now you're going to see what you should have been experiencing all along. You better dust off your checkbook while you're cleaning your house."

Ben flinched; he was now sitting at his dining room table. He couldn't help but resent the attitude—even from a friend—that he *should* suffer because of his absence. Besides, he thought, no one could ever know how miserable he had been. "Well, I'm not thinking about money right now. That's the problem. Everybody always connects being a parent to money. I just want to get to know my daughter again. I feel like there's a lot I can teach her. Maybe she can teach me some things too."

"Yeah, right. Not about money." Ramsey chuckled. "You have to purchase the right to teach your children, brother."

"Well anyway, I'm down for whatever." Ben was trying his best to conclude this discussion.

Ramsey got the hint. "So, what time is she coming?"

"Her plane gets in at five. I'm kind of sweating bullets." Ben caught a whiff of his hands still smelling of wax. "I've been cleaning for days, it seems like. I didn't realize how filthy I really am. Listen, I'd better go. I still have a few things to do before I pick her up at the airport."

It had been over a year since Ben had last seen Makeba. He thought back to the moment she had walked out of his hotel room. He had spent the night trying not to feel too sorry for himself. The television had been on, but he only remembered lying in his bed, looking at the pictures of his daughter and crying.

It was all such a surprise. He had come to Philadelphia that day to promote his new book. He had been happy, almost delirious about the reception it had gotten. Ben had to admit to himself that he had tried to slip quietly into town, do the book signing and head back to Minneapolis. But Makeba had walked herself back into his life. Reasserted herself, like children often do. Ben had thought that night that there was no way a father could, indefinitely, forever, deny what was true. And that's what he had been doing. Denying. For nearly ten years he had buried himself, dug deep into the ground and tried to disappear. He was in Minnesota for Christ's sake.

And now so was Makeba. Ben walked up to the gate. He was about three minutes late. He saw her as soon as he passed the check-in counter. She looked up and smiled at him.

She transformed to mist. A slate-infused mist with a strong, heat-generating smile. Ben moved toward her. He opened his arms and drew in his breath, inhaling her. And she settled, nestled really, in the heart of his grasp. And this time, all the hesitancy, the stuttering, halting energy, was gone. They melted into each other. Not lovers. Father and daughter. Spirit to spirit. Suddenly the world became narrow. The lights dimmed. Everyone left, rushed out to their appointed flights, back to their cars. Somewhere. Everywhere.

And there were no public announcements. Nothing was there except them and they spoke nothing audible to each other. No admonitions. No pleas. No shame. And Ben rolled himself backwards, regressing beyond all of his sophisticated escapism and into the space where he understood completely the nature of parenthood. The solid-gold quality of stewardship. Suddenly he understood how people could sacrifice *their own lives* for those of their children. Indeed, maybe it wasn't even a sacrifice. Maybe it was a privilege. To feel like this. To feel expanded, multiplied, exponential.

"If you hadn't come soon, I was going to catch the next flight out of here," Makeba lightly whispered. Her face rested in the curve of his shoulder so he heard only the suppressed giggle.

"Do you think I'll ever be on time for anything? Believe me, I was racing to get here as fast as I could."

"Don't worry about it. I was just kidding." Makeba now stepped back, allowing Ben to see her. Her hair had been straightened and curled. It turned up and under her chin from the sides.

"Well, anyway you're here. At least I don't have to talk to you on the telephone for a while." Ben grabbed her bag and pointed her toward the baggage claim area. Now there were people around them again. Moving walkways with people gliding by. But Ben and his daughter walked on solid ground. Their movement was much slower, more deliberate than everyone else's.

"Oh, so you don't like talking to me on the phone, huh?" Ben sometimes forgot how sarcastic and wry Makeba could be. Over the past year they had talked on the telephone nearly every day, sometimes more than once.

"You know I love talking to you. But my phone bill . . ."

Makeba burst into laughter. "Your phone bill must be as high as your car payment or your rent."

"That's what I'm saying. It's definitely cheaper to have you here."

"Now there's a welcome I didn't expect."

"You know what I'm talking about." Ben smiled. And she smiled.

"This way I know what I'm worth to you." Makeba flipped her head back to show even more teeth. "So let's see now, how much am I really worth? The phone bill has to be at least two hundred a month and that's for twelve months. Hmmmm. And the plane ticket cost three hundred and fifty. Yeah, now we're talking. And that's not including any gifts I might happen to get while I'm here."

Ben laughed out loud. It wasn't a nervous laugh. He was bounding. They were moving through the airport. It wasn't that he had money. Actually, he didn't. Having one book that did moderately well barely took care of the basics. The difference was, Makeba was now in that category. Her emotional needs—because that's all he could really attend to now—were of central importance to him now.

"The phone bill is more like three-fifty a month if you want to know the God's honest truth."

"Good."

He laughed again. "Is it that you *like* spending my money?"

"Your money? I thought you were supposed to be my father."

"Not supposed to be, Makeba. I *am* your father. The guy that married your mother is *supposed* to be your father. But, for good or for bad, I really am."

Makeba fell instantly silent. Ben knew he had brushed past the safe zone. But in the year they had been talking, he had had to stifle his resentment, his shame at having his place filled by someone else. She had had a rough life, and yet, there was a man in her house who performed the function of father. And she loved him. Sometimes she would call Ben when she was upset with her stepfather and Ben would feel stronger, keener as he silently listened to her complain. But if he ever contributed, was outraged or joined her anger, she would immediately turn on him. It presented a dilemma for him. On some level he had great respect for this man. On the other, as he became privy to the way he had raised Makeba, he was saddened. Angered. How dare someone undermine the self-esteem of another person! Of someone you claim to love *like* a daughter.

They were now at his car, a red '89 Jetta. "You know, one of the things I've been thinking about is what makes a father. I mean, you say you're my father. I know you are on some level. I mean I do remember you. I remember a lot about the things that we did. But like I said in my journal, it's all unclear. But anyway, the thing that bugs me is, how important is biology? I mean . . . you know . . . I don't really know you. I call somebody else 'Dad.' "

There it was. Ben felt his gut drop. He became the windshield. The steering wheel. The tires. The axle. He was rolling down I-35W toward his house. He was everything in motion except himself.

She continued. "Don't get me wrong. Even though I don't know why, I know that I love you. There *is* something genuine in you that is me. I know we're a lot alike. You're always disorganized and confused. You have a hard time making decisions. You're a dreamer. We are a lot alike. I know that you are my father. But my dad . . . ah . . . my daddy has been there for me. He's taken pretty good care of me. I know he's a pain, but he's been there."

"I know." What else could he say? She wasn't trying to be mean. She was just saying what was true. And then they were downtown. And then into his garage. Now he was taking her bags out of the trunk. And he couldn't stop thinking, wondering. Where were they going? There was nothing new in what she was saying. She said the same things periodically on the telephone. But she was with him now. And he realized that the scar she carried was just that: a scar. It would not go away with a telephone call—not even a hundred telephone calls. It was a scar. The mark of Mates perhaps. No. No. He couldn't call Mates into this again. He was a shadow now and even when he was real, he was only guilt. And guilt could be erased through action. And he was acting. And maybe even scars over time could be healed. Yes. Yes. That's right. Some scars do go away. There is that possibility. Sometimes when you hurt yourself and you look at the results,

240

you say, "That's a nasty scar," and you think it's going to be like that forever. But then, ten years later, you're lying in bed with someone and they touch you on that spot and you look and you realize only you can see it. Only you know it was once a nasty scar. But. But. You really never forget it. Even though no one else can see it. You still know it was there.

And then just as he was bending down to grab her suitcase, a Samsonite number with fabric on the sides like a carpetbag, she touched him on the arm. He turned around. The top of her head came just to the level of his eyes, so he had to look down. She extended her hand. He took it. "I forgive you. I want you to know that. I don't know why. People tell me I'm stupid. But I forgive you."

And even though he knew her well enough—or rather he knew himself well enough—to know that if she was like him, that statement was an intention, a desire. She *wanted* to forgive him. She had never said that before. She had to say it before it could become a possibility. And even though he understood that, he accepted her intention, her desire, as absolute joy. As redemption.

And then they were outside. In the park. Walking. Hand in hand. And the weather was nonexistent. And there were no people, only things to do. Only places to see. Restaurants to eat in. And there were birds there. And they sang. And the waning sun waited while they walked, thrilled to be late for the setting. And the moon looked on, anxiously awaiting its turn to christen.

And eventually the moon did present itself. Nearly full. Contented. And they talked about books she'd read and Geri and Lena and Helen and Hannibal, whom Makeba barely remembered, and Ramsey, whom she remembered well.

It was now nearly midnight of the first day Ben had breathed clearly in years. He remembered Makeba mentioned that thing about wanting to breathe freely. Without hesitation. Without the threat of Mates. Without shame. Just breathe like anyone would who was in the process of making amends. His mind was so clear now that he felt disconnected from everything else in his life. This night, as they sat on his couch in his apartment, it was as if it was a first date in the

1800s where you would linger as long as possible in the parlor. Hoping.

And in a way he *was* hoping. Hoping that this was truly a beginning. That they would bond in the most perfect of ways. That he might tell her a bedtime story and she might slowly slip into the folds of sleep and he might kiss her gently on the cheek, stand back and admire his Makeba as he had once done.

That was the thing. Sitting next to her now or across from her at the restaurant, he was struck by the complexity of his own memory. He looked at her. He saw the frayed jeans. The thick shoes. The fatigue-green T-shirt. Her softly blemished face. The glow of a young woman. A smart, alert young woman. He saw all these things with his eyes but in his mind she was still nine or ten. Still a gangly, precious little child. Or she was two and he was teasing her. Holding out a ball, offering it to her. Waiting until she reached for it, only to pull it away. Only to entice her into the same game again. Suddenly he was remembering things he had not been able to remember before. No matter how hard he had tried to tell the story about their separation, there was always so much information that was lost. Gone. He couldn't remember it. He couldn't make it up. He had to be here at this moment thinking it.

Oh, how wonderful it was to return home. That was what he thought. "I'm really glad you did what you did. You know that, don't you?"

"Yes. I know." Makeba was tired. She had been completely enswirled in the vague familiarity of the smell of the man who sat next to her. The man who truly was her father. And her journey to Minnesota had been harder than riding the train into the city that fateful day. She had hated explaining to her mother and stepfather that she had to do this. They reminded her over and over that Ben hadn't really lifted a finger to find her. That she was the one who was making all the effort. And this was true. But it was her life that she was trying to save. "Somebody had to get you straight." She yawned. "I think I'm going to bed."

"Do you like your room?"

"Yes. What are we doing tomorrow?" She slowly got up.

"Mall of America sound good to you?"

"Sounds fine. Well . . . ah . . ." She still didn't know what to call him. There wasn't enough room in her head to call two people Daddy. Maybe in time. But now, there was no appropriately affectionate name. And she was beginning to feel affection. The hours on the telephone. His willingness to listen to her ramble. To push her to *do* something with her life. There were moments when he *felt* like the real daddy. But it would be too much to give right now. "I'm heading to bed. Good night." She reached down to an expectant father and kissed him on the cheek.

And then it was them eating a breakfast of pancakes which he made for her, using a recipe he had learned by watching her mother. And then they were driving. Strolling through the ridiculously large megamall. They watched the kids in Snoopy World. Shopped. Went to see a movie. And all the time, Ben knew he was doing an abnormal thing. He was trying to remove the scar. To be unblemished again. He wanted it off of him. Off of her. He was scrubbing as hard as he could. And it was easy. She was making it easy.

She was making it easy because she needed it more than he did. And suddenly Ben understood that they really were bound together. Children who are separated from their fathers and their fathers who are missing, both need the same thing. Each of them must come to see that they need each other to live a whole life. A life without doubt and shame. That what had passed for living before their reconnection was just not acceptable. It had nothing to do with money. It had to do with salvation.

When they returned from the mall, Ben was tired and retired to his bedroom to take a nap. But instead of sleeping, he lay there, fully dressed, thinking about how lucky he was. He had recovered something very valuable that had been lost. He wanted to sleep but he couldn't shut off his dancing mind. His daughter was in the next room reading. Her presence in his home had changed it instantly. He got up from the bed, opened his bedroom door and saw Makeba sitting at the dining room table. But she wasn't reading. She was writing.

Ben wanted to interrupt her. To say something more. To let her know again, how happy he was. But instead, he stepped back into the bedroom, closed the door and eased himself back onto the bed.

His mouth still moving. His mind still keen. His heart still full. He had covered the distance. Had been lost in it. They would be okay. Whether she stayed in Minneapolis or moved to San Francisco. Whether he moved to be with her or not. They could survive anything now because they had survived. He knew it as surely as he knew that Mates would always be a shadow in his life. He had faced everything. He was alive. He was a father.